DREAM
A LITTLE
DREAM

THE SILVER TRILOGY
BOOK ONE

DREAM A LITTLE DREAM

KERSTIN GIER

Translated from the German
by Anthea Bell

HENRY HOLT AND COMPANY
NEW YORK

Henry Holt and Company, LLC
Publishers since 1866
175 Fifth Avenue
New York, New York 10010
macteenbooks.com

First published in the United States in 2015 by Henry Holt and Company, LLC.
Originally published in Germany in 2013 by Fischer Verlag GmbH
under the title *Das erste Buch der Traüme.*

Library of Congress Cataloging-in-Publication Data
Gier, Kerstin.
[Erste Buch der Traüme. English.]
Dream a little dream / Kerstin Gier ; translated from the German
by Anthea Bell. — First American edition.
pages   cm. — (The Silver trilogy ; book 1)
"Originally published in Germany in 2013 by Fischer Verlag GmbH under the title
Das Erste Buch Der Traüme."
ISBN 978-1-62779-027-7 (hardback) • ISBN 978-1-62779-028-4 (e-book)
[1. Dreams—Fiction. 2. Demonology—Fiction. 3. Supernatural—Fiction.
4. Schools—Fiction. 5. Moving, Household—Fiction. 6. London (England)—
Fiction. 7. England—Fiction. 8. Horror stories.] I. Title.
PZ7.G3523Dre 2015   [Fic]—dc23   2014033756

Henry Holt books may be purchased for business or promotional use. For information
on bulk purchases, please contact the Macmillan Corporate and Premium Sales
Department at (800) 221-7945 x5442 or by e-mail at specialmarkets@macmillan.com.

First American Edition—2015 / Designed by April Ward

Printed in the United States of America by R. R. Donnelley & Sons Company,
Harrisonburg, Virginia

1 3 5 7 9 10 8 6 4 2

For E.
It's always nice to dream with you.

What if you slept
And what if
In your sleep
You dreamed
And what if
In your dream
You went to heaven
And there plucked a strange and beautiful flower
And what if
When you awoke
You had that flower in your hand
Ah, what then?

SAMUEL TAYLOR COLERIDGE

DREAM A LITTLE DREAM

1

THE DOG WAS SNUFFLING at my bag. For a drug-tracking dog it was a surprisingly fluffy specimen, like a golden retriever, and I was just going to tickle it behind the ears when it bared its teeth and uttered a threatening "Woof!" Then it sat down and pressed its nose hard against the side of my bag. The customs officer seemed to be as surprised as I was. He looked twice from the dog to me and back again before reaching for the bag and saying, "Okay, then, let's see what our Amber's found in there."

Oh, great. Less than half an hour on British soil, and I was already under suspicion of drug smuggling. The genuine smugglers in the line behind me probably couldn't believe their luck. Thanks to me, they could stroll through the barrier at their leisure, with their Swiss watches and designer drugs. What customs man in his right mind was going to pick a fifteen-year-old girl with a ponytail out of the line, instead, for instance, of that nervous-looking guy with the shifty expression back there? Or the suspiciously pale boy with tousled hair on the plane who had gone to sleep before we even reached the runway to take off? No wonder he was grinning so gleefully. His pockets were probably stuffed full of illegal sleeping pills.

But I decided not to let myself get upset. Beyond the barrier, after all, a wonderful new life was waiting for us, with exactly the home we'd always dreamed of.

I cast a reassuring glance at my little sister, Mia, who had already reached the barrier and was bobbing impatiently up and down on the balls of her feet. This was only the last hurdle standing between us and the aforesaid wonderful new life. Everything was okay. The flight had gone smoothly, no turbulence, so Mia didn't have to throw up, and for once I hadn't been sitting next to a fat man stinking of beer and competing with me for the armrest. And although, as usual, Papa had booked us on one of those cheapo airlines, the plane hadn't run out of fuel when we had to circle above Heathrow while we waited to land. There'd also been that good-looking dark-haired boy in the row in front of me on the other side of the plane, who turned around to smile at me remarkably often. I'd been at the point of saying something to him, but then I'd seen he was leafing through a magazine for football fans, moving his lips as he read, so I hadn't. The same boy, incidentally, was now staring rather curiously at my bag. In fact, everyone was staring curiously at my bag.

Wide-eyed, I looked at the customs man and smiled my very nicest smile. "Please . . . we're in such a hurry, the plane came in late, and we were waiting for ages at baggage collection. And my mom is waiting out there to meet my little sister and me. I promise, word of honor, there's nothing in my bag but dirty laundry and . . ." At that exact moment I remembered what else was in the bag, so I fell silent for a second. "Well, anyway, there aren't any drugs in it," I finished in a rather subdued voice, looking reproachfully at the dog. Stupid animal!

The customs man, unmoved, heaved the bag up onto a table. A colleague of his unzipped it and folded back the top. Everyone standing around probably realized instantly what the dog had smelled. Because, to be honest, it didn't really take a dog's sensitive nose to place it.

"What in hell . . . ?" asked the customs man, and his colleague held his nose while he began clearing my clothes to one side with his fingertips. It must have looked to the spectators as if it was my things that stank to high heaven.

"Cheese from the Entlebuch Biosphere reserve in Switzerland," I explained as my face probably turned much the same color as the burgundy bra that the man was inspecting. "Five and a half pounds of unpasteurized Swiss cheese." Although I didn't remember it smelling quite so bad. "Tastes better than it smells—honest."

The silly dog, Amber, shook herself. I heard people chuckling, and you could bet the genuine smugglers were rubbing their hands together with glee. I thought I'd rather not know what the good-looking dark-haired boy was doing. Probably just feeling thankful that he hadn't asked me for my phone number.

"That's what I call a brilliant hiding place for drugs," said someone behind us, and I looked at Mia and sighed heavily. Mia sighed too. We really were in a hurry.

However, it was naïve of us to think that only the cheese still stood between us and our wonderful new life—in fact, the cheese just lengthened the period of time during which we firmly believed we did have a wonderful new life ahead of us.

Most girls probably dream of other things, but Mia and I wished for nothing more fervently than a real home. One we'd stay in for longer than a year. With a room for each of us.

This was our sixth move in eight years, meaning six different countries on four different continents, starting at a new school six times, making new friends six times, saying good-bye to them six times. We were experts at packing and unpacking, we kept our personal possessions to a minimum, and it's easy to guess why neither of us played the piano.

Mom was a professor of literary studies (with two doctoral degrees), and almost every year she held a post as a lecturer at a different university. We'd been living in Pretoria until June, and before that we'd lived in Utrecht, Berkeley, Hyderabad, Edinburgh, and Munich. Our parents had divorced seven years ago. Papa was an engineer and as restless as Mom, meaning he went to live in different places just as often. So we couldn't even spend our summer vacations at one and the same place; it always had to be wherever Papa was working at the time. Right now he was working in Zurich, so this last vacation had been comparatively good (several trips to the mountains of Switzerland and a visit to the biosphere, home of the cheese), but unfortunately not all the places where we'd happened to find ourselves were as nice as that.

Lottie, our au pair, sometimes said we ought to be grateful that our parents' work meant we saw so much of the world, except, to be honest, once you've spent a summer on the outskirts of an industrial area of Bratislava, it's easy to keep your gratitude within bounds.

Starting this fall, Mom would be teaching at Magdalen College, Oxford, fulfilling a great dream of hers. She'd wished for a teaching post at the University of Oxford for decades. And the little eighteenth-century cottage she'd rented just outside the city fulfilled a dream of our own. We were going to settle down at last and have a real home. In photos the house had looked romantic and comfortable, and as if it were full of wonderful, scary mysteries from the cellar to the attic. There was a large garden, with old trees and a summerhouse, and from the second-floor windows you had a view right down to the Thames, at least in winter. Lottie was planning to grow vegetables, make her own jam, and join the Women's Institute. Mia wanted to build a tree house, get a rowboat, and tame an owl, and I dreamed of finding a chest full of old letters in the attic and solving all the cottage's mysteries. We also definitely wanted to hang a swing in one of the trees—a swing made out of a rusty old iron bedstead where you could lie and look up at the sky. And we were going to have a real English picnic at least every other day, and the house would smell of Lottie's homemade cookies. Maybe of cheese fondue as well, because the customs officers had chopped our nice Entlebuch Biosphere cheese into such tiny little pieces that there was nothing else to be done with it.

When we finally got out of customs and into the main arrivals hall of the airport (incidentally, it turned out that there was no law against bringing a few pounds of cheese into Great Britain for one's personal use), it took Mom less than a minute to pop our dream of English country life like a soap bubble.

"There's been a slight change of plan, mousies," she told us after we'd all hugged and said hello, and in spite of her radiant smile, you could see her guilty conscience written all over her face.

KERSTIN GIER

Behind her, a man was approaching with an empty baggage cart, and without looking closely, I knew who he was: the change of plan in person.

"I hate changes of plan," muttered Mia.

Mom was still smiling for all she was worth. "You'll love this one," she said, untruthfully. "Welcome to London, the most exciting city in the world!"

"Welcome home," said Mr. Change of Plan in a deep, warm voice, heaving our bags up into the cart.

I hated changes of plan too, from the bottom of my heart.

ON OUR FIRST NIGHT in London I dreamed of Hansel and
Gretel. Or, to be precise, I dreamed that Mia and I were
Hansel and Gretel and Mom had taken us into the forest and
left us there. "It's for your own good!" she said before she
disappeared among the trees. Poor little Hansel and I wandered helplessly around until we came to a mysterious gingerbread house. Luckily I woke up before the wicked witch
came out of it, but I felt only a second of relief, and it occurred to me that my dream wasn't all that far from the truth.
Mom had said, "It's for your own good!" about seventeen
times yesterday. I was still so furious with her that I felt like
grinding my teeth nonstop.

I did realize that even people over forty have a right to a
full and satisfactory love life, but couldn't she have waited
until we were grown up? A few years weren't going to make
much difference to her now. And if she absolutely had to
spend time with Mr. Change of Plan, wouldn't a weekend
relationship be enough for her? Did she have to turn our
whole life upside down? Couldn't she at least have asked us?

Mr. Change of Plan's real name, incidentally, was Ernest Spencer, and he had driven us here in his car last night, making conversation all the time in such a cheerful, casual way, you'd have thought he didn't even notice that Mia and I were so disappointed and furious that we were fighting back tears and didn't say a word. (And it was a long drive from the airport into the city.) Not until Ernest was taking our baggage out of the trunk of the car did Mia get her voice back.

"Oh no," she said, with her very sweetest smile, handing him back the plastic bag with the dismembered cheese in it. "This is for you. A present from Switzerland."

Ernest exchanged a delighted glance with Mom. "Why, thank you both. That's really nice of you!"

Mia and I grinned at each other quite happily—but that was the only good moment of the evening. Ernest went home with his stinking, ruined cheese, after kissing Mom and assuring us of how much he was looking forward to tomorrow evening. Because we were invited to his house then, to meet his children.

"We're looking forward to it too," said Mom.

You bet your life.

The moment we first laid eyes on him, we were suspicious of Ernest I'm-just-like-my-stuffy-old-first-name Spencer. He'd even brought presents, which showed he was in dead earnest about Mom. Normally the men in Mom's life don't show any interest in sucking up to Mia and me—far from it. They'd always done their best to ignore us as much as possible. But Ernest had brought me a book about secret messages and codes and how to decipher them, which really did look very interesting. Only with Mia he didn't get it quite right; he gave her a book called *Maureen the Little Detective*, but now that she was nearly thirteen, she was a few years too old for it. However, the mere fact that Ernest had asked about our interests made him different.

And Mom was besotted with him—don't ask me why. It couldn't be his looks. Ernest had a large bald patch, enormous ears, and teeth that were far too white. It was all very well for Lottie to insist that Ernest was a handsome man; we just couldn't go along with her opinion. Maybe he did have nice eyes, but with ears like that who was going to look into his eyes? Not to mention that he was ancient—over fifty. His wife had died more than ten years ago, and he lived in London with his two children. Mia the little detective and I had Googled to check up on him at once. Google knew all about Ernest Spencer because he was one of those star lawyers who are always getting into the papers, whether it's outside the Royal Courts of Justice or on the red carpet at a charity gala. And his late wife had been two hundred and first, or something like that, in line to the throne of England, so he moved in the top circles of society.

By all the laws of probability, Ernest and Mom should never have crossed each other's paths. But a mean trick on the part of fate, and Ernest's special subject—international commercial law—had taken him to Pretoria six months ago, and he and Mom had met at a party. Idiots that we were, we'd even encouraged her to go to it, so she'd have a nice evening and get to know people.

And that had landed us in this mess.

"Keep still, dear!" Lottie was tugging at the hem of my skirt, but it was no use; it was too short.

Lottie Wastlhuber had come to us twelve years ago as an au pair and stayed on ever since. Which was a good thing, because otherwise we'd have had to survive on sandwiches. Mom usually forgot about meals, and she hated to cook. Without Lottie, no one would have braided our hair into funny German styles, but then again, no one would have given birthday parties for our dolls or decorated the Christmas tree with us. In fact, we probably wouldn't even have had a Christmas tree, because Mom didn't think much of customs and traditions. She was also terribly forgetful, the very image of an absentminded professor. She forgot absolutely everything: fetching Mia from her flute lessons, the name of our dog, and where she'd parked the car. We'd all have been lost without Lottie.

Not that Lottie was infallible. She'd bought my school uniform a size too small, the same as every year, and also the same as every year, she was trying to blame it on me.

"I just don't see how anyone can grow so much in a single summer," she wailed, doing her best to button the blazer up over my breasts. "And then there's all *this* up here! You did it on purpose!"

"Yes, sure!" Although I was as cross as I could be, I had to grin. Lottie might have congratulated me. "All *this* up here" might not be especially impressive for someone nearly sixteen, but at least I wasn't flat as a board anymore. So I didn't think it was so bad if I had to leave the blazer unbuttoned. Along with the skirt being too short, it gave me kind of a cool look, and it did show off as much of my figure as possible.

"It looks much better on Liv," complained Mia, who was already dressed in her own outfit. "Why didn't you buy mine a size too small as well? And why are all school uniforms dark blue? And why is the school called Frognal Academy when it doesn't have a frog on its crest?" She sullenly patted the embroidered crest on the breast pocket of her blazer. "I look dumb. Everything here is dumb." She turned slowly on her own axis, pointing to the unfamiliar items of furniture around us and saying in an extra-loud voice, "Dumb. Dumb. Dumb. Dumb. Right, Livvy? We'd been looking forward so much to the cottage in Oxford, and instead we end up *here*. . . ."

"Here" was the apartment where Ernest had dropped us off last night, on the third floor of a rather grand block somewhere in the northwest of London. It had four bedrooms, gleaming marble floors, and a whole lot of furniture and other stuff that didn't belong to us. (Much of it was gilded, even the sofa cushions.) According to the nameplate beside the doorbell, it belonged to some people called Finchley. They obviously collected china ballerinas. There were ballerinas all over the place.

I nodded. "We don't even have our favorite things here," I said in a voice just as loud as Mia's.

"Shh," said Lottie, glancing anxiously over her shoulder. "You both know perfectly well that this is only temporary. And the cottage was a catastrophe." She had given up tugging at my uniform. It didn't do any good.

"Yes, so Mr. Spencer says," said Mia. (We were supposed to call him by his first name, but we pretended we'd forgotten.)

"Your mother saw the rat with her own eyes," said Lottie. "Do you two really want to live in a house where there are rats?"

"Yes," Mia and I replied in chorus. First, rats are better

than their image (we'd found that out when we saw *Rata-touille*), and second, you could bet the rat was just as much of an invention as the rest of it. We weren't as dumb as all that—we knew exactly what was going on here. Mom had laid it on just a tiny little bit too thick to convince us last night. Apparently the cottage had smelled of mold, the heating didn't work properly, there'd been crows nesting in the chimneys, the neighbors had been rude and noisy, and the surroundings looked dismal. Furthermore, public transport wasn't good, and the school where we'd originally been going to go had a bad reputation. That, said Mom, was why she'd had to back out of the rental agreement and find this apartment instead—on a temporary basis, of course. (Like everywhere else we'd ever lived.)

Well, yes, Mom admitted, all that had happened behind our backs, but only because she hadn't wanted to spoil our vacation with Papa. Anyway, she said, it was for our own good—she'd be commuting to Oxford every day so that we could go to an excellent school here, and also—"to be honest, mousies!"—wouldn't it be cooler to live in London than out in the country?

Of course none of this had anything at all to do with the fact that Mr. I-know-what's-good-for-you Spencer just happened to live in this part of London himself and wanted to have Mom as close to him as possible. Also entirely by chance, the school we'd be going to now just happened to be the school where Ernest's own children went. The kids we were going to meet at dinner tomorrow.

There was nothing short of a disaster on the way, that was clear. The end of an era.

"I don't feel well," I said.

"You're only nervous." Lottie patted Mia's shoulder reassuringly with one hand while she put a strand of hair back behind my ear with the other. "That's perfectly normal on your first day in a new school. But believe you me, there's no reason for you two to have an inferiority complex or anything. You're both very, very pretty girls, and clever as you are, you don't have to worry about keeping up with your studies." She smiled lovingly at us. "My wonderfully clever, wonderfully beautiful, blond elfin girls."

"Yup, wonderfully clever, wonderfully beautiful, blond elfin girls, and me with braces on my teeth and nerdy glasses and a nose much too long for me," muttered Mia, ignoring the fact that Lottie was feeling so emotional that her big, brown, round eyes had gone a little damp. "Two girls of no fixed address."

And with a totally deranged mother, probably the oldest au pair girl in the business, and a whole heap of shattered dreams of life in the country, I added silently, but I couldn't help responding to Lottie's smile. She was so sweet, standing there beaming at us, full of optimism and pride. Anyway, none of this was her fault.

"You'll only have to wear the braces for another six months. You'll easily see that through, Mia-mouse." Mom had come in from the next room. As usual, she'd heard only the part of the conversation that she wanted to hear. "Those are really attractive school uniforms." She gave us a sunny smile and began rummaging around in one of the moving company's boxes labeled SHOES.

Of course Mom's shoes had arrived in this stuffy old apartment, while my crates of books were gathering dust in some container belonging to the same firm, along with my secret notebooks and my guitar case.

I glared at Mom's slender back. It wasn't surprising that Mr. Spencer had fallen for her. She looked pretty good for a professor of English literature. She's a natural blonde, long legs, blue eyes, great teeth. She was forty-six, but you wouldn't guess that except in bright daylight when she'd drunk too much red wine the evening before. On good days she looked like Gwyneth Paltrow. Although her new haircut was frightful. She must have been to the same hairdresser as Duchess Camilla.

Mom dropped the shoes she didn't need on the rug behind her. Our dog, Butter—full name Princess Buttercup, formerly known as Dr. Watson (the name Dr. Watson dated from before we'd realized that she was a girl)—snapped up a jogging shoe and dragged it off to her improvised sleeping place under the coffee table, where she began chewing it with relish. None of us stopped her; after all, she wasn't having an easy time either. I bet she'd been looking forward to the cottage with the garden as much as we had. But of course no one had asked her opinion. Dogs and children had no rights in this household.

Another jogging shoe hit me on the shin.

"Mom," I said fretfully, "do you have to do that? As if it wasn't chaotic enough here already?"

Mom acted as if she hadn't heard me and went on rummaging in the box, while Lottie gave me a reproachful look. I stared grimly back. If I wasn't even allowed to speak my mind anymore, this really was the end.

"There they are." Mom had finally found the shoes she

wanted—a pair of black pumps—and held them trium-
phantly aloft.

"That's all that matters, then," said Mia venomously.

Mom slipped the shoes on and turned back to us. "Right,
as far as I'm concerned we can go," she said cheerfully. She
didn't seem a bit bothered that Mia and I were looking at her
in a way that could have curdled milk.

Lottie hugged us. "You'll be fine, dears. I mean, it really
isn't your *first* first day at school."

I RAISED MY CHIN and straightened my shoulders as well as I could in the tight-fitting blazer. Lottie was right—this really was not our first time at a new school. We'd been through much worse already. At least this time we knew the language of the country and could speak it, which had not been the case in Utrecht, for instance. Although Mom insisted that anyone who knew German and English could understand Dutch as well (yes, sure, and the Earth is flat, Mom!).

Because people could speak English almost everywhere our respective parents took us, they'd decided to turn Dad's German surname of Silber into Silver for Mia and me, and that was one thing at least to make life easier here in London for us. And we certainly needn't be afraid of meeting a millipede in the toilet, like in Hyderabad. (I still sometimes dreamed of that creature—it was longer than my forearm, and worse than that, it had looked at me with its horrible millipede eyes.) No, everything here was so hygienically germ free that you could even sit on the seat of the toilet without worrying. The Frognal Academy for Boys and Girls was a private school in Hampstead, a posh part of London, which meant that the kids didn't have to be searched for weapons in the morning with metal detectors, as in the junior high I attended in Berkeley, California, three schools ago. And certainly there must be nicer students here than the girl who'd been assigned to show me around, who was staring at me as if I smelled bad. (Which I didn't—I'd showered for quarter of an hour longer than usual on account of that cheese.)

I could only hope Mia had a nicer "big sister" to show her the ropes.

"Is Liv short for Livetta or Carlivonia?" mine asked.

Is it what? Was she trying to make a fool of me? No one in the world was called Livetta or Carlivonia, were they? On the other hand, her own name was Persephone.

"Olivia," I said, feeling annoyed with myself because, under Persephone's critical eyes, I kept wishing Lottie had bought my school uniform in the right size after all. And that I had my contact lenses in, instead of wearing the nerdy glasses that, along with my stern ponytail, were supposed to correct the impression given by the too-short skirt and the too-tight blazer. Which they did.

The headmistress had wanted Persephone to be my big sister because, as a glance at our schedules showed, we had almost all the same classes. Just moments ago, in the headmistress's office, she had been giving me a friendly smile; in fact, her eyes had been positively shining when the headmistress told her that I'd lived, among other places, in South Africa and the Netherlands. But the light in them went right out again when she asked were my parents diplomats or did they own a diamond mine and I had to say no, neither of those was right. Since then she had switched off the smile and kept wrinkling up her nose instead. She was still wrinkling it up. She looked like one of those grumpy monkeys in Hyderabad who stole your breakfast if you didn't watch out.

"Olivia?" she repeated. "I know at least ten Olivias. My friend's cat is called Olivia."

"Well, you're the first Persephone I've ever met." *Because that's a name you wouldn't even call a cat.*

Walking on, Persephone tossed her hair back. "In our family, we all have names out of Greek myths. My sister is called Pandora, and my brother is Priam."

Poor things. But a lot better than Persephone, all the same. Since she was looking at me as if she expected an answer, I said quickly, "And all your names begin with *P*. How, er . . . practical."

"Yes, and they go with our surname. Porter-Peregrin." Persephone Porter-Peregrin—good heavens above!—tossed her hair back again and pushed open a glass door that had posters and notes stuck all over it.

A glittering movie poster in particular caught my eye. The film was called *Autumn Ball*. Under the gilt letters of the title, a couple were dancing through a sea of colorful leaves, he in white tie and tails, she in a pink tulle evening dress. The showing was on October 5, and tickets could be bought at the secretary's office. I loved movies, but I wasn't going to waste my money on silly high school romances like that. You always knew how the film was going to end after five seconds.

There was no more peace and quiet on the other side of the glass door. We were suddenly surrounded by students all streaming through the halls at the same time. At Frognal Academy the lower, middle, and upper school were all under the same roof, and I automatically looked for Mia's shock of blond hair. It was the first time in years that we'd been at the same school, and I'd made sure to impress upon Mia that she ought to mention, in passing, that her big sister could do kung fu—just in case any of the students tried anything funny.

But Mia was nowhere to be seen. I had some difficulty following Persephone through the crowd. The personal part of our conversation seemed to be over now; obviously she didn't want any more than necessary to do with someone who shared her friend's cat's name, and whose parents weren't diplomats and didn't own any diamond mine either.

"Lower school canteen." Now and then she pointed somewhere and cast words over her shoulder in a singsong tone, without bothering about whether I heard them or not. "Middle school and upper school cafeteria both on the first floor. Toilets there. Computer rooms are lilac. Natural science labs, green."

Another glass door covered with posters. Once again, the words *Autumn Ball* stood out with tasteless prominence. This time I stopped to take a closer look. Yes, it looked like a film of the worst kind. The girl in the picture was looking soulfully at the guy she was dancing with, while he seemed to be forcing a smile, looking a little envious of the tiara she was wearing, when all he had was a nasty side-parted hairstyle.

But maybe I wasn't doing the film justice and it wasn't the usual high school garbage with the malicious blond cheerleader, the charming but superficial football captain, and the impoverished, beautiful outsider with a heart of gold. For all I knew, *Autumn Ball* was a spy thriller and the pink tulle dress, the soulful smile, and the silly tiara were just camouflage so that the girl could outwit the boy with the side part and get the key to a safe full of secret papers that she could use to save the world. Or else the guy was a serial killer and had it in for high school girls. . . .

"Forget it!" Persephone had obviously noticed that I wasn't behind her anymore and had come back. "The ball is for the upper school. If you're younger, you only get to go if someone invites you."

It was a few seconds before I caught on to what she meant (I had to come a long way back from the serial killer). Persephone used the lag time to take a lip gloss out of her pocket and pull off the top.

God, how silly of me. *Autumn Ball* wasn't a movie but plain reality. I couldn't help laughing at myself a little.

Beside us, a few of the students began playing with a grapefruit, throwing it back and forth. "It's a traditional ball to commemorate the year when this school was founded. Everyone has to wear Victorian costumes. I'll be going, of course." Persephone was touching up her lips. At first I admired her for doing it without a mirror; then I realized that it was a colorless lip gloss, so it didn't matter if she smeared it right up to her nose. "With a boy who knows my sister. She's on the ball committee. Hey, stop that, you idiots." The grapefruit had shot past overhead, just missing her. What a pity.

"But there's a Christmas party for all the classes," Persephone added graciously. "You and your little sister can . . ." At this point she stopped talking—indeed, she stopped breathing. She just stared past me, like a Hyderabad monkey turned to stone while putting on lip gloss.

I turned around to find out what had made her stop breathing. Well, at least no UFO had landed. Instead I saw a group of older students, all standing out from the crowd in a

similarly striking way. They were four boys, and almost everyone in this corridor was staring at them. They were deep in
conversation, and while they were strolling casually along,
they did so in step with each other, as if in time to music that
only they could hear. All they needed was slow motion and a
wind machine to blow the hair away from their faces. They
were coming straight toward us, and I wondered which of
them had turned Persephone into a pillar of salt. As far as I
could judge at first glance, it could have been any of them,
provided she fancied the tall, blond, athletic type. (I didn't,
myself. I had a weakness for dark-haired, brooding guys who
read poetry and played the saxophone and liked to watch
Sherlock Holmes films. So far, unfortunately, I hadn't met
many like that. Oh, all right, I hadn't met *any* boy like that
yet. But they must be out there somewhere!)

The most conspicuously good looking was the second
from the left, who had golden-blond curls framing a perfectly
proportioned, angelic face. Even at close quarters, his face
might have been made of porcelain, without any pores showing in his skin—in fact, unnaturally perfect. Compared with
him, the other three looked more normal.

Persephone uttered a hoarse, "Hi, Japscrsch."

She got no answer. The boys were much too absorbed in
their conversation to honor us with so much as a glance. And
presumably none of them was really called Japscrsch.

The grapefruit came flying back, and it would certainly
have hit Persephone Pillar of Salt right on the nose if I hadn't
lunged forward to intercept it. To be honest, it was more of a
reflex action than a deliberate good deed, and the stupid thing
was that one of the guys from the Club of Casual Blonds (the
one on the extreme left) had the same idea or the same reflex

himself, so our shoulders collided in midair as we jumped to catch it. But it was in my hand that the grapefruit landed.

The boy looked down at me. "Not bad," he said appreciatively. His sleeve had slipped up as he reached for the grapefruit. He quickly pulled it down again, but not quickly enough for me. I'd read the words tattooed inside his wrist: *numen noctis.*

He grinned at me. "Basketball or handball?"

"Neither. I just felt hungry."

"I see." He smiled, and I was about to rethink the kind of guy I fancied and throw him over in favor of the tall, tattooed type with pale skin, tousled honey-blond hair, and slate-gray eyes, when he added, "You're the cheese girl from the airport. What sort of cheese was it again?"

Okay, so I didn't rethink. "Entlebuch Biosphere cheese," I said with dignity, stepping away from him. He wasn't all that good looking anyway. His nose was too long, there were dark shadows under his eyes, and his hair looked as if it had never known a comb. I knew who he was too: the guy who had fallen asleep so unnaturally fast on the flight from Switzerland. Although he now seemed wide awake. And extremely amused.

"Entlebuch Biosphere cheese. That's right," he repeated, with a mean kind of chuckle.

I looked past him with deliberate lack of interest.

The porcelain angel had moved away, but one of his friends had stopped beside Persephone. He looked familiar to me too, but I had to stare at him for at least five seconds before I worked out why, and then I almost squealed out loud. Incredible! It was Ken standing in front of me! The life-size, flesh-and-blood version of the Barbie doll's boyfriend that our great-aunt Gertrude had given Mia for Christmas. Shaving Fun Ken, to identify him properly. (Aunt Gertrude's presents were always good for a laugh. She'd given me a set of iron-on beads.)

Persephone, anyway, had come around from her rigidity far enough to be able to breathe and roll her eyes again. Her cheeks were unnaturally red, but whether with anger or lack of oxygen I couldn't tell. The boys who had been playing grapefruit-ball had deliberately disappeared.

"New friend of yours, Aphrodite?" inquired Shaving Fun Ken, pointing to me.

Persephone's cheeks went a little darker red. "Oh, hi, *Jasper*! I only just noticed you," she said in a voice that sounded almost normal (in her case, that was tremendously blasé), only a little shriller than before. "My God, no! Old Cook the headmistress gave me the job of keeping an eye on her. New student—Olive something or other. Her parents are missionaries or some such thing."

Or some such thing. I looked at her incredulously through glasses that were evidently suitable for a missionary couple's daughter. Was that the only alternative to diplomats and diamond-mine owners that occurred to her?

Shaving Fun Ken looked me up and down, rubbing his stubbly chin. I absolutely needed to show him to Mia: the likeness was astonishing. (*Ken has a date with Barbie. His three-days' beard is bothering him. Help him to shave it off.*)

"What's your name?" he asked.

"Didn't you hear her? Olive Something Or Other," I said. (*Barbie is rather annoyed by the way Ken is behaving. He normally has better manners and doesn't look quite so lecherous. So she has no intention of telling him her real name.*)

Once again he stroked his chin. "If your parents are missionaries, I bet you're still—"

"We'd better get moving," the boy from the plane interrupted him, taking his arm quite roughly. "Come along, Jasper."

"I suppose it's okay to ask." Obviously Shaving Fun Ken could hardly take his eyes off me. "Nice legs, anyway. For a missionary's daughter."

I opened my mouth to say something (as if he was likely to know a single missionary's daughter, the big show-off), but before I could, Persephone had clutched my sleeve with her hand. "We'll have to get moving ourselves. We have chemistry with Roberts, and she won't like it if I'm late on the very first day."

I stumbled as she hauled me forward, but all the same I was glad to be moving, because I couldn't think of the perfect put-down of an answer.

ABOUT ME:
My name is Secrecy—I'm right here among you, and I know *all* your secrets.

3 September, 6 p.m.

School has begun again—so welcome back, all my regular readers. And for anyone new to this blog: Don't even try to find out who I am, because so far no one has managed it.

So now the annual mystery at Frognal Academy begins again: Who's going to the Autumn Ball, and who with? Since the ball committee has done away with the election of a Ball King and a Ball Queen (Did any of you ever understand why? It's not as if an election like that has anything to do with discrimination, does it?), I've decided to carry on that fine old tradition and have an internal election here. You're welcome to send me your suggestions by e-mail at secrecy.buzz@yahoo.com.

Of course, the burning question is, who will get to go as Arthur Hamilton's partner? For you new students, Arthur is the best-looking boy in this school—or, for all I know, in the entire Western Hemisphere. And now that Colin Davison has left, he's also the new captain of our basketball team. Officially,

Arthur is going out with Anabel Scott, who did her A levels last year and just left for finishing school in Switzerland, but—boys, please skip this bit; it's only for the girls—unofficially he's definitely up for grabs. And I don't say that just because, in principle, I don't expect long-distance relationships to last. Okay, her relationship status on Facebook is still the same, but be honest: Have any of you seen the two of them together since the end-of-term ball? And why does Anabel always look as if she were about to burst into tears?

But who'd be surprised if she did?? Not me, anyway. By now everyone must have realized that since the tragic death of Anabel's ex-boyfriend Tom Holland, Anabel and Arthur have no longer been the dream couple who could make any of us green with envy just from looking at them. For new students: Oh dear, what a lot of this story you've missed! Poor Tom died in a car accident in June. And never mind ex! I've suggested here, more than once, that the electricity between him and Anabel was still working. Everyone saw it too, except maybe Arthur. But when Anabel had that dramatic outburst of tears at Tom's funeral, he must have noticed. (And incidentally, it wasn't Arthur who comforted Anabel, it was Henry Harper—just to refresh your memory and confuse you a bit more. ☺)

So what do you think? Who will be Arthur's new girlfriend? Bets taken here!

See you soon!

Love from Secrecy

"MY BIG SISTER'S NAME is Daisy Dawn Steward!" said Mia, and crumbs flew out of her mouth with every consonant. "Her hobby is Taylor Lautner, and she talked about him and nothing else all day."

I could easily trump that. "*My* big sister is called Persephone Porter-Peregrin. And she didn't talk to me at all after she'd dragged me off to the first classroom. But I guess that wasn't so bad, because her hobby seems to be wrinkling up her nose."

"Funny sort of names, like racehorses," said Lottie. She didn't say anything about having Taylor Lautner for a hobby—she'd hung up a poster of him herself the year before last. On the inside of her wardrobe. She said it was because wolves are so cute.

In spite of the tartan curtains with gold thread running through them, and the china ballerinas everywhere, it was quite comfortable in the kitchen of the strange apartment. Late summer rain was beating against the window, and the air was full of the comforting smell of vanilla and chocolate.

Lottie had been baking our favorite cookies: vanilla crescents made to her grandmother's recipe. Along with the vanilla crescents, we were drinking hot cocoa with whipped cream and chocolate sprinkles on top. Lottie had also given us towels to rub our hair dry after the rain had drenched it. The full charge of loving care, butter, and sugar really did cheer us up for the time being. Lottie obviously felt sorrier for us than she liked to admit. Normally it was against her principles to bake Christmas cookies before December, and she was very strict about the traditional Christmas stuff. Too bad if anyone so much as hummed "Silent Night" in June. Lottie was having none of that. It brought bad luck, or so she said.

For some time we were happy enough filling our faces with cookies and doing a running commentary on imaginary horse races: "Persephone Porter-Peregrin instantly takes the lead on the inside. She's won almost all the derbies here at Ascot this year. She leaves her rival Vanilla Crescent behind her right away. . . . But what's this? Daisy Dawn, starting number five, comes up to the front—this is thrilling— on the straight she's neck and neck with Persephone and— yes! You wouldn't believe it! The outsider Daisy Dawn wins by a nose!"

"It's not as if vanilla crescents were Christmas biscuits like gingerbread, strictly speaking," Lottie was muttering in German, more to herself than us. Way back when she first came to us, Papa had insisted on a German au pair so that we'd learn to speak his mother tongue better. That was because when he spoke German to us himself, we were inclined to reply either not at all or in English (well, I was; at the time Mia couldn't say anything except "dadadada"), and that was not his idea of a proper bilingual upbringing. As Lottie could speak hardly any English at all at that time, we always had to do our best to speak German to her, and Papa was delighted.

"So you can eat them all the year round." Lottie was still rather afraid that Baby Jesus might bear her a grudge over those vanilla crescents. "But only in exceptional cases, of course."

"We're very, very exceptional cases," Mia assured her. "Two kids in a one-parent family, no home and no hope, totally lost and strangers in this big city."

I'm afraid she wasn't exaggerating all that much. We'd found our way home only with the help of some friendly passersby and a nice bus driver. As we didn't remember the number of the building where we were to live for the time being, and all the buildings around here looked the same, we'd probably still have been wandering around in the pouring rain, like Hansel and Gretel in the forest, if Buttercup hadn't been standing at the first-floor window barking like crazy. Now the clever dog was lying on the corner bench in the kitchen with her head on my lap, hoping that a vanilla crescent would find its way into her mouth by some miraculous means.

"It's a fact—you two don't have an easy time," said Lottie, sighing deeply, and just for a moment I had a guilty conscience. To make Lottie feel better, we could have told her that it really hadn't been too bad at school. Our first day at school in London had gone a lot better than, for instance, our first day in Berkeley, California, where a girl gang had threatened to force my head into the toilet. (It had only been threats on the first day; on the fifth day they actually did it. That was also the day when I signed up to learn kung fu.)

Today's first day hadn't been at all like that or like various other memorable first days at assorted new schools. Apart from Persephone and Shaving Fun Ken, none of the Frognal Academy students had struck me as unpleasant, and even the teachers seemed to be okay. I didn't have the feeling that I wouldn't be able to keep up in any subject, the French teacher had praised my good accent, the classrooms were bright and pleasant, and even school lunch had been quite good. The girl who sat next to me in French had taken over from Persephone, entirely unasked, in showing me around, took me to the cafeteria at midday, and introduced me to her friends. I learned from them that the mushy peas were better avoided and that the Autumn Ball would be cool because after the stuffy, official part of it there was going to be a band playing that unfortunately I'd never heard of before. Anyway, as first days at a new school go, mine had been pretty good. Mia's too.

So we really ought to have told Lottie all that, but it was nice to have her so sympathetic and concerned for us—especially as the day wasn't over yet. The worst still lay ahead of us: dinner at Ernest's place, when we were going to meet his son and daughter. They were seventeen-year-old twins, and if you believed what Ernest said about them, they were models of talent and virtue. I hated them already.

Lottie seemed to be thinking of this dinner date as well. "I've hung up your red velvet skirt and white shirt for this evening, Mia. And I ironed your mother's blue tea dress for you, Liv."

"Why not go the whole hog and make it the little black dress with fake gemstones all over it?" I said sarcastically.

"Yes, worn with kid gloves and all," agreed Mia. "Oh,

come on, this is only a stupid dinner. On a perfectly ordinary Monday. I'm wearing my jeans."

"You're doing no such thing," said Lottie. "I want you two showing yourselves in your best light."

"What, in Mom's blue tea dress? What are you wearing, then, Lottie—your Sunday-best dirndl?" Mia and I giggled.

Lottie looked majestic. She wasn't taking jokes about traditional dirndl skirts and dresses any more than she'd have us go against Christmas customs. "I would, because you can never go wrong in a dirndl. But I'm staying here with Buttercup."

"What? You're making us go on our own?" cried Mia.

Lottie didn't say anything.

"Oh, I see—Mr. Spencer hasn't invited you," I concluded after working it out, and I suddenly had a sinking feeling inside me.

Mia widened her eyes indignantly. "That stupid, snobby . . ."

Lottie immediately began defending Ernest. "It wouldn't be the right thing to do. After all, you don't take the nanny to a . . . a *family occasion* like this."

"But you're part of our family!" Mia was crumbling up a vanilla crescent, and Buttercup hopefully raised her head. "Talk about arrogance!"

"No, that's not it at all," Lottie contradicted her. "Mr. Spencer's behavior toward me is always perfectly correct. He's very nice, a real gentleman, and I'm sure his feelings for your mother are genuine and honorable. He really did his best to find a solution when it turned out that the cottage wouldn't do. We wouldn't have found this apartment without his help, and you'd never have been accepted by the Frognal

Academy—it's said to have a waiting list miles long. So you'd better start liking him." She looked sternly at us. "And you'll dress properly this evening."

The trouble was, Lottie couldn't look stern any more sucessfully than Buttercup could look ferocious. They both had such cute brown eyes. I loved Lottie so much at that moment, I could have burst with it.

"Okay," I said. "If you'll lend me your dirndl."

Mia had a fit of giggles. "Yes, you can never go wrong in Lottie's dirndl."

"I didn't say you can't go wrong in *my* dirndl, I said in *a* dirndl." Lottie turned up her nose, threw back her brown curly hair (it looked just like Buttercup's), and went on in her native German. "I don't want to disillusion you, my loves, but you simply don't have enough on your hips to look good in a dirndl, understand?"

I wanted to laugh, but somehow it just turned into a funny snort. "Oh, Lottie, I do love you!" I said, much more seriously than I meant to.

I'D EXPECTED ERNEST SPENCER to live in a bigger, more showy sort of house, and I was almost disappointed when the taxi stopped outside a comparatively ordinary sort of brick building in Redington Road. Traditional-style sash windows with white frames, several gables and bow windows, hidden behind tall hedges and walls, like most of the houses here. It had stopped raining, and the evening sun was bathing everything in golden light.

"It looks very pretty," whispered Mia in surprise as we followed Mom up the paved path to the front door, past flowering hydrangeas and box trees clipped into globe shapes.

"So do you," I whispered back. She did; she looked good enough to eat, with the cute braids on which Lottie had insisted, in exchange for the jeans that Mom, much to Lottie's displeasure, had said we could wear. Probably, for one thing, because she wanted to wear her freshly ironed blue dress herself.

Mom had pressed the doorbell, and we heard three

melodious notes inside the house. "Please be *nice*, you two! And try to behave yourselves."

"You mean we're not to throw our food about the way we usually do, belch, and tell improper jokes?" I blew a strand of hair away from my face. Lottie would have braided my hair too, but I had deliberately spent so long in the bathroom that there wasn't enough time for it. "Honestly, Mom, if any of us has to be warned to be on our best behavior, it's you!"

"Exactly! *We* have perfect manners. Good evening, sir." Mia bobbed a curtsy to a large stone statue beside the front door, a mixture of eagle (head down to rib cage) and lion (the rest of him), and rather stout into the bargain. "Allow me to introduce myself. My name is Mia Silver, this is my sister Olivia Silver, and the one with the heavy frown looking more like a wicked stepmother is our real mom, Professor Ann Matthews. May I ask whom I have the honor of addressing?"

"This is Frightful Freddy, also known as Fat Freddy." The front door had been opened, without a sound, by a tall boy a little older than me, wearing a long-sleeved black T-shirt and jeans. I heaved a sigh of relief. Thank goodness Mom had put the silly tea dress on herself; I'd have felt totally ridiculous in it.

"My grandparents gave him to my parents as a wedding present," said the boy, patting Frightful Freddy's beak. "Years ago, Dad wanted to move him to the far corner of the garden, but he weighs about a ton."

"Hello, Grayson!" Mom kissed the boy on both cheeks and then pointed to us. "These are my two mousies, Mia and Liv."

Mia and I hated being called mousies. It was as if Mom was letting everyone know that our front teeth were a little too large, which was possibly true.

Grayson smiled at us. "Hi. Good to meet you."

"I bet," I muttered under my breath.

"You have lipstick on your cheek," said Mia.

Mom sighed, and Grayson looked a bit baffled. I couldn't help noticing that he looked very like his father if you took no notice of his hair. The same broad shoulders, the same self-confident bearing, the same noncommittal politician's smile. That was probably why he seemed so familiar to me. Admittedly he didn't have ears as enormous as Ernest's, but they might yet catch up with his father's. I'd once read that ears and noses are the only parts of the body to go on grow-ing into old age.

Mom walked energetically past Grayson, as if she knew her way around the house very well. There was nothing we could do but follow her. Only, we stopped in the corridor, at a loss, because she had disappeared.

Grayson closed the door behind us and passed the back of his hand over his cheeks. In fact, Mia had invented the lipstick bit.

"Is there at least something delicious to eat?" asked Mia, after we had stared at each other awkwardly for a couple of seconds.

"I think so," said Grayson, smiling again. I've no idea how he managed it. I couldn't bring myself to smile back, anyway. Stupid show-off. "Mrs. Dimbleby has left quails on a baking tray ready to go into the oven."

Exactly what we might have expected! "Mrs. Dimbleby?" I repeated. "I assume she's your cook? And Mr. Dimbleby will be your gardener, I'm sure."

"She's our cook and housekeeper." Grayson was still smil-ing, but from the way he looked at me (one eyebrow slightly raised), I could tell that he'd registered my ironic undertone. Incidentally, he hadn't inherited Ernest's blue eyes. His were light brown, a striking contrast with his fair hair. "As far as I know, Mr. Dimbleby sells insurance. Dad does the gardening himself—he says it's relaxing." The eyebrow went a little farther up. "And I hear that you girls have a nanny. Is that right?"

"Well, we . . ." Bloody hell. Luckily Ernest interrupted us, with Mom clinging to his arm as if it were a life preserver. Just like yesterday he was beaming at us as if we were the best things he'd ever seen.

"Good, Grayson's already taken your coats. Welcome to the Casa Spencer. Come along through. Florence is waiting with the starters."

Neither Grayson nor Mia and I explained that we didn't have any coats with us. (How could we, when our fall and winter clothes were still in the moving company's crates somewhere?) Mom cast us a last warning glance before we followed her and Ernest in silence through a double door into the living and dining room. It was a pretty place, with wooden floorboards, windows down to floor level, an open hearth, white sofas with embroidered cushions, a piano, and a large dining table from which there was a lovely view of the garden. It looked spacious but not enormously large, and surprisingly . . . well, *comfortable*. I'd never in my life have thought of Ernest having such unstylish sofas, getting on in years a bit, with covers torn at the edges and brightly colored cushions that didn't match. There was even an amusing fur cushion in the shape of a ginger cat. The cushion stretched as we passed it.

"This is our cat, Spot." A girl had just glided past us to

put a plate down on the dining table. She had to be Grayson's twin sister; they had the same light-brown eyes. "And you must be Liv and Mia. Ann's told us so much about you. That's a lovely way you've done your hair." She seemed to smile as easily as her brother, but it looked better on her, because she had dimples in her cheeks, a snub nose that went with the dimples, and a pretty, freckled complexion. "I'm Florence, and I'm really pleased to meet you." She was small and delicately built, but with voluptuous breasts, and her face was framed by shining, chestnut-brown curls falling in ringlets to her shoulders. Mia and I could only gawp at her. She was simply stunning.

"What a pretty dress, Ann," she said to Mom in a voice as sweet as honey. "Blue suits you so well."

Suddenly I seemed to myself not just dry as a stick, long-nosed, and plain simplistic in the way my mind worked but also dreadfully immature. Mom was right: we were being downright bad mannered. We'd hit out with dark looks and said rude things just to punish her. Like naughty toddlers flinging themselves on the supermarket floor and throwing tantrums. Meanwhile Florence and Grayson showed no weak spots but were behaving like grown-ups. They didn't react to our rudeness. They were smiling, paying compliments, and carrying on a polite conversation. Maybe they really were glad that their father had met our mom. Or maybe they were just pretending to be glad. Whichever way it was, they were doing far better than we were.

Feeling ashamed of myself, I decided that from then on I'd be just as well brought up and polite. Although that, as it turned out, wasn't going to be so simple.

"There's only something small for a starter." When

everyone was sitting down, Florence smiled warmly at Mia and me from the other side of the table. "Mrs. Dimbleby bought far too many quails. I hope you like quails with celeriac purée."

Oh no—here we went. Celeriac. Eeugh! "That sounds . . . interesting," I said in as politely adult a tone as I could manage. *Interesting* was always a useful word.

"I'm afraid I'm a vegetarian," claimed Mia, proving cleverer than me, as she often did. "And I have this silly allergy to celeriac."

Also, you're stuffed full of Christmas cookies, I added silently.

"Oh dear, never mind. I'll make you a sandwich if you like." Florence smiled so radiantly, it positively hurt your eyes. "You're staying in the Finchleys' apartment, aren't you? Is Mrs. Finchley still collecting those charming china figurines?"

I wondered whether I could say "Yes, they're so interesting" again without sounding negative about it, but once again Mia had chipped in ahead of me. "No, these days she's collecting the most dreadfully vulgar-looking dancers."

I quickly looked down at the plate with my starter on it, so as not to giggle. What on earth *was* the stuff on it? I could identify the thin, red slices as some kind of meat, but what was the mushy pile beside it?

Grayson, who was sitting beside me, seemed to have read my mind. "Chutneys are Mrs. Dimbleby's specialty," he told me quietly. "This one is green-tomato chutney."

"Oh. Ah. Interesting." I put a lavish forkful into my mouth and nearly spat it all out again. For a moment I forgot my good intentions. "Are those *raisins* in it?" I asked Grayson incredulously. He didn't reply. He had taken his iPhone out of his jeans pocket and was looking at the display under the table. I'd have looked too, purely out of curiosity, but I had enough to do swallowing the weird chutney stuff. As well as raisins, it contained onions, garlic, curry power, ginger, and—yes, no doubt about it, that was cinnamon. And something that, when I bit it, felt like crunchy buttons of some kind. Mrs. Dimbleby had probably stirred in everything that needed to be used up. If that was her specialty, I hated to think what the thing she didn't cook so well would taste like.

Mia grinned at me maliciously as I washed the chutney down with a gulp of orange juice.

"But aren't the Finchleys coming back from South America next month, Dad?" asked Florence.

"Yes, they are. They'll be needing their apartment back from the first of October." Ernest glanced briefly at Mom and took a deep breath. "In fact, that's exactly what we wanted to discuss with all of you this evening."

The display of Grayson's iPhone flickered. When he noticed me looking curiously at it, he held his hand farther under the table, as if he was afraid I might read the message with him. I wasn't even particularly interested in his text message. I thought the tattoo on the inside of his wrist was far more intriguing. Black lettering, half hidden by the sleeve of his T-shirt.

"You're one of that blond boy group from school," I whispered. "That's why I thought you looked familiar."

"What?"

"We've met before. I saw you and your friends in school today."

"Really? I don't remember that."

Of course not. He hadn't so much as looked at me. "Never

mind. Pretty tattoo." *Sub um* . . . Unfortunately I couldn't make out the rest of it.

"What?" His eyes had been following my glance. "Oh, that. It's not a tattoo, only felt pen. Er . . . notes for Latin."

Yes, sure. "Interesting," I said. "Show me!"

But Grayson wasn't about to do any such thing. He pulled the sleeve of his T-shirt down over the "notes" and turned back to his iPhone.

That was *really* interesting. Without thinking, I put another forkful of chutney into my mouth. Bad mistake—it tasted even worse the second time. But at least I could now identify the crunchy buttons as walnuts.

"You see, it's like this. . . ." Ernest was looking solemn and had taken Mom's hand. Mom was smiling in a forced way at the pretty arrangement of blue hydrangeas in the middle of the dining table. No doubt about it—something serious was coming.

"Ann . . . your mother . . . well . . ." Ernest cleared his throat and began again. This time he wasn't stammering. Instead he sounded as if he were addressing the Economic and Social Committee of the European Court of Justice. "Ann and I have decided to take the fiasco over at the cottage as a sign from Fortuna to consolidate our relationship and dispense with the problem of who lives where by, so to speak . . . merging."

After this announcement there was silence for a good five seconds, after which I had a terrible coughing fit, because as I gasped for air, a raisin had gone down the wrong way. It was some time before I had dealt . . . no, sorry, *dispensed* with the coughing fit. My eyes were streaming, but I could clearly see that Florence, sitting opposite me, had stopped smiling. Even the sun had stopped shining in through the window, having disappeared behind the roof of the house next door. Grayson, to be sure, was still busy with his cell phone under the table. He was probably Googling the meaning of *consolidate*, although it was only too obvious.

"Lottie says you should always explain yourself as simply as possible so that people can understand you," commented Mia.

"Yes, what, exactly, are you saying, Dad?" Florence's voice was no longer sweet as honey. It sounded rather like the way the chutney tasted. "You mean that you and Ann are looking for a *shared* apartment? Now? At once? But you've only known each other for six months."

"So to speak . . . well, no, not really." Ernest was still smiling, but tiny beads of sweat were standing out on his bald patch. "After thinking it over at length . . . At our age, time is a precious . . ." He shook his head, obviously furious with himself for being so tongue-tied. "The house is large enough for us all," he said at last, firmly.

"And you two grew up here," said Mom to Grayson and Florence. The corners of her mouth were quivering slightly. "We didn't want to ask you to face moving house in your last year at school."

No, sure. Moving house wasn't good for the emotional balance of young people. Anyone could tell that from Mia and me. Mia made a funny sound, like Buttercup when you stepped on her paw by accident.

"We're supposed to move into *this* house?" she asked quietly. "And all of us live here together?"

Ernest and Mom, who were still holding hands, exchanged a brief glance.

"Yes," said Ernest firmly. Mom just nodded.

"But that's ridiculous!" Florence pushed her plate away. "This house is only just large enough for us—where do you think we can put three extra people?"

Four! I felt like saying. She'd forgotten Lottie. But I could only get out a kind of croak—there was still something lodged in my throat.

"This house is enormous, Florence," said Ernest. "It has six bedrooms. If we move around a bit, we'll all fit in perfectly well. I thought Grayson could have the gable room at the front of the house, you can have your old room back again, and then Mia and Liv can—"

"What?" Florence's voice wasn't far from being a screech now. "Those are *my* rooms up under the roof—I'm certainly not giving them up and sharing a bathroom with Grayson again. Grayson! Say something, why don't you?"

Grayson was looking confused. He hadn't even looked up from his iPhone. Imagine that, when the world was coming to an end up above the table! He certainly had strong nerves! "Er . . . yes," he said. "Why can't Florence stay on the top floor under the roof? There are plenty of rooms on the second floor."

"Grayson, have you been listening *at all?*" Florence stared at him, stunned. "They're planning to *move in here* next month! Tell them we don't have room for them! The gable room is Granny's room, my old room is Dad's office, the corner room is our guest room, and I've put all my winter clothes in the built-in cupboard in your room. . . ."

"Flo, darling, do please listen." The beads of sweat on Ernest's forehead seemed to have grown a little larger. "I can understand that you feel you won't have quite as much space to yourself, but—"

"But *what?*" spat Florence.

Even in all this upheaval, I couldn't help being grateful to her for having stopped being so grown-up and polite. I liked her a lot better with that hysterical voice and eyes flashing with fury. Mia and I were looking back and forth at her and Ernest as if they were playing tennis. Mom fixed her eyes firmly on the flower arrangement again, and Grayson was staring at his iPhone as if spellbound. Maybe he was Googling "patchwork family" and "first aid."

"—it wouldn't be forever," said Ernest. "Look, this time next year you twins will be moving out to study somewhere, then you'll be home during university vacations at the most, and—"

Florence interrupted him. "And so you won't be lonely you're bringing a woman and two substitute children into the house? Can't you wait until we've left?"

Yes, or even a few years longer.

Now it was Ernest's turn to sound chillier. "I realize that you have to get used to this new situation, as we all of us here do. But I have already made up my mind." He passed the back of his hand over his forehead. "We just have to move things around a little. If Grayson moves into the gable room—"

"Which belongs to Granny!" Florence was shouting in such a loud voice that the ginger cat jumped off the sofa and several feet into the air. He was quite a fat cat. "Have you told Granny about your plans? No, of course not! She's on a cruise on the other side of the world—very practical, isn't it?—and she doesn't know the first thing about all this!"

"Florence—"

"Where's she going to sleep when she comes to stay?"

"Don't be ridiculous. Your grandmother lives twenty minutes away—she doesn't need a room here at all. She can simply drive back to her own house after visiting us. But if you like, you can have the gable room, Grayson can just stay in his old room, Mia can have the corner room, and I'll clear the study out for Liv." Ernest smiled at Mom. "I work much too hard anyway. I'll avoid doing that at home in the future."

Hesitantly, Mom returned his smile.

"Wait a moment—if Liv and Mia are going to be on the second floor too, then who gets my rooms in the attic?" Florence looked penetratingly at Mom. "You, by any chance?"

"No," said Mom, sounding scared. "I don't need much space. Honestly, as far as that goes, I can manage with very little. All I have is a few crates of books. No, your father thought the rooms up there would be just right for Lottie."

At this Florence went right off her rocker. "The *nanny*?" she cried shrilly, digging her forefinger into the air so hard that she almost poked Mia's forehead. "These two are far too old for a nanny . . . and I'm supposed to give up my attic rooms to her and share a bathroom with three other people? Honestly, this is the end!"

"Lottie is much more than a nanny. She also does almost all the housework, the shopping, and the cooking," said Ernest. "And as . . . well . . . a very important emotional factor, she cannot, at the moment, be excluded from these considerations."

"Meaning what?"

"Meaning that we need Lottie," I said quietly.

"Not forever, of course," Mom made haste to say. "You are quite right, Florence. Mia and Liv are indeed much too old for a nanny. Maybe Lottie will stay another year, maybe only six months. . . ." She saw Mia's lower lip beginning to tremble and added, "We'll just have to see how much longer we need her."

I reached for Mia's hand under the table and squeezed it. *Don't cry*, I begged her silently. Because I was afraid that if Mia started crying, I'd have to join in too.

"And how about Mrs. Dimbleby?"

"Mrs. Dimbleby has been wanting to work shorter hours for years," said Ernest. "She'll be glad if she's needed here for only one or two days a week."

"Grayson! Did you hear that?" cried Florence.

Grayson raised his head. He actually was still busy with his iPhone. "Yes, of course," he said.

But Florence didn't seem to believe him. Once again, at high volume, she summed up the evening's revelations for her own benefit. "Dad doesn't just want Ann and her children to move in here, all of us to clear out of our rooms, *and share a bathroom between four of us*"—at this point her voice rose to such a pitch that I felt as if the windowpanes were beginning to rattle—"he also wants to fire Mrs. Dimbleby and give her job to Ann's nanny instead! And the nanny is getting my rooms up in the attic."

"Oh," said Grayson. "That's not a great idea. We'd have to go through her bedroom to get to our billiard table in the attic."

Florence groaned. "Don't you understand what Dad just said? They'll be moving in here in three weeks' time. . . ."

"Two weeks' time, to be precise. I'm taking a day off work for it," said Ernest. "And there are some painting jobs to be done first."

"They'll be moving in here, bag, baggage, and nanny!"

"And dog," added Mia.

"And dog," repeated Florence. She seemed to have exhausted her strength; she wasn't shouting anymore. The word *dog* came out as hardly more than a whisper. But as if on cue, the ginger cat arched his back in front of the dining table and mewed out loud. Florence's shouting seemed to have attracted him rather than putting him off.

Ernest smiled. A little wearily, maybe, but it was definitely a smile. "That's all clear, then. So now we can fetch the quails in from the kitchen, can't we, Spot? Will you lend me a hand, Ann?"

Mom stood up with such alacrity that she almost brought the tablecloth with her. "Nothing I'd rather do," she said.

The cat followed them into the kitchen.

GRAYSON, FLORENCE, MIA, AND I stayed behind in the dining room in silence. I guess you'd feel rather like being quiet if an avalanche had just rolled over you. I'd worked it out that Ernest and Mom would be moving in together, but even I had been surprised to realize they were planning to do it so soon. They must have been really sure they were right for each other.

Grayson's cell phone vibrated in the silence.

"Only too clear, all of it," said Florence bitterly after a minute. "Oh, and thanks a million for your support, Grayson."

"'Scuse me." Grayson was staring at his display. "But this is all decided anyway, right? And weren't you saying yesterday how happy you are for Dad?"

"Well, I am. But no one could have guessed they'd want to move in together right away. I mean, they hardly know each other. She's an *American*. She could be after Dad for his money or I don't know what, or she could be a psychopath, or . . ."

". . . or hopelessly disorganized, or a kleptomaniac, a Republican, a Jehovah's Witness, or anything," I suggested.

"That isn't funny," said Florence.

"Do you have anything against Jehovah's Witnesses?" asked Mia, all pretended innocence.

Grayson pushed his chair back and stood up, his eyes still fixed on his cell phone. He obviously hadn't taken in a word anyone was saying. "I'm just going out to clear something up. Tell Dad I'll be right back. And I'd like at least three quails. I'm ravenous."

"You're . . ." Florence watched his retreating form indignantly. "Don't you notice anything?"

I cleared my throat. "I need to go to the toilet. Where, exactly . . . ?"

"Well, seeing you're going to be at home here any moment now, you ought to be able to find the way yourself," said Florence sharply.

"You're right," I said. It couldn't be all that difficult. I followed Grayson out into the corridor.

"Do tell me, is your dad an internationally wanted terrorist or a serial murderer?" Mia was asking behind me in her sweetest voice.

I didn't hear what Florence replied to that.

The first door I opened was a broom cupboard, but the second, right beside the way to the stairs, was the guest toilet. I looked for the light switch.

"Not tonight, for heaven's sake. I already told you." The window stood ajar, and I could hear Grayson's voice. He was obviously outside the house, talking on his cell phone. I didn't switch the light on but went over to the window so that I could hear him better.

"Yes, I know it's the new moon tonight, but can't we put the whole thing off until tomorrow evening for once? There's all hell let loose here, and I don't know whether I'll be able to sleep at all tonight. . . . Yup, I do realize that we can't put off the new moon just because of me, but . . . No, of course that's not what I want. Okay, if you say so, Henry, I'll try to . . . I hope I can find it. I suppose it was your idea, was it? I thought so. . . . No, I'll tell you tomorrow. If I don't go back indoors this minute, my sister will murder me. . . . Yes, thanks for your sympathy. See you later."

Hmm. *Interesting.* I sat on the toilet lid in the dark and entirely forgot what I was really there for. Contrary to all common sense, I felt a delicious sense of anticipation inside me. What had taken Grayson's mind off our very own family tragedy so much this evening? What kind of transaction could take place only when the moon was new? And what did those words in Latin on Grayson's wrist mean? It was clear as day that my future stepbrother had a secret—and I just *loved* secrets.

I got back to the dining room in an inappropriately cheerful mood, just ahead of Grayson. And just before the Jehovah's Witness and the serial murderer, in an atmosphere of family harmony, brought in the quails.

The rest of the evening went comparatively undramatically. At least, until the moment when I knocked over my glass with such a sweeping movement that my shirt was drenched with orange juice from the collar to the hem. As Ernest had only just refilled the glass, adding ice cubes as well, my teeth immediately began to chatter.

"I've been waiting for that all evening!" said Mom in her

I-can-be-witty-too voice. "Knocking over glasses is one of my girls' specialties."

"Oh, Mom! Last time that happened to me, I was seven years old! Ew, what's that?" There was an ice cube melting inside my bra. (If I'd listened to Lottie's advice and done up the two top buttons of my blouse, that wouldn't have happened.) I quickly fished it out and put it on my plate, never mind whether that was the polite thing to do or not. Judging by the way Florence and Grayson were looking at me, it wasn't.

"Exactly," said Mia. "If it's anyone's specialty, it's mine."

"Cola! All over my computer keyboard," Mom remembered. "And black currant juice on pure-white tablecloths. And assorted smoothies, usually spilled on carpets."

I dared not wring out the blouse, or I'd have drenched the Persian rug. It looked expensive.

Ernest looked at me sympathetically. "Florence, be a good girl and get one of your tops for Liv. She's freezing. She can't go home like that."

"I get the idea!" Florence crossed her arms. "First I have to give them my rooms, now it's my clothes, right?"

You had to hand it to Florence for staying there at all until then. After all that drama, she could have marched out of the dining room, slamming the door behind her, to fling herself on her bed in floods of tears. At least, that's what I'd have done in her place. However, up to this point she'd been nibbling a quail peacefully, and she'd even taken part in the conversation, if not at any length. Or maybe she'd simply been afraid of leaving her dad alone with Mom. Ernest and Mom themselves had been doing their level best to pretend they'd forgotten all about the last hour. They'd talked about anything and everything except the changes that were going to take place. And I'd been concentrating on Grayson's sleeve, hoping it would ride up again and show those mysterious words. But although Grayson had consumed no fewer than four poor little mini-birds in a pretty brutal way, eating them with his hands (every time a bone cracked, Mia jumped—I think she was on the point of becoming a vegetarian for real), his wrist had been covered the whole time.

"Florence!" said Ernest reproachfully.

"Dad!" replied Florence in exactly the same tone of voice.

"It's okay," I said. "It will dry again." *By the day after tomorrow or thereabouts.*

"Nonsense. You're wet through. Florence will now go upstairs and find you a sweater."

"Florence has no intention of doing any such thing," said Florence, looking him in the eye.

"*Florence Cecilia Elizabeth Spencer!*"

"What are you going to do about it, Dad? Send me to bed without any dessert?"

"It's okay." Grayson put down the quail leg he'd just been gnawing and stood up. "She can have one of my sweaters."

"Wow, how chivalrous," said Florence.

"There's really no need," I said, my teeth still chattering, but Grayson was already out of the room.

"He has this terrible urge to keep everything on an even keel and avoid conflict," said Florence, to no one in particular.

"I like your middle names." Mia was looking at Florence, wide-eyed. "You're really lucky, you know? Mom gave Liv and me the names of her favorite aunts as middle names. Well, she forced them on us. *Gertrude* and *Virginia*."

For a split second Florence's face cleared.

"My aunts are named after Gertrude Stein and Virginia Woolf," said Mom. "Two great women writers."

"With shitty names," added Mia.

Mom sighed. "I think it's about time we left. It's been a wonderfu—" She stopped short and cleared her throat. That seemed to be overdoing it, even to Mom herself. "Thank you for the delicious meal, Ernest."

"Yes, thanks a lot," said Mia. "Now we'll appreciate Lottie's cooking more than ever."

I could have sworn that the corners of Ernest's mouth twitched as he stood up and gave Mom his hand. "Mrs. Dimbleby did make a dessert, but I'll quite understand if you'd rather get home. It's later than I expected, and the children have school tomorrow. I'll call you a taxi. It'll be here in a couple of minutes."

"Here." Grayson was back. "Freshly washed." He handed me a gray hooded sweater, and while Ernest was phoning for a taxi, I went into the guest toilet and changed out of my blouse. The sweater did smell of soap, but also a bit of crisply broiled quails. Delicious, really.

When I came out again, everyone else was standing in the corridor waiting for me. Everyone but Florence, who was nowhere to be seen. She was probably already packing her things.

Grayson grinned at me wearily. "Really suits you. At least six sizes too large."

"I like oversize," I said, crumpling up my blouse in my

hands. "Thanks. I'll give it back to you when . . . well, sometime."

He sighed. "Looks like we'll be seeing each other quite often."

"I guess there'll be no avoiding it." Oops. I hoped that hadn't sounded full of happy anticipation. I cast a last glance at his wrist, but too bad: the mysterious words were still hidden by his sleeve.

THIS TIME MOM abandoned Hansel and Gretel (otherwise known as Mia and me) not in the forest, as I dreamed our first night in London, but in the corridor of Ernest's house before she disappeared through a doorway with the words "It's for your own good."

"Did you hear that?" Mia asked. "There are quails cackling somewhere around here."

"Right you are!" The door of the broom cupboard opened, creaking, and out came . . . Lottie. She was waving a hatchet about. "I could do with a bit of help. Someone has to stretch their necks out so that I can slaughter them."

"And if you don't do it right, *Nanny*, Dad will throw you out and get Mrs. Dimbleby back." Florence was skating gracefully along the corridor in a glittery black tutu. She performed a pirouette in front of the coat and hat stand, and gave us a nice smile. "Looking for the gingerbread house, were you? The witch will be so pleased to see you. Grayson, show these two the way, will you?"

Grayson, who was leaning on the wall beside the coat

stand, looked up from his iPhone for a moment and pointed to the door behind which Mom had disappeared. Its handle was a gigantic vanilla crescent. "Along there, mousies," he said, and Mia set off at once.

I wanted to call "Don't be so stupid, Hansel!" after her, but something seemed to be sticking in my throat, and before I knew it, Mia had taken hold of the vanilla crescent, whereupon a claw appeared out of nowhere, then grabbed her by her collar, and she disappeared.

"And now I have to share my bathroom with only one little quail," said Florence, laughing. "Be a good little girl, Liv. Just follow your sister."

"No, don't," whispered Lottie behind me. "It's only the first of September, far too soon for Christmas baking." She pointed to a door beside the broom cupboard. It was painted green. "You'll be safe in there."

"Don't you dare!" screeched Florence. She skated straight toward me. I flung myself on the green door, tore it open, and slipped through, and it latched behind me a tenth of a second before Florence began thundering on it from the other side. Only at that moment did I realize that it was all just a dream, and a silly dream at that. (Besides being easy to interpret, except maybe for the skates. What was my unconscious mind trying to tell me about those skates?) All the same, my heart was still thudding rather fast with agitation.

Hesitantly, I looked around me. I was in another corridor, one that seemed to go on forever, with countless doors to the right and left. The door I'd come through was painted deep green and had dark, old-fashioned metal fittings, a letter box in the same material, and a pretty brass doorknob in the shape of a lizard. I decided to go back, because now that

I knew I was only dreaming, I wasn't afraid of Florence anymore. I felt extremely keen to show her how good I was at kung fu. In a dream, of course, I'd be even better at it than in reality. But just as I was turning the lizard knob, I caught sight of a movement in the corner of my eye. Another door, next to this one, had opened, and someone had come out into the corridor. It was Grayson. Although he was only a few feet away, he didn't seem to have noticed me. He carefully closed the door behind him and muttered something that I couldn't make out. Then he took a deep breath, opened the door once more, and disappeared again. I let go of my door in order to take a closer look at Grayson's. It was just like the white-painted front door to the Spencers' house, including the steps outside and the heavyweight stone statue that was half eagle, half lion. When I came closer, the statue blinked its eyes, raised one clawed foot, and said in a surprisingly squeaky, high voice, "No one can come in unless they say my name three times backward."

Aha, a riddle. I loved riddles. Although this one could have been a little harder to crack. "You're Frightful Freddy," I said.

The statue lowered its beak majestically. "Just Freddy, if you don't mind."

"Oh, but that's too simple," I said, disappointed, and almost annoyed by the failure of my dream mind to think up anything better. "Ydderf, Ydderf, Ydderf."

"That's right," squeaked Freddy. "You can come in."

"Okay." I pushed the door open. When I stepped through the doorway, I wasn't in the front hall of the Spencers' house, as I'd expected, but in a meadow. Although it was night, and quite dark, I could make out trees and rocks sticking up above the ground. A little way ahead of me, Grayson was sweeping the beam of his flashlight over the ground.

This version of the dream was definitely cooler than my Hansel and Gretel variation just now.

"Is this a *cemetery*?" I asked.

Grayson swung around, shone the flashlight on my face, and let out a small sound of alarm.

I smiled at him.

"What the hell are you doing here?" He rubbed his forehead with his free hand. "Go away again, would you?"

"Yes, it *is* a cemetery," I said, answering my own question. Because a little way off I could see the outlines of assorted stone crosses, columns, and statues. My power of vision was sensational in this dream, and improving by the second. "We're in Highgate Cemetery, aren't we?"

Grayson ignored me. He lowered the beam of the flashlight to a gravestone on the ground.

"How cool. I know it only from photos, but I've always thought I'd just love to see it," I said. "Except not by night."

Grayson grunted in annoyance. "Me neither. This is a totally crazy meeting place," he said, although more to himself than me. "As if the whole thing wasn't weird enough anyway. What's more, no one can see more than a meter ahead."

"I can." I had to stop myself jumping up and down in my enthusiasm. "I can see in the dark like a cat. Only in this dream, I'll admit, but it's great. In the normal way I'm blind as a bat without my glasses or contact lenses. So what are we looking for?"

"*We* are not looking for anything." Grayson sounded distinctly annoyed. He was shining his flashlight on the inscriptions on the gravestones beside the path, whether they were vertical or lying flat. They seemed to be ancient. Many of them were cracked or covered with ivy. Mist drifted, true to form, over the ground, and the wind made the leaves of the trees rustle. There were sure to be rats here too. And spiders. "*I* am looking for the tomb of Christina Rossetti," he added.

"Girlfriend of yours?"

Grayson snorted, but at least he answered this time. He sounded resigned, as if he'd decided to make the best of my presence. "Christina Rossetti was a Victorian woman poet. Haven't you ever had to analyze one of her poems? *Where sunless rivers weep their waves into the deep* . . . blah, blah, blah, something about a star and shadows and a nightingale."

"*She sleeps a charmed sleep: Awake her not.*" A figure emerged from the shadows of a weeping willow and came toward us, declaiming poetry. It was the boy who'd jumped for the grapefruit in school today, only I'd been quicker off the mark and caught it first—the character with tousled hair from our flight. Nice of him to turn up in this dream, because in the meantime I'd entirely forgotten him. "*Led by a single star, she came from very far to seek where shadows are her pleasant lot.*"

Hmm, not bad—so at least in dreams there were boys who could recite poetry.

"Henry," said Grayson, addressing the newcomer with relief.

"Where on earth have you been? The Rossetti grave is back there." Henry pointed to somewhere behind him. "I told you to take your bearings by the creepy angel with a cowl on."

"They all look creepy in the dark." Grayson and the new

arrival performed a kind of kindergarten finger game by way of saying hello, a mixture of high fives, hooking their fingers together. Sweet. "Thank God you're here, or I'd have been wandering around the place forever."

"That's what I thought. Jasper didn't find it either. Arthur's looking for him. Who's that with you?" Henry's eyes didn't seem to see as well in the dark as mine, because he hadn't recognized me. But now he groaned out loud. "Oh no, why do I have to go dreaming of the cheese girl? Just now I met my cat Plum, who was run over when I was twelve. He rubbed around my legs purring."

"Oh, how cute," I said.

"Not cute at all. He looked just the way he was when I last saw him: all-over blood and with his guts coming out. . . ." Henry shook himself. "Compared with that, you're a positively welcome sight. All the same, go away, will you? I really don't know what you're doing here. Get out!" He waved one hand as if shooing an annoying fly away. "I said *get out*, cheese girl!" When I didn't move, he seemed to be annoyed. "Why doesn't she disappear?"

"Could be because I don't answer to the name of *cheese girl*, idiot," I told him.

Grayson cleared his throat. "I'm afraid she . . . er . . . came here with me, Henry." Judging by his tone of voice, he seemed to find this somehow embarrassing.

"You know my cheese girl?"

"Looks like it." Grayson rubbed his forehead with the back of his hand again. "She's my new little sister. I only found that out this evening."

"Oh, shit!" Henry looked dismayed. "You mean . . . ?"

Grayson nodded. "I told you all hell was let loose at home.

Talk about a super dinner party. Florence did her nut when Dad told us his professor, her two daughters, their nanny, and their dachshund were going to move in with us. In two weeks' time."

"Buttercup is not a dachshund," I said indignantly. "Or at least only about a tenth of her is."

Neither of them paid me any attention at all. "Hey, I'm really sorry about that." Henry had put an arm sympathetically around Grayson's shoulders. They were going back the way Henry had come from, walking side by side down an overgrown gravel path, and I was scurrying along in their wake.

"Then your dad is really serious. No wonder you dream of her." Henry turned around to me. "Although you really could have done worse. She's kind of sweet, don't you think?"

Grayson turned his own head. "And she's still following us."

"Yes. Only, she feels it's a little bit creepy here," I said. "And what's more, I'd like to know what you two are up to."

"You'll have to send her away," Henry told Grayson. "Very firmly! It worked for me with Plum just now. He dissolved into crinkly drifts of smoke. Or of course you could turn her into a gravestone or a tree, but telling her to go away ought to be enough for a start."

"Okay." Grayson had stopped and was waiting for me to catch up. As he did so, he sighed deeply. "What are we really doing here, Henry? This is all *crazy*."

"I know."

Grayson looked around. Then he whispered, "Aren't you frightened?"

"Yes, I am," said Henry seriously. "But I'm even more afraid of what will happen if we *don't* bring it off."

"This is a nightmare," said Grayson, and Henry nodded.

"No need to exaggerate, boys," I said. "You're going for a nice nocturnal walk in a famous cemetery, and what's more, I'm with you—other people might enjoy a dream like this."

Grayson groaned. "You're still there."

"Just send her away," said Henry. "Concentrate on making her disappear."

"Right." Grayson looked firmly into my eyes. This was only a dream, so I looked equally firmly into his. I wouldn't have dared to stare at him so hard earlier at supper, and I'd been concentrating more on his wrist, anyway. But now I had to admit that my future stepbrother was very good looking, in spite of his family likeness to Ernest and Florence. Everything soft and round about Florence was hard and angular in her brother, particularly his chin. Best of all were his eyes, which were caramel colored in the dim light here. Grayson's glance blurred slightly and wandered slowly from my eyes to my lips.

Aha! Lovely dream. Really lovely dream. I just hoped Lottie didn't turn up with her hatchet at this point.

Henry cleared his throat. "Grayson?"

"Er . . . yes." Was that a touch of pink on Grayson's cheeks? He shook his head. "Please, Liv, be a good girl and go away."

"Not unless you tell me what's written on your wrist," I said, to cover up for my own embarrassment. "*Sub um . . .* and how does it go on?"

"What?"

"*Sub umbra floreo,*" Henry replied, stepping in for Grayson.

"You have to be firmer about it, Grayson, and you really have to want her to disappear."

"But I do!" Grayson assured him. "Only, she's kind of so . . ."

"I know what you mean," said Henry. Then he stopped short. "Is that by any chance your sweater she's wearing?"

Dismayed, I looked down at myself. Sure enough, I really was wearing Grayson's hooded sweater. Over my nightie. I'd felt so cold when I went to bed that I'd put it on again. Apart from that and my nightie, all I had on were my fluffy gray polka-dot socks. Typical of my dreams: I was never properly dressed for the occasion.

Grayson groaned. "Yes, it could well be my sweater," he admitted. "Oh God, how I hate my unconscious mind. Why does it do these things to me?"

"Oh, come on, it could be a whole lot more embarrassing. Think of poor old Jasper and Mrs. Beckett in her bikini." Henry laughed. "Hurry up. Jasper and Arthur will be waiting for us. That's if Jasper made it here at all."

"I hope he didn't," muttered Grayson. "Then at least we'd have a reprieve until the next new moon. . . ."

"*Sub umbra floreo*—what's that supposed to mean?" I asked. " 'Planted under the flowers?' "

Henry chuckled.

"Look, I only studied Latin for six months," I said, slightly wounded, "and that was ages ago, so I don't remember a lot about it."

"We noticed," said Henry.

Annoyed, Grayson shook his head. "This is too much. Go away, Liv!" he said firmly. "Get out of here! Clear off! *Er . . .* begone!"

Henry looked at me with interest. He was probably expecting me to dissolve into smoke.

"Okay," I said, when nothing of the sort happened and Grayson's face assumed an expression of despair. "If you don't want me hanging around, I will clear off. Have fun." I turned and marched along the gravel path. Glancing back over my shoulder, I saw that Grayson and Henry watched me for a couple more seconds, and then they went on in the opposite direction. As soon as they did that, I took two steps sideways and got into cover behind a large tree trunk. Did they think they could shake me off as easily as that? Oh no, not now. Just when the dream was getting really interesting.

THIS WAS FUN! While I was stalking Grayson and Henry, I felt like Catwoman. Or James Bond. Or a cross between the two of them. Coolest of all were my improved powers of vision. There wasn't a streetlight switched on anywhere, and even the moon wasn't shining in the sky, but I could still see everything. I could avoid overhanging branches and stones lying on the path. The soles of my fluffy socks meant I was walking so quietly that I could get really close to the two of them, keeping an eye open all the time for the nearest hiding place. I was just surprised that I hadn't woken up yet. Normally the phase of a dream when I knew for certain I was dreaming never lasted long, particularly not when it was as entertaining a dream as this one.

"There you two are!" The beam of Grayson's flashlight had found two more figures: Arthur and Jasper, I assumed. With a judo roll worthy of the movies, I hid behind a gravestone, just in case they, too, had developed catlike powers of vision. I cautiously raised my head so that I could peer over the top edge of the gravestone. Like I said, I was having fun.

"You'll never believe it, but Jasper was standing right outside the gate and couldn't get in." That was Arthur, if my guess was right.

"It was locked." The rather fretful voice of Shaving Fun Ken, who, to my delight, was wearing plaid flannel pajamas. At least I wasn't the only one unsuitably dressed. I'd also seen the other boy, Arthur, in school that morning. He was the one with the blond curls who looked like an angel. Positively uncannily beautiful.

"I was going to climb the wall, but a night watchman with a dog came along, and there was barbed wire. . . ."

"This is a dream, Jasper!" said Henry impatiently. "You don't have to come in through the gate. And you don't have to be afraid of night watchmen, because everything you see while you're alone is only a figment of your own imagination. How often do I have to explain that to you?" He looked around, and I quickly ducked my head. "I hope your night watchman won't bother us here. We've just had to shake off other . . . er . . . distractions."

I supposed that meant me. What a cheek!

"Don't worry. We dealt with the man and his dog," said Arthur.

"Yes, it was cool," said Jasper. "Arthur made a fireball appear out of nowhere and—"

"We'd better hurry," Henry interrupted. "We've already lost too much time, and for all we know Jasper will wake up again before we have our answer."

"Not this time," said Jasper, with some pride in his voice. "I took one of my mother's migraine tablets. They always knock her out flat for two days."

"All the same, let's start," said Grayson. "The fact is, I'm not sure whether I closed my bedroom door properly, and around three in the morning Spot is always scratching at the carpet like mad, wanting to go out . . . Did you see that?" He pointed into the mist. "What was it?"

"Only the wind," said Henry. A gust of wind had indeed set the branches of the trees moving, but for a moment I felt as if I'd seen a scurrying figure in the drifting mist.

"I only thought . . ." Grayson stared into the darkness.

"There's enough room here." Arthur had gone a few steps farther, into the shade of an old cedar tree. The others followed him. Suddenly their mood seemed to be rather apprehensive. I was all agog, biting my lower lip. What was going to happen now? I very much hoped there wouldn't be any skeletons or half-putrefied zombies in this dream, because that sort of thing always terrified me in movies. On the other hand, we were in a cemetery, so I supposed it was only to be expected. For a moment I wondered whether my dream was straying too far into the realm of cliché, but never mind. Just as long as it went on being exciting. (But if possible without any spiders.)

"Five have broken the seal, five have sworn the oath, and five will open the gate, as it is written. We have come, as on every night of the new moon, to renew our solemn oath." Arthur had picked up a stick and was drawing something on the ground with it as he walked around in a wide circle. Where the end of the stick touched the ground, the grass went up in flames.

I was impressed.

The others stood around the fire. Then, in an unctuous voice, Arthur intoned a kind of singsong. From behind my gravestone, unfortunately, I could catch only fragments of it because the flames were crackling so loudly: ". . . *custos opacum* . . . know that we have aroused your anger . . . you rightly have doubts of us . . . swear that Anabel is sorry for what happened . . . she is suffering . . . do everything in our power to fulfill our oath . . . do not punish her any more . . ."

"Or us, either," said Jasper. "We can't help it. . . ." He fell silent when he noticed the disapproving faces of the others.

"Come and speak to us," Arthur went on, and the flames burned higher. "*Foedus sanguinis* . . . *interlunium* . . . you who have a thousand names and are at home in the night . . . we need . . ." The rest of it was lost in the crackling.

What did they need? Who was Anabel, and what was she sorry for? And what oath were they going to fulfill? I was almost bursting with curiosity, but I dared not get any closer in case they discovered me. Particularly as Henry was looking straight in my direction. The flames reflected in his eyes looked really scary. No, I couldn't steal any closer to them. Not unless I really was a cat . . . Just a moment! This was a dream, after all. I could be anything I liked, even a cat. I'd often turned into an animal in a dream. (Not always of my own free will. I shuddered to remember the dream when I'd been a mouse and Lottie had chased me with a broom.)

"*Custos opacum* . . . we humbly ask you to show us who is to fill the empty place . . . *non es aliquid absconditum* . . . please . . ."

I narrowed my eyes and thought as hard as I could of the barn owl I had once been allowed to hold in a wildlife park in Germany. Owls could see at night even better than cats, and above all they could fly without a sound. When I opened my eyes again, I found myself at an airy height several yards above the ground, with my claws around a branch of the cedar tree.

This was a great dream! It had missed the part where I'd have had to learn to fly and taken me straight to the right place, at the perfect observation post. I squinted past my beak and down to the ground. The four boys were standing just below me, and now I could also see what Arthur had been drawing on the ground: a large, five-pointed star, a pentagram with a circle around it. The grass was still burning half a yard high in some places; in others the flames were already going out.

"We have come together on this night of the new moon, O Lord of Shadows and Darkness, so that you can tell us the name of her who is to complete our circle again, so that we can keep our part of the pact," cried Arthur.

O Lord of Shadows and Darkness—well, now it all sounded somehow more menacing and less ridiculous. But I was glad that he was speaking English and not Latin. It meant that at least I could understand him. I couldn't wait to see whether the Lord of Shadows and Darkness was going to turn up now in person.

At first the flames only burned higher, and then the earth rose up in the middle of the pentagram and, with a dull growl, something pushed up out of the ground. Okay, so now it was getting *really* creepy. My cedar tree was shaking. Terrified that some kind of zombie was going to crawl out of the ground (you could bet that the Lord of Shadows and Darkness didn't look cute), I instinctively closed my eyes and wound my arms around a branch. I was entirely forgetting that I was an owl and didn't have any arms. A stupid mistake. When I opened my eyes again, I no longer had claws and feathers, and I was crouching rather awkwardly in human form in the branches of the cedar, complete with nightie, hooded sweater, polka-dot socks, and the certainty that my weight was far too much for the thin branches. They cracked, giving way under me, and although I reached for anything that came my way as I fell, I dropped like a stone into the middle of the pentagram and right onto what had come up from the ground. It wasn't a zombie, only a polished stone slab about the size of a kitchen table.

By all the laws of nature known to me, I ought to have broken every bone in my body when I hit the stone slab, but luckily the laws of nature didn't seem to apply in this dream. A few cedar needles trickled down onto my head, and a cone landed in my lap, but I hadn't suffered any harm at all.

I could move without any pain and look at the totally astonished faces of the boys around me as they looked at me, wide-eyed.

All the same, it was rather embarrassing and kind of beneath my dignity. I didn't feel a bit like Catwoman now, which was not a good way for my dream to turn out. Far from it. I quickly closed my eyes, hoping that I could simply turn back into an owl and fly away. Unfortunately I couldn't manage to concentrate on owlishness—no wonder, with everyone staring at me like that. In frustration, I pulled the cedar needles out of the sweater and tugged my nightie down over my knees.

The four boys were still looking horrified. Henry and Grayson maybe a little less so than the other two.

"I was a barn owl a moment ago, honest," I assured them.

Shaving Fun Ken put out his hand and briefly touched my arm.

"I . . . I don't understand this," he said. "What does it mean? I thought he'd give us a name and not throw a whole girl on the altar just like that. . . ."

"Who are you?" asked Arthur. At close quarters, and in this light, he looked more than ever like an angel come to life. An eerie angel.

A sudden gust of wind rustled the leaves of the trees standing around and blew Arthur's fair curls out of his face. "Tell me your name or . . . *abeas in malam crucem!*"

Or . . . what? *Disappear in a bad cross?* What a shame I'd spent so little time learning Latin. Stupidly, I'd thought no one ever needed it. For a moment I was tempted to answer in an equally unctuous tone (and neatly show off by slipping in the only Latin saying that I knew), something along the lines of "I, O unworthy one, am the cousin of the Lord of Shadows and Darkness, and *in dubio pro reo*," but unfortunately Grayson and Henry knew who I really was.

Jasper seemed to remember me, too.

"That . . . that's the missionary's daughter who was being shown around school today by Pandora Porter-Peregrin's little sister!" he said, sounding quite agitated. "Don't you recognize her, Henry? Imagine her with heavy black-framed glasses and a ponytail. . . ."

Henry said nothing. Grayson sighed. The wind blew through the branches of the cedar tree, bringing more cedar needles and cones down on me. Lightning flashed on the horizon, and for a split second I had the feeling, once again, that I could make out a figure in the mist.

"You mean this girl really exists?" asked Arthur. "And she goes to our school? Are you sure?"

"Yes," said Jasper firmly. "She's new. The funny thing is

that when I heard she's a missionary's daughter, it made me think at once she must still be a virgin. Is that right, Henry? You were talking to her as well. Don't you recognize her?"

Henry still said nothing. He and Grayson were looking at each other as if they were having a silent conversation. Lightning flashed across the sky once again.

"That's a sign," said Arthur. "She could be the Chosen One! Anyone know her name?"

Thunder rolled in the distance.

"The Chosen One," I repeated, injecting as much contempt as possible into my voice. "Oh, very original. Although I have to admit that this trick with the stone slab was very . . . By the way, who pushed it up out of the ground?" I slid off the slab of granite, because I got the impression that Arthur was staring under my nightie. In fact, I felt as if they were all coming rather too close to me. The fitful flames bathed their faces from below in orange light and sent shadows dancing over their skin.

Yet another flash of lightning. And another crash of thunder, closer this time.

"We can easily find out her name tomorrow—Pandora's little sister will be thrilled if I ask her." Jasper laughed in a self-satisfied way. "She's always practically fainting away with delight if I even look at her."

Grayson muttered something, but so quietly that it was swallowed up by Jasper's laughter, the rustling of the leaves, and the crackling of the flames.

Meanwhile, Arthur was solemnly holding his stick aloft. "We understand, Commander of the Night. We thank you for your answer. And we will not disappoint you again."

"I'm sorry, Arthur, but she is definitely not . . . er . . . ," said Grayson, rather louder than before. He rubbed his forehead, and by now I knew him well enough to realize that he always did that when he felt embarrassed. "It's all my fault that she's here. Her name is Liv, and she is my father's girlfriend's daughter. And obviously . . ." He paused for a moment, shooting me a nasty look. "Obviously I can't stop thinking about her. I'm sorry I wrecked our ritual."

Arthur did not reply to that. He lowered his stick, put out his hand, and reached for a strand of my hair, then let it slide slowly along his fingers. I flinched away.

"You really mean it?" asked Jasper. "Your dad's girlfriend is a missionary?"

Grayson sighed again.

Henry was looking at me thoughtfully. "It really is a strange coincidence that she fell into the middle of our circle during the ritual, Grayson," he said quietly as another flash of lightning lit up the sky.

"Sorry," said Grayson, with a remorseful shrug of his shoulders. "Maybe we ought to just start all over again."

"No need to apologize." Arthur ran his thumb over the strand of my hair that he was holding. Normally I'd have rapped his knuckles, but for some reason I couldn't move. This dream had clearly gone out of control. Any moment now, I realized, it would change into a nightmare. And I didn't like that idea a bit.

"I don't believe in coincidences," said Arthur.

"Nor do I. Not since . . ." Jasper's self-satisfied look had gone away. He looked anxious now instead. "Not since, well, you know what happened," he finished quietly. "If you know her well, Grayson, all the better. Then it will be easier for us—"

A mighty crash of thunder yet again. That did it. I had to do something before all this mystic playacting in the cemetery finally became a nightmare and my cousin the Lord of Shadows and Darkness emerged from the mist and struck me down with Lottie's hatchet.

"Take your paws off me, Gandalf," I said firmly, snatching my hair away from Arthur's fingers. "All this stuff is extremely interesting, but now I really have to go. I'm not supposed to be out in a thunderstorm." I meant that to sound casual, but sad to say, it didn't. Even Jasper, dim as he was, had to realize that I was frightened.

Only then did I notice how tall they all were. Over six feet, every one of them, and as I watched them they seemed to be growing taller every second.

Lightning bathed the cemetery in glaring light. I swallowed. The outer flames of the pentagram were flaring up again, and out of the corner of my eye it looked as if the drifting mists in the dark were growing arms and legs. . . .

"I'm warning you, I can do kung fu," I said. An even mightier roll of thunder followed my words, the ground shook again, and I lost my balance and fell over.

"Ouch," I said out loud, rubbing my hip bones. My feline powers of vision were gone in an instant. I'd landed on a hard marble floor. Somewhere to the left, I saw a small, formless something in the dim light. I groped for it and held it before my eyes. It was one of Mrs. Finchley's stupid, grinning ballerinas. I had pushed it under my bed so that I didn't have to keep looking at it. But now I was amazingly glad to see its blurred shape in front of me.

I was awake.

Thank heavens.

"PUT LOTTIE'S IPAD DOWN, LIV," said my mother. "You know perfectly well that I won't have that sort of thing at meals."

"I have to look something up for school. If I had a smartphone like everyone else, I'd have done it long ago." Much to our annoyance, Mia and I only had ancient, clunky cell phones for emergencies, obsolete SIM-card models passed on from our father. Useless and embarrassing.

I entered *"sub umbra floreo"* into the search field.

"Latin?" asked Mom, who could obviously read at a distance better than I'd expected. "What subject do you need that for?"

"For . . . er . . ." The search engine was spewing out any number of hits. I let my finger run down them. *Sub umbra floreo*—"I flower in the shade." The inscription was part of the coat of arms of Belize. Hmm. "Geography," I said. "Where exactly is Belize?"

"In Central America. Next door to Guatemala. Its former

name was British Honduras." Sometimes Mom was faster than the iPad, and she knew at least as much as Wikipedia.

"Aha." I wondered where my unconscious mind had fished up the motto of the state of Belize. I was fairly sure that today was the first time I'd ever heard of the country. So how could I dream of it? It was really odd, all the stuff you could subconsciously snap up and store away.

Another odd thing was that I could still remember almost every detail of last night's dream. Even as a child I'd had vivid dreams (I fell out of bed quite often, and for a while I went sleepwalking. Lottie liked telling the story of how she found me standing beside her bed and ordering an orange sorbet in Spanish). But normally my memories of a dream disappeared much faster than I liked, sometimes just seconds after I awoke, never mind how exciting or important or funny the dream might have been. So for a while I got into the habit of writing down particularly interesting dreams right away. I always kept a notebook and a pen on my bedside table. (I had to hide the notebook in a safe place during the day, because of course I didn't want anyone else reading it.) But there'd been no need to write last night's dream down.

Moreover, I'd been woken in the night not by a genuine thunderstorm but by the sound of the garbage men out in the street, and the clanking of bins and other containers. My heart had still been in my mouth as I struggled up from the floor and tried to sort my thoughts out. Crazy as the dream might have been, it had seemed to me so real that I'd switched on the golden lamp on my bedside table and taken a surrep-titious look at the soles of my fluffy socks, to see if they showed traces of earth from the cemetery, then checked to see if I had resin on my hands or cedar needles in my hair. Of course there was nothing of the kind.

By then I could laugh at myself. At least I couldn't accuse myself of a lack of imagination.

"Please can I have another piece of toast?" asked Mia, as I typed "Christina Rosetti" into the search field. It was her grave that Grayson had been looking for in the dream. I spelled the name wrong, but there were any number of hits.

"That's your fifth piece of toast," Mom said to Mia. And she told me, "Didn't you hear what I said? No iPads at meals. Put it away."

She was too late, because the display had just revealed some surprising facts: Christina Rossetti really was a poet of Victorian times, died 1894, buried in London—and in Highgate Cemetery at that.

This was getting a little sinister.

I closed the cover of the iPad and pushed it a little way away from me.

"Would you rather I was anorexic?" asked Mia. "Anorexia is a great danger to girls of my age, particularly in unstable family remonstrances."

"Circumstances," said Mom, automatically correcting Mia as she handed her the bread basket.

But it wasn't as sinister as all that, when you came to consider it carefully. I ignored my goose bumps and opened up the iPad again. There was sure to be a logical explanation. And after all, my mother was a lecturer in English studies, so it was more than likely that I'd heard her mention the name of Christina Rossetti, particularly as she was a contemporary of Emily Dickinson, and Mom and I both loved Emily Dickinson's poems. The information about where she was buried must have lodged itself somewhere in my unconscious mind, and last night it had made its way into my dream. Simple.

On the other hand . . . I couldn't remember the precise wording of the poem that Grayson and Henry had quoted in my dream, but it had rhymed and it sounded genuine. And good. If my unconscious mind had made that up all by itself, I was probably a genius.

"Mom, do you know anything about Christina Rossetti?"

"Yes, of course. I have a lovely illustrated edition of *Goblin Market*. In one of my crates of books."

"Did you maybe read it aloud to me when I was little?"

"I could have." Mom took the iPad away from me and closed the cover. "But you really only liked poems with happy endings. The poetry of Christina Rossetti is rather gloomy."

"Like the atmosphere in this apartment." Mia looked at the kitchen doorway through which Lottie had disappeared just now. After her second cup of coffee, Lottie always disappeared into the bathroom for a quarter of an hour—every morning without fail. "Have you told Lottie that you and Mr. Spencer will soon be throwing her out, or do we have to do it?"

"No one is going to throw Lottie out," said Mom. "Her time as an au pair in this family is simply coming to an end— and Lottie has known that for a long time. You two aren't children anymore, even if the way you act is anything but grown-up. I was really ashamed of you last night. . . ."

"Ditto." Mia had spread about half a pound of marmalade on her toast and was trying to cram the whole thing into her mouth, before it sagged and gave way in the middle.

"But where will Lottie go if she can't work for us

anymore?" I asked. Christina Rossetti and my crazy dream were forgotten for the time being. "She hasn't studied or trained for anything. If you and Papa hadn't persuaded her to stay on after her first year as an au pair with us, then she'd have studied and had a career. She gave all that up for us. And now she's old, she has to be told that she isn't wanted anymore. I call that shabby."

Mom laughed briefly. "Good heavens, Liv, don't be such a drama queen! First, it was Lottie's own decision to stay on, and if you ask me, not a bad one. She's seen a great deal of the world, she's learned foreign languages, and goodness knows she's not earned badly in all these years—all your father's maintenance payments for you two have gone toward her salary. Second, she's only thirty-one—and if that's old, then what would you call me?"

"Ancient," said Mia with her mouth full.

Mom sighed.

"What did Lottie say when you told her she was going to be fired?"

"I'm sure she cried." Mia looked as if she were going to cry herself. "Poor old Lottie."

"Nonsense," said Mom. "Of course Lottie will miss you, but she's looking forward to new challenges."

"Oh, sure." Did she think we were stupid?

"Anyway, it's not going to be as soon as all that," said Mom. "She'll certainly be staying with us until Easter, probably until the end of the school year. We'll see. And she has plenty of time to think what she'd like to do next."

"Buttercup will pine away if Lottie isn't here anymore," said Mia. "Remember how Lottie had to go to Germany when her granny died? Buttercup didn't eat for seven whole days."

I looked at the door, but Lottie's quarter of an hour wasn't up yet. "Poor Lottie, I expect she's trying to be brave. This will break her heart."

"You may be taking yourselves a little too seriously," said Mom. "Can't you envisage someone enjoying her life even without you?"

"Yes. I bet that's been *your* dream ever since you met Mr. Spencer," said Mia.

Mom rolled her eyes. "Seriously, mousies, don't be so selfish. Lottie might meet a man, settle down, and have children of her own."

Mia and I looked at each other. I was pretty sure we were thinking exactly the same thing.

"That's a great idea!" said Mia, her eyes shining. "If we want Lottie to be happy, we just have to find her a husband."

Mom laughed at that. "Right," she said. "Have fun."

10

MY LOCKER AT SCHOOL was number 0013 and was thus in a prime position right where the corridor began. However, I suspected that it was available only because no one wanted the number thirteen. Good thing I wasn't superstitious. I didn't believe in unlucky numbers any more than I believed in horoscopes, or four-leaf clovers and chimney sweeps that brought you luck. So far as I was concerned, mirrors could be broken on Friday the thirteenth, and on the same date hordes of black cats could cross my path—whether from left to right (lucky) or the other way around (unlucky), it made no difference to me. (Lottie had told us about the black cats; she also touched wood three times on the slightest provocation. She thought my disbelief in any kind of extrasensory perception was because of my star sign and that those born like me under Libra, with Sagittarius in the ascendant, were skeptics. They always wanted to find explanations for everything, and that, said Lottie, was why I had doubted the existence of Santa Claus and the Tooth Fairy even as a toddler.)

The locker was wonderfully large. I unloaded what felt

like a hundred pounds of textbooks, exercise books, and files into it, as well as my sports bag, and I'd still have had room for a picnic basket and a tennis racket. Not that I'd have needed one; this term I'd signed up for track and field sports, in the absence of anything I considered a real alternative. I'd really have liked something typical of Great Britain, but the sports on offer at Frognal Academy, unfortunately, weren't as British as the coat of arms on the school gates suggested. In my year you couldn't opt for rowing, field hockey, cricket, or polo—very disappointing.

When I closed the door of the locker, I almost dropped my English books in a fright. I was looking straight into the face of Shaving Fun Ken, who was grinning at me for all he was worth, showing his white teeth. I immediately had every detail of my crazy dream in front of my eyes again, including the sight of Shaving Fun Ken in plaid flannel pajamas.

"Hi, Liz," he said, putting out his hand. I was so startled that I actually shook it. "We had the pleasure of meeting yesterday," he said, "but I entirely forgot to introduce myself. I'm Jasper. Jasper Grant." When I didn't react, he laughed. "Yes, that's right. *The* Jasper Grant." Extraordinarily, he was laughing exactly as he'd laughed in my dream: a sort of self-satisfied chuckle.

I withdrew my hand and tried not to show how confused I felt.

"But I hope you don't believe everything Aphrodite Porter-Peregrin told you about me," he went on. "The fact is, Madison didn't dump me, I dumped her."

What? I finally came back to my senses. "That really sets my mind at rest," I said sarcastically. "I admit I'd wondered."

"Well, you know how it is. Somehow it's always kind

of embarrassing to a girl when you say you're tired of her."
Jasper's glance moved down over me, stopping briefly at my
legs. "Although I bet no one's ever told you that, have they,
Liz?" he said in an ingratiating tone of voice. "I can imagine
you'd look stunning without those glasses . . . wouldn't she,
Henry?" He waved to someone behind me. "See who's here."
This time he sounded positively triumphant. "Little Liz."

Slowly, I turned around. Henry was standing in the
milling throng right behind me, paler and with his hair unti-
dier than ever.

Henry, then. And he'd had that name in my dream, too.
The odd thing was that I could have sworn the name had
never been mentioned during that business with Persephone
and the grapefruit. So how on earth had I managed to name
him Henry so accurately in my dream?

And why was I getting goose bumps now?

"*Jasper*," said Henry, slowly and meaningfully.

On the other hand, perhaps Grayson had mentioned his
name during their phone conversation, when I was eaves-
dropping. In addition, Henry was quite a common name,
and he kind of looked like a Henry.

"What about it?" Jasper grinned at Henry. "I suppose it's
all right to renew old acquaintances." He put an arm around
my shoulders. "Liz is still stunned to think Jasper Grant remembered her name, right?"

"Yes, particularly as you got it wrong," I said, freeing
myself from his grip. "My name is Olivia."

"That's a pretty name too! A very sweet name for a very
sweet girl," Jasper said, not in the least deterred. Even the
genuine Shaving Fun Ken must have a larger brain inside his

plastic skull. "But I think you ought to wear your hair loose. I'm sure it would suit you much better, particularly when it's a little untidy. Don't you agree, Henry?"

Henry obviously preferred not to reply. He had opened locker number 0015, but he was still looking at me over the top of its door with the same thoughtful expression as in the dream.

I shook my head and tried to pull myself together.

Advice on my hairstyle from Shaving Fun Ken, silly looks from Bed-Head Henry—there really were better ways to begin the day. Clutching my books, I pushed past the two of them.

"Wait a minute," Jasper called after me, but I pretended I couldn't hear him. *You'd better get out of here*, I told myself, *or you'll never stop thinking about that stupid dream!*

But that was easier said than done. Everything, absolutely everything, today seemed bent on reminding me forcefully of my dream. The English lesson was about Victorian litera-ture, and everyone was given a writer whose life and work he or she would introduce to the class in the coming weeks. In my shock at seeing Christina Rossetti on the list (was she following me around?), I entirely forgot to volunteer to sponsor Sir Arthur Conan Doyle and was very nearly landed with Emily Brontë. Luckily at the last moment it occurred to the boy who had opted for Elizabeth Barrett Browning that poetry was girlie stuff. I was very glad we were able to swap, because last year, in Pretoria, my English teacher had given me a bad grade because I didn't see *Wuthering Heights* the same way she did. (I'd defended Heathcliff's behavior by putting it down to his underprivileged background.

Dickens's David Copperfield had also had a bad time as a boy, said the teacher, but he had turned out all right.)

Music was my third class, and it might have made me think of other things, but the teacher's name was Mrs. Beckett, and I was sure that I'd heard her name in my dream as well. In addition, the subject of Gregorian chant reminded me forcibly of Arthur's singsong chant as he was conjuring up the Lord of Shadows. *Custos opacum . . . Come and speak to us.* The dream had its hooks firmly into me, like a catchy tune that was particularly hard to get out of my mind.

In French, which was my next class, Persephone Puffed-Up unexpectedly sat down beside me. "Hi, Liv! I hope you don't mind Julie and me changing places. I mean, I'm your big sister, so I have to look after you." Ignoring my astonished expression, she produced a sugary-sweet smile. "What an achievement, Liv—first day at this school, and you're already in the Tittle-Tattle blog."

"In the what?"

"And those glasses really suit you—I meant to say so yesterday. There's something so . . . so retro about them."

Silly frump. I knew myself that those heavy-framed glasses were a bad buy. I'd chosen them only because, being so huge, they performed the optical illusion of making my nose look shorter. In retrospect, maybe that shouldn't have been the deciding argument for choosing them, but now I had them, so I needed to make the best of it.

"Thank you. Emma Watson wears the same model," I said.

"Oh, I didn't know that Emma Watson wore glasses."

She didn't, but who was to know?

Persephone leaned a little closer and whispered, "Is it true that your mother is going to marry the Spencer twins' father?"

Oh my God. I hadn't even thought of that. No one had said a word about getting married so far. But the way things were going, it probably couldn't be ruled out. "Well, in any case, they're . . . they're a couple," I said stiffly.

"Crazy. Then you'll be moving in with them?"

I nodded.

"Crazy!" said Persephone even more enthusiastically. "The Tittle-Tattle blog is always up to date with the latest developments. Wow! I bet there are advantages to being Grayson Spencer's future little sister." She patted my hand. "Of course he can't take you to the Autumn Ball himself, but he and Florence are sure to try pairing you off with one of their friends. The only question is who?"

"What's a tittle-tattle blog?" It sounded somehow improper. And why couldn't Grayson go to the ball with me? That was a purely theoretical question, of course.

"You're too young for Jasper—you're only fifteen, right?—and probably not pretty enough for Arthur, but then, who *is* pretty enough for Arthur?" Persephone sighed deeply, and I couldn't help feeling that she wasn't talking to me anymore, she was thinking out loud. And without stopping to take a breath or bothering about my confused expression. "That leaves Henry Harper—but could anyone get him to go to a dance? However hard I try, I can't imagine him in evening dress. Last year, anyway, he was conspicuous by his absence from the Autumn Ball, and he wasn't at the end-of-year ball either. Of course I know about the rumor that he and Anabel Scott . . . but I mean, *hello?* No one really believes it, Tittle-Tattle or no Tittle-Tattle."

My God, what on earth was the matter with her? And was it catching? I instinctively edged a little farther away from her, but Persephone moved to close the gap between us again. "Then again, Secrecy always has a good nose for these things. She knew when it was all over between Madison and Jasper—even before they knew it themselves."

Mrs. Lawrence, the French teacher, had come into the classroom and asked for quiet, but unfortunately Persephone wasn't about to let that stop her. "If Florence has her way, I bet you'll have to go with Emily Clark's pimply brother," she said, still thinking aloud. "But better to go to the ball with Sam the Pimple than not at all. I went with Ben Ryan last year, and it didn't bother me. I'm so fed up with waiting for Jasper to remember my name, or even register my existence at all. As a girl, I mean. This year I'm going with Gabriel. He owes Pandora a favor—he's on the basketball team too—and believe you me, I'll make sure it's the best evening of his life. Because of course the boys talk in the locker room, and Gabriel will say such enthusiastic things about me to Jasper that he'll be pale with envy and never call me Aphrodite again, and—"

"I said *un petit peu de silence, s'il vous plaît,* and that means you too, Persephone!" Mrs. Lawrence was standing in front of us, frowning, and she looked really annoyed. All the same, I'd never been so glad to see a teacher in my life.

"*Pardon, madame.* Liv is new, so she has a lot of questions," said Persephone with an apologetic flutter of her eyelids. "Hush for now, Liv," she hissed in a loud stage whisper. "We can talk about it later." With that, she leaned over her books again, and I looked at my watch, feeling exhausted. Wow! She'd mentioned at least thirty-seven names and the same number of facts in just two minutes, and I didn't understand a word of it. However, I did know one thing for certain: I wouldn't be going anywhere with Emily Thingummy's pimply brother.

The Frognal Academy Tittle-Tattle Blog, with all the latest gossip, the best rumors, and the hottest scandals from our school.

ABOUT ME:
My name is Secrecy—I'm right here among you, and I know *all* your secrets.

4 September, 8:30 a.m.

Good morning, darlings!

To wake you up right away, here's a photo I managed to take just now. Voilà—the new owner of locker number 0013.

So what do you think of Liv Silver, Class Eleven, our new student at Frognal Academy? Her father is a famous German nuclear physicist, and her mother, a professor of literature who will be lecturing at Oxford, is soon going to marry Grayson and Florence Spencer's father. At least, they're all moving in together in October. Liv's little sister, Mia, is in Class Eight, and they both have the same exciting hair color. It's probably known as moonlight blond, and it's exactly the color of the streaks that Hazel Pritchard got the hairdresser to put in her own hair at the price of ninety pounds. Only, in the Silver sisters' hair it's natural and comes for free—chance would be a fine thing, don't you agree, Hazel? I've heard some criticism of the glasses both sisters wear, but personally I think they're kind of stylish. Hey, Grayson, soon you'll have three sisters—congratulations. And what a good thing Emily isn't the jealous type. . . .

Next week the basketball season starts again, a good opportunity to take a closer look at Arthur and Co. After the Frognal Flames played so outstandingly well last season, winning the Schools' Cup, to everyone's surprise, I'm expecting a full house in the spectators' stands this season encouraging our boys. Aesthetically speaking, those sloppy shirts they wear are the worst (even polo kit has more sex appeal), but all the same I don't object to the sweaty sight of our Four Musketeers: Arthur Hamilton, Henry Harper, Grayson Spencer, and the three-point king, Jasper Grant.

So have a good day here at school—oh, and if you want it to be a *really* good day, mind you steer clear of Mr. Daniels. He must have ordered a pound of raw onions with his doner kebab at the Turkish restaurant last night.

See you soon!

Love from Secrecy

THE FROGNAL ACADEMY LIBRARY had fourteen computer
desks, with access to the Internet included, and all fourteen
of them were empty. Presumably because everyone but me
had a tablet or a smartphone and could update their Facebook status at five-minute intervals. But there wasn't much
going on around here at midday in any event; there wasn't
anyone around except for one of the smaller boys sitting in a
corner reading. I chose a screen right at the back, where I
couldn't be seen from the door, just in case it came into
Persephone's head to look for me here. She'd obviously decided to be best friends with me from now on. It had nothing
to do with a sudden liking for my company, but I guess
my connection with the Spencers made up for the absence
of diamond mines or diplomatic parents in the family. It would
have been much nicer if she'd gone on ignoring me, and
above all much quieter. She even followed me to the toilets,
where she kept on nattering. I'd slipped out of the cafeteria
and come here on the pretext of looking for my sister—I

thought I'd rather do without lunch than spend another minute with Persephone.

And now I had three-quarters of an hour for valuable research. First I wanted to check whether Persephone really had found her information about the merging of our family with the Spencers in a blog. And sure enough, searching for the terms "Grayson Spencer," "Liv Silver," and "Frognal Academy" led me straight to a page that called itself the Frognal Academy Tittle-Tattle Blog, written by someone who gave her name as Secrecy. The latest entry was time stamped eight thirty that morning. I held my breath for a moment as I recognized the lead item: a photograph of me just as I was opening my locker.

Oh, shit.

I quickly read the text under it twice running, to make sure that my eyes hadn't deceived me. Then I took a deep breath. Moonlight blond, indeed! This girl Secrecy (or was Secrecy a boy?) was very well informed—except that the bit about Papa was wrong: he was neither famous nor a nuclear physicist, and as an engineer he worked mainly on the development of hybrid cars. But the rest of it was right—and how horrifying was that? She or he had been lying in wait for me near the lockers to take that photo. *I'm right here among you, and I know* all *your secrets.*

I scrolled down to earlier entries and began reading. The style and content reminded me a little of the trashy magazines I loved to look at in the dentist's waiting room, except that the blog wasn't devoted to celebrities, actors, and the European aristocracy but was all about the students and teachers of Frognal Academy and their families. Secrecy apparently knew everything. She revealed clandestine relationships and knew who was splitting up from whom and why. Her articles were pitiless and malicious. And admittedly, also *very* entertaining.

It was just about miraculous that no one seemed to have found out who she was yet—half the people she had exposed in her blog must entertain murderous feelings about her, that was for sure. And the other half would want to pluck out all her hairs one by one, at the very least. But she also had any number of fans, judging by the comments.

"Don't even try to find out who I am, because so far no one has managed it"—that read to me like a personal challenge. I just couldn't resist puzzles and mysteries. In any case, someone who knew Florence or Grayson well must be hiding behind the name of Secrecy, because only they knew about Mom and Ernest's plans. And only since yesterday evening at that. Or had Secrecy simply happened to eavesdrop on a conversation by chance? Did she have undercover informers? Did she have up-to-date bugging methods? Was she hacking into private e-mail accounts?

Someone put a hand on my shoulder, and I jumped. I'd been so deep in thought that I hadn't paid any attention to the movements I'd seen out of the corner of my eye.

To my relief, however, it wasn't Persephone who had tracked me down, but Grayson. Thanks to Secrecy, I now knew that Grayson was an outstandingly good basketball player, that he was deputy editor of the students' magazine *reflexx*, and that he had broken the heart of a girl called Maisie Brown last year because he'd taken Florence's best friend, Emily Clark, to the Autumn Ball instead of her. (Ah, that would almost certainly be Emily with the pimply brother—I was beginning to get an idea of the situation.)

"Hi," whispered Grayson.

"Hi," I whispered back.

Then I noticed that he wasn't on his own. A little way off, Jasper was perched on the edge of a table, and Henry was leaning against some shelves beside him, with his arms crossed.

For a second I felt I'd gone back into my dream, and I saw myself dropping out of the cedar tree right in front of their feet again. *I was a barn owl a moment ago, honest.*

Luckily my arm was lying over my notebook, so Grayson couldn't read what I had been writing, but he'd had a good chance to see what was on the screen.

"Don't you like your paparazzi photo?" he asked, still in a whisper. "You got off lightly—she snapped me with an icicle on my nose."

I giggled. I must definitely look for that photo later. Jasper and Henry were openly watching us, but at least they couldn't hear what we were saying so long as we stuck to whispering. I closed my notebook and leaned my elbows on it.

"How do you know Secrecy is a she?" I asked.

Grayson shrugged his shoulders. "Well, a boy wouldn't be able to write so knowledgeably about the lace and frills on ball dresses."

"Unless he does it on purpose to be taken for a girl."

"Hmm. I never thought of that." He scratched his nose, and I noticed that the words had disappeared from his wrist. They really had been felt pen. "What are you doing here?"

"Hiding from Persephone Porter-Peregrin, my new best friend. How about you?"

"We, er . . . incidentally, these are *my* best friends. I think you've met Jasper and Henry." He sighed. "And this is Arthur."

Sure enough, Arthur had appeared behind Henry and Jasper. "You can talk out loud, Grayson," he said. "Our dear Miss Cooper has gone for lunch and is leaving the library in good hands." Smiling, he came toward us. Henry and Jasper left their observation posts and strolled closer too.

"Hi. You must be Grayson's new little sister. Liv, is that right?"

I nodded. My God, Secrecy was right, he really was the best-looking boy in the Western Hemisphere. Those angelic golden curls! They'd have made any other boy look like a girl, but they suited him perfectly. In daylight he didn't look at all uncanny, more the opposite. My short-term memory made the information I'd just picked up from the Tittle-Tattle blog into a kind of Wanted poster up beside his head before my mind's eyes.

ARTHUR HAMILTON, AGE 18.
Captain of the basketball team. In a (long-distance) relationship with Anabel Scott. Favorite subjects: sports and math. Favorite color: blue. Cautioned by the police for violent behavior last winter. Father: managing director of a large advertising agency. Family has their own private cinema at home.

"So how do you like it at Frognal?"

"Seems to be very . . . interesting here," I said.

"She's just discovered the Tittle-Tattle blog," said Grayson.

Arthur laughed. "Yes, *interesting* is the right word." He exchanged a brief glance with Henry, who was leaning against some bookshelves with his arms folded again. It seemed to be his favorite position. I'd gleaned a large amount of information about him, too, by now:

HENRY HARPER, AGE 17. Forward with the Frognal Flames. Son of a prominent London businessman on his third marriage. Will have to share his inheritance with a whole crowd of siblings and half siblings— that's if there's any of it left, because last winter his father fell in love again, with a Bulgarian lingerie model / call girl who he hopes will be wife number four. Candidate for a scholarship to St. Andrew's. At present unattached. Attractive gray eyes, and always has a kind of funny look.

I quickly looked away and pretended I had to search for something in my files. When Henry looked at me, I always felt as if he could read my thoughts.

"Do you like basketball, Liv?" asked Arthur. "We're having a little party at my house on Saturday evening to celebrate the start of the season—it'd be good if Grayson brought you with him. Then you could meet a few people. And we have a little pool, so bring a bikini if you'd like to swim."

I blinked suspiciously. Was he serious? I mean, he'd only that moment met me.

"How about it—will you come?"

On the other hand, why wouldn't people simply be nice? What's more, I'd be fascinated to see his family's private cinema. "If Grayson will take me, then I'd like to," I said.

"Of course we'll have to ask your mother first," said Grayson, joining the conversation. Turning to his friend, he went on, "She's rather strict about Liv not staying out late."

What on earth did he mean? Mom wasn't at all strict—quite the opposite. She was always telling me the things she'd done when she was my age. Even in Pretoria, which wasn't the safest place in the world, I'd been allowed to stay out as long as I liked on the weekend. Luckily for her, I'd never wanted to stay out very long.

"Er, yes," I said, with an inquiring look at Grayson. Why did he make a claim like that? "My mom is extremely . . . strict."

"Well, I think that's a good thing," said Jasper. "For girls."

Before anyone could find out exactly what he meant by that, the bell rang for the beginning of the next class.

"It's only a harmless little party," said Arthur as I put my things together and got to my feet. "I'm sure your mother won't object."

No, far from it. She'd be over the moon to think I was making friends so quickly. And with the most popular clique in the whole school. That was really something else—and so much better than getting my head dunked in the toilet.

"And you'd have your new, responsible big brother looking after you on the way," said Henry.

"I can look after myself, thanks," I said.

"Yes, right!" Jasper gave a chuckle of amusement. "After all, you can do kung fu."

I'd already turned to move away, but now I froze in mid-movement. *What had he just said?*

Jasper chuckled even louder. "Why are you looking so surprised? You said so yourself in the cemetery, don't you remember? Or is that another of those night-watchman things?"

The others were certainly looking at him in surprise, except for Henry, who was looking at me. Much more attentively than I liked.

I tried to keep a neutral expression on my face, but I was afraid I didn't do very well. I had goose bumps all over. This wasn't possible. . . . It couldn't be possible.

"In what cemetery?" I asked, far too late in the day.

"Oh, never mind me," said Jasper cheerfully. "I'm talking nonsense."

"So you are," said Grayson with a wry grin, and Arthur rolled his eyes and laughed. Only Henry didn't move a muscle.

Okay. Don't panic. I can think all this over later. Get away from here first.

"I must be going." I ignored Henry's penetrating gaze, jammed my things under my arm, and made for the door. "Double period of Spanish."

"*Que te diviertas*," said Arthur behind me.

"See you later," Grayson murmured, and the last thing I heard before I closed the library door behind me, struggling hysterically for air, was Henry's voice, saying, "Jas, you really must stop helping yourself to your mother's supply of pills."

12

RIGHT, SO LET'S KEEP CALM and take another look at the facts, I told myself. I'd been having a confused dream, set against the background of Highgate Cemetery, about conjuring up some kind of spirits, in the course of which I had landed, unfortunately, on an altar in the middle of a burning pentagram. So far, so crazy. But not what you'd describe as unusual for a dream. But if Jasper could remember something I had said in the dream—well, that *was* unusual. Indeed, it was downright impossible. Jasper *couldn't* have had the same dream as me.

But then how did he know what I'd said in my dream in the cemetery?

What was it that Sherlock Holmes said? "When you have eliminated the impossible, what remains, however improbable, must be the truth." Only, what remained if you *couldn't* eliminate the impossible?

It wasn't just that one remark that made me wonder what was going on. This very morning I'd had an odd feeling when Jasper made his silly remarks. And then there was the fact that I'd known Henry's name. Plus Christina Rossetti, and Grayson's "tattoo"—were they all mere chance and the work of my own brilliant unconscious mind? Hardly.

No, there was obviously something wrong with that dream. It hadn't just been an unusually clear dream, it had been about things that I couldn't know, places where I had never been before—and the worst of it was that I wasn't the only one to have dreamed it. That was where the owl came into it. I'd felt flattered by the interest Grayson's friends were taking in me, and by Arthur's invitation, but I no longer thought they were just being nice. They wanted something from me—and it wasn't because of my charms. It was all to do with that dream.

However, as I said, that was impossible. And whatever I thought about it, whenever I followed any train of thought, I came up against the word *impossible* like a wall that couldn't be crossed. Twelve hours later I had a bad headache but still no satisfactory explanation.

I'd been in bed for hours now, afraid of going to sleep. I'd persuaded Lottie to lend me her iPad, but even the Internet, which usually knows everything, couldn't come up with any answers. Dreams, I gathered, were as individual as thoughts. Or as Carl Gustav Jung, according to the Internet *the* expert on dreams and the way to interpret them, had put it, dreams didn't take sides; they were nothing to do with how consciousness works, but spontaneous products of the unconscious mind. Jung, as I discovered, also went on about what he called archetypal dreams arising from a collective unconscious, and those were to do with our ancient tribal and human history. The word *collective* made me feel hopeful, but as I read on, I realized that try as I might, I couldn't really classify my cemetery dream as the archetypal sort, if only because there weren't any archetypes involved. No meetings with an old man, no falling down holes in the ground, no flowing water . . . and as for wise messages from the ancient wisdom of humanity, in my dream anyway they were a total loss.

As it got later and later, I went from website to website with less and less of a plan in mind. The search engine offered me some lines of verse by the poet Rilke:

> *They say life is a dream, but that's not so;*
> *Or not a dream alone. Dreaming is part of life,*
> *Strange and confused, where we can never know*
> *How truth and seeming both together flow.*

My idea precisely. Rilke said just what I thought, at least about dreams being strange and confused. I yawned. I was tired to death, and so was the charge of the iPad. It gave up just as, in searching for the words "door" and "dreams," I had landed on the website of a carpenter's workshop promising me, "If you're not happy with ready-made goods, we'll make you the door of your dreams."

I propped my chin on my knees and wrapped my arms around them. Maybe I was simply losing my mind? At least that would have been a logical explanation—and oh how I longed for a logical explanation.

And for sleep. Just as soon as I'd done a little more thinking . . .

I must have gone to sleep sitting up, because on my way to the bus stop with Mia in the morning I couldn't remember coming up with a single clear idea. I hardly remembered my dreams, either, only that they'd been entirely disconnected, something about a tram and some bears. Just before waking, I dreamed of visiting Aunt Gertrude in Boston, where we had to eat fish soup, and Emma Watson was there too, wearing my glasses. As if that wasn't strange enough, I saw my green door with the lizard doorknob from the last dream right in the middle of Aunt Gertrude's dining room wall with its blue and gold wallpaper. Aunt Gertrude seemed much annoyed by it. She said, several times, that the door didn't go with her color scheme at all, and would I kindly also eat the cuttlefish so that they wouldn't have died in vain. The next thing I knew, I was awake.

"This is a really spectacular case." Mia, in a very cheerful mood, was hopping along beside me, jumping over the cracks between the paving stones. And unlike me, she was wide awake. "But this Secrecy person won't stay anonymous for long, not now that Mia Silver, private detective, is on the case." Yesterday's discovery of the Tittle-Tattle blog had excited Mia even more than me. She loved mysteries at least as much as I did, and Secrecy was a great challenge to our inborn curiosity.

A red double-decker bus braked a few yards ahead of us, and Mia began to run while I was still checking the number.

"Don't we have to wait for the 603 bus?"

"No, the 210 goes the same way," claimed Mia, already half inside the bus.

"How sure of that are you?"

"Seventy percent," said Mia, undisturbed. "Come on! I want to sit on top this time."

Sighing, I followed her into the bus and up the stairs,

where she slipped smoothly as an eel past a man wearing a hat, to make sure of getting us two seats at the front.

"I'll murder you if we're on the wrong bus," I said.

"Show a little more confidence in Mia Silver, private detective, please." Mia contentedly stretched her legs out in front of her. "I'll have solved this case by Christmas," she solemnly assured me. "You can be my assistant if you like. And my decoy, of course."

"I don't know about that, Mia Silver, private detective—Secrecy seems to be up to all the tricks."

"So am I." The bus had begun moving, and sure enough the view from up top was great. You felt you were hovering high above the road.

"Up to now, anyway," I said, "no one's been able to work out what his or her game is."

"Okay, but even Secrecy isn't infallible," Mia retorted. "For instance, she was dead wrong about Papa's profession."

"Yes, I thought that was odd myself. Can there be a famous nuclear physicist with the same surname?"

"No!" Mia's face wore a mischievous grin. She glanced quickly around the bus. Then she bent over to me and whispered, "You can put the famous nuclear physicist bit down to me. I told Daisy the Chinese secret service was interested in Papa's work. It kind of sounded more interesting to me than the truth."

I couldn't help smiling. "Ah—then could Daisy Dawn be Secrecy?"

"No, stupid, she didn't come to Frognal until last year, and the blog had already been running for three years by then. But you can bet she passed the story on. To someone who then passed it on to Secrecy. I can't wait to unpack the box with my detective gear in it. Think how useful we'll find the ballpoint pen with the mini-camera built into it. . . ."

My little sister was in her element. Oh well, at least one of us was happy. I was still just confused. On one hand I was relieved that nothing special had happened in the night, on the other hand—and to my own surprise—I was actually a little disappointed. Even in the light of day I didn't think what had happened was any less mysterious. But however terrifying the whole thing might have been—maybe the dream itself held the answers to all my questions.

13

I WAITED FOR MIA at the gate when school was over for the day, watching the students streaming past me in their dark-blue uniforms. Was Secrecy among them, taking photos on the sly? Just in case she was, I leaned against a post by the wall in as fetching a pose as I could manage, with a slight smile on my face. There'd be nothing worse than being photographed with my mouth open, or with a grumpy expression, unless maybe I was also dribbling.

I straightened my glasses. It had been a pleasingly uneventful day, no upsetting encounters with people out of my dreams, no further mentions of me in the Tittle-Tattle blog, no time to brood on stuff that couldn't be possible. Even Persephone couldn't get on my nerves too badly, because we only had two classes together on Wednesdays. From now on, Wednesday was going to be my favorite day of the week.

Standing at my observation post, I saw Arthur and Jasper leaving the school grounds together, closely followed by Henry, who was with Florence and another girl and was deep in an obviously interesting conversation. Henry briefly glanced my way but didn't really seem to notice me in the milling throng. Half a minute later, when the crowd of students was thinning out, and only a few came strolling through the gateway, Grayson appeared. He was looking down at the ground as he pushed his bicycle right past me, and he jumped when I said, "Hi."

"Oh . . . it's you," he said, not very enthusiastically.

His reaction hurt my feelings a little bit. "Yes, it's me. I'm sure it's going to be great to share a bathroom with you in the near future." I changed the leg I was standing on. What a good thing I'd assumed that casual but attractive pose.

Grayson had stopped and was looking all around him carefully. Very carefully. *Too* carefully.

"The coast's clear; the Chinese secret service has knocked off work for the day," I said after about twenty seconds. Grayson stopped.

"Er, Liv, you don't by any chance have that hooded sweater I lent you here, do you? I'd like to have it back."

"Of course." I felt slightly irritated. Didn't he have anything else to wear? "But no, I don't by any chance have it here right now. We'll be seeing each other at Arthur's party on Saturday, and I'll give it back to you then, freshly washed and dried."

Grayson checked out our surroundings yet again. Then he said, "Well, about Saturday evening . . . I'd rather . . . you see . . . I mean, you can simply say your mother's forbidden you to go to Arthur's party."

Now my feelings were more than a little bit hurt. "But why would I do that?"

"Because it . . . because I . . ." Grayson passed his hand over his forehead—by now I was familiar with that gesture of his—and looked at me as if hoping I would finish his sentence for him.

I wasn't going to give him an easy way out. I made myself look sad. "Because you don't want me to go to the party?"

He nodded.

Oh, charming! "Well, I suppose that's that, then," I said, shrugging my shoulders. "It's just that—Mom was so thrilled to think you and your friends were being so nice to me." And sure enough, Mom had said exactly what I'd expected. "How delightful of Grayson and his friends. Of course you must go. I'm really glad you're getting to know people so quickly!"

Grayson let out a funny kind of snort. "Listen, we're not being all that nice to you. It'd be much better for you to steer clear of us." He mounted his bike.

"Okay, I'll tell Mom," I said, adding with a touch of malice, "although maybe you'd rather tell her the reasons yourself."

Grayson didn't seem to like that idea at all. He looked far from happy. "Don't forget my sweater, will you?" he said as he was about to ride away. "I'd be really glad to have it back tomorrow. You needn't bother about washing it."

"Okay," I said slowly.

"What was all that about?" Mia had appeared like a jack-in-the-box. The two of us watched Grayson cycle away. "First he seems so nice, then he doesn't want to take you to this party? In your place I'd go anyway."

"I will, too," I agreed. "What a . . ." I tried to find the right word.

"An idiot," said Mia bluntly, linking arms with me. We strolled over to the bus stop side by side.

"How was your day?" I asked.

"Not bad, really. Even if those girls get on my nerves. If I ever turn out like that, brain-dead on account of some boy and scribbling hearts all over my exercise books, I just hope someone shoots me."

"I'll remind you of that."

"Seriously! I'm so glad we're immune to boys, Livvy."

"Maybe not absolutely immune, but at least hard to infect," I admitted. It was a necessity. If you move every year like us, you have to be careful not to go falling in love, or you get your heart broken saying good-bye. And who'd want a thing like that to happen? "But maybe Mom is right, and someday when the ideal man for you comes along . . ."

"He'll just have to wait until I'm through with college!"

I nudged Mia in the ribs. "I bet Aunt Gertrude always said that too," I suggested, trying to scare her. "And look what became of her."

"So? I'm certainly not about to sit in a horrible house with four cats, making crochet doilies. As a famous private detective, I'll be solving the most interesting cases in the whole world."

"Then maybe you can start by telling me exactly why Grayson is so keen to have his sweater back." I was still feeling sore over that.

"Could be it's his favorite one," said Mia thoughtfully. "Or he's hidden a love letter in it. Or he's just an idiot."

"Yup. I'm afraid he is." So I was going to keep his sweater out of pure malice.

Only, that evening, when I was putting on my nightie and I saw Grayson's sweater lying on the gold-upholstered bench in front of the bed, it did occur to me that there could be something else behind it. That Grayson might have a special reason for wanting it back in such a tearing hurry. I picked it up and buried my nose in it. It was just the sort of thing to be someone's favorite, made of wool that was heavy but soft as butter, slightly roughened on the inside. And it still smelled slightly of Grayson, or rather Grayson's soap.

The pockets were empty, and to be on the safe side I felt the seams as well. No sign of anything hidden there.

Maybe . . . It was a crazy thought, but the night before last I'd been wearing the sweater in bed, and then I met its rightful owner in my dream. Could that be why Grayson was suddenly so keen to have it back? Was there some connection between the sweater and the dream? Strange as that might sound, I was going to wear it again that night, anyway. Just to find out what happened.

Or if anything at all did happen.

THE SHINY GREEN DOOR attracted my eyes in a bleak street lined with gray, shabby terraced houses. I had no idea what I'd been dreaming up to this point, but the moment I saw the door I was sitting on a bicycle, pedaling hard to pull a heavily laden trailer behind me. Uphill.

The door! In my dream last time it had led me to the cemetery.

Mom overtook me. She, too, was riding a bike with a trailer. "Feeling tired is no excuse," she called to me.

"What are we doing here?" I asked.

"Moving house," replied Mom, looking over her shoulder. "Same as usual."

"I see." I braked and got off my bicycle to take a closer look at the green door. Yes, no doubt about it, this was the same door as last time, and it was also the door that had turned up in Aunt Gertrude's dining room. Suddenly it was all as clear as day: if I wanted to find out the meaning of these mysterious dreams, then I had to open it. And go through the doorway.

If I was brave enough.

"No dawdling, mousie!" cried Mom. "We have to go on! We always have to go on."

"But without me today," I said. The lizard doorknob felt warm when I turned it. I took a deep breath and went through the doorway.

"Olivia Gertrude Silver! Come back this minute!" I heard Mom calling a moment before I slammed the door in her face. Just the same as last time, I was standing in a corridor that seemed to go on and on forever. Fascinated, I looked at all the doors. They looked like the windows of an Advent calendar and were equally individual in their size, shape, and color. There were plain, white-painted doors, there were the front doors of modern houses, and others that looked like the doors of elevators, nothing decorative about them. Others could have been shop doors, or the magnificent portals of castles and palaces.

The bright-red door opposite seemed to be a new one, or at least I couldn't remember seeing it here on my last visit. It was a very striking door with a showy golden doorknob shaped like a crown; you wouldn't forget it in a hurry. I didn't find Grayson's door, which had been right next to mine before, until I'd gone a little farther down the corridor. So the doors here obviously didn't stay in the same spot but played a kind of hide-and-seek. Next to Grayson's door I saw one painted pale gray, with glass panes in it and ornate lettering. The lettering said MATTHEWS' MOONSHINE ANTIQUARIAN BOOKS. BOOKS TO LAST YOU A LIFETIME. OPEN FROM MIDNIGHT TO DAWN. That sounded enticing. For a moment I was tempted to press the handle down and explore the inside of the antiquarian bookshop, but then I reminded myself why

I was here, and I went on to Grayson's door. It looked just the same as in my last dream, a perfect copy of the front door of the Spencers' house. Frightful Freddy spread his wings and squeaked, "No one can come in unless they say my name three times backward."

"Ydderf, Ydderf, Ydderf," I replied, whereupon Freddy folded his wings and curled his lion's tail around his feet.

"You may enter," he squeaked solemnly.

I hesitated. Somehow I felt I'd better arm myself for what was to come. Whatever that might be. Maybe I ought to imagine Lottie's hatchet out of the last dream. Or at least dream that I had a sharp knife in my pocket. Or hang some garlic around my neck, or . . .

"What are you waiting for?" inquired Frightful Freddy.

"I'm on my way." If things got too dangerous, I could always just wake up. That had worked last time. (And this time, for safety's sake, I had padded the floor beside my bed with cushions.) Taking a deep breath, I went through the doorway. Instead of darkness and the spooky peace of the cemetery, I walked into bright light, the noise of a lot of people shouting, and metallic clanking. My foot missed a step, and I lost my balance and reached for the nearest thing I could grab, which turned out to be the shoulder of a red-headed girl.

"Watch out," she said, but she paid me no further attention. Instead, she leaned forward and shouted, "That was a foul, ref! Do you have tomatoes for eyes or what?"

I'd regained my footing, and I looked curiously around. Aha—a sports hall. I was standing on the steps between the tiers of seating for spectators, all of them full, and a basketball game was in progress on the court in front of me. It wasn't difficult to guess that the boys in the black and red stripes were the Frognal Flames. Arthur was just catching a ball passed to him by Grayson, and he passed it on to Henry, who dribbled it skillfully past the member of the opposing team who was marking him and then threw it to Jasper. Jasper leaped up in the air right under the basket, and as he came down he shot the ball through the hoop. The crowd shouted with glee. According to the scoreboard, the Frognal Flames were eighteen points in the lead. It looked like it was about to be a landslide victory. Two of the spectators kindly moved up a bit to make room for me in the front row, right behind the substitutes' bench. If I turned around, I could still see Grayson's door at the far end of the tiers of seats. However, apart from me, no one seemed bothered by the sight of a front door in the middle of the wall of a sports hall. And the spectators took no notice of me, either, as if it were perfectly normal to turn up at a basketball game barefoot and in a nightdress. I didn't know just what I'd been expecting, but I felt a sense of relief. In any case, this was more comfortable than being in a cemetery by night, with people reciting gruesome incantations to conjure up spirits.

I watched the game, feeling almost relaxed. At first it looked as if the opposing team didn't have the slightest chance against the magnificent form of the Frognal Flames, but then Grayson began passing poorly and losing the ball, and the other team was catching up. I didn't understand basketball, but as far as I could judge, Grayson was suddenly playing incredibly badly. He missed the basket, didn't pass the ball to members of his own team, and committed foul after unnecessary foul. The spectators booed him. Someone shouted, "Go home, Grayson, you total loser!" and threw an empty soda can onto the court. Grayson looked absolutely miserable, but he went on systematically making every wrong move in the game. The other team's fans were yelling with delight, shouting, "Number Five's our man!"

I could hardly bear to watch, but it wasn't until the score was 63–61 in favor of the other side that the coach of the Frognal Flames substituted another player for Grayson, looking at him icily as he trotted off the court, his shoulders stooped. In all the noise I couldn't make out what the coach was saying to Grayson, but there was contempt all over his face. Grayson seemed to be near tears and was obviously trying to apologize, but the coach had already turned away to shout tactical orders over the court. From then on he ignored Grayson.

The Flames seemed to be doing better again without Grayson, but it looked as if it was too late for the team to reverse the damage. Grayson dropped onto the substitutes' bench, looking terribly ashamed of himself, and the other players moved away from him as if he had an infection.

He buried his face in a towel.

Although it was only a dream, I felt really sorry for him. I leaned forward and patted him on the shoulder from behind. "Hey, it's only a game," I said, trying to console him.

Very slowly, he raised his head and turned around to me. "It's not only a game," he said, "it's *the* game. And I've botched it!"

"Well . . ." Unfortunately he was right. He really had botched it. "But all the same, it's just a game between two high school teams."

"A game in which I've failed." His eyes wandered along the rows of spectators. "Of course you had to be here to see it too. And Emily won't even look my way, she's so ashamed of me."

"Silly cow," I said spontaneously, following the direction of his eyes. "Which one is she? The dark-haired girl in the blue sweater beside Florence?" I hesitated for a moment. "And is that by any chance *Henry* coming down the steps? Hang on a moment!" I turned to look back at the court, where Henry was just passing the ball to Jasper. Then I looked at the steps again. No, I hadn't made a mistake. There was Henry waving to me. "Grayson? Does Henry by any chance have an identical twin brother?"

But Grayson had buried his head in his towel again and didn't hear me. Or was pretending not to hear me.

I looked once again from the Henry in his basketball shirt to the Henry coming toward me in jeans and T-shirt from the other side of the hall, and then from one to the other again, before shrugging my shoulders. After all, it was a dream; I didn't have to take it literally.

"Sorry, could you move up a bit? Thanks." Henry squeezed into the second row and sat down right behind me. "Hi, cheese girl. Good game?"

"Depends how you look at it. You two are losing," I said, as if it were normal for there to be two of him. "And do stop calling me cheese girl."

Henry watched his alter ego sinking a three-pointer in the basket and whistled appreciatively through his teeth. "Hey, I'm playing pretty well!" He leaned so far forward that his head was almost level with mine. I tried not to let that make me nervous. This was good practice. Training for reality.

"Okay, cheese girl, I'll call you Liv from now on." Henry's voice was soft and deep, right beside my ear. "I have an idea it was Grayson who made a mess of the game, right?"

Grayson's head emerged from the towel. "I made a *total* mess of it," he agreed. It didn't seem to bother him that there were two Henrys here. "I let the coach down, and the team, and you . . . and Emily and Florence and my father and . . . listen to what they're saying!"

The opposing team's fans were still chanting. "Grayson Spencer, the losing Flame, send the Frognals a sympathy card!" And "The fire of the Flames is going out, Spencer the loser's a layabout."

Grayson was pale as death.

"The first couplet doesn't rhyme," I said.

Henry nodded. "And the meter of the second one's all wrong. Idiots."

That didn't seem to cheer Grayson up. He disappeared under his towel again. I suspected that he was shedding tears into it.

"I'm afraid he has this dream quite often," said Henry sympathetically.

"What, about sniffling into a towel?"

"No, of being a total failure on the basketball court, so that we all lose and everyone turns against him."

"Has it ever happened, then? In real life, I mean?"

Henry shook his head. "No, never. Grayson is brilliant at all kinds of sport. Last season he went on playing even with a badly bruised shoulder and scored eight points. What are you actually doing here?" That last bit came out so unexpectedly that I didn't have time to think my answer over properly.

"I wanted to see the game—what do you think?" I felt a little uncomfortable under his piercing gaze.

He grinned broadly. "Barefoot and in a nightdress? And isn't that Grayson's sweater you're wearing again? I told him he'd better get it back. It's rather too large for you, I'd say."

"Well, and you're here twice—that's rather too often, I'd say," I replied, imitating his mocking tone of voice. But secretly I was annoyed. I really could have worn something else. The nightdress was old and ugly, and with Grayson's sweater over it I probably looked as if I'd run away from some kind of madhouse. But I could always alter that—after all, this was a dream. I briefly narrowed my eyes, and when I opened them again I was wearing my favorite jeans, sneakers, and a red T-shirt with I AM PROTECTED BY THREE INVISIBLE NINJAS on the front of it. I was also wearing mascara and a touch of lip gloss.

So it worked.

"You're really good," said Henry, standing up. "Or, alternatively, I am. It all depends." He looked at me with his head to one side. "How about going for a walk?"

"But we can't leave poor Grayson in the lurch." Particularly not now, when the fans of the Frognal Flames were joining in with their opponents' chanting. "Bad, worse, Spencer's the worst!" they were yelling, and, "Never trust Grayson Spencer!" A white-haired old lady in a Chanel suit was standing at the top of the tiers of seats, in the back row, shouting, "Grayson Ernest Theodore Spencer, I am severely disappointed in you!" and angrily waving an umbrella in the air.

Henry climbed over the seat beside me and shook Grayson by the shoulder. "Hey, Grayson! Pull yourself together. This is only a nightmare."

Grayson lowered the towel. "You can say that again," he muttered.

"No, really, you're only dreaming it. Or do you seriously think Tyler Smith of the stupid Hampstead Hornets could bring off a spectacular dunk like that? Look at him!"

"Well," said Grayson doubtfully, "people sometimes rise above themselves in the heat of a game. . . ."

"But Tyler Smith? Not in a hundred years." Henry straightened up again. "Do me a favor—dream something else! Something nicer! But wait until we're out the door, okay?"

Grayson looked at us undecidedly. "You mean this is a dream?"

"Of course it's a dream," I said. "Or do you think there could really be two of Henry here?"

"Hmm, yes, that *is* odd," admitted Grayson.

"Come on!" Henry reached for my hand. "We must go, Liv."

"Grayson can come as well." My heart was beating a little faster, and I didn't know why.

"No, I can't." Grayson shook his head. "I'm not backing out now! I'd never let the team down. It would be cowardly and unworthy."

"But, Grayson, none of this is really happening." I had to shout over my shoulder, because Henry was already leading me up the steps, and the noise in the hall was terrible.

"Grayson will be fine by himself," Henry assured me.

"But . . . it sounds as if they're going to kill him any moment now!" We'd reached Grayson's door, and I turned back again. "Listen to that!"

"I'm not deaf!"

"Burn him now, burn the traitor. Burn him now, not a day later!" chanted the mob, while Henry flung the door open and pushed me out into the corridor on the other side. He energetically slammed the door behind us, and the shouting and noise in the hall fell silent at once.

"You're a fine kind of friend," I said reproachfully.

"And you're still here." I didn't know if he was saying that to me or to Frightful Freddy, who now spread his wings and fluffed up his feathers slightly.

"No one can come in unless they say my name three times backward."

"Yes, sure, maybe next time, Fatty," said Henry. He had obviously forgotten to let go of my hand, and I decided not to remind him. Not yet, anyway, because it felt rather good.

Surreptitiously, I glanced at Henry sideways. The lighting conditions in this corridor were like the light on a summer evening when the sun has just sunk beneath the horizon and it isn't really light or really dark. There were no windows or lamps anywhere, so it wasn't clear where the light came from. But it made Henry look rather good. I hoped it did the same for me, because he was subjecting me to a thorough examination as well.

"You're still here," he repeated.

"Is that a good thing or not? And shouldn't we go back in again and help poor Grayson?"

"Don't worry about Grayson. He's fine. He won't even remember his dream tomorrow morning."

"How about us?"

"That's what I'm trying to find out." He smiled at me. "Coming for a little walk?"

"We've been doing that for some time." And in fact we had. We strolled down the corridor side by side, holding hands. A brand-new experience for me, both in a dream and in real life. I didn't mind if it went on a little longer.

"Let's hope Lottie doesn't come around the corner with her hatchet," I murmured.

"What?"

"Oh, nothing." Only now did I see that several other passages branched off this corridor, all lined with doors and all of them infinitely long. We ought to have passed my door long ago, but it must have changed places again. "If we were in Grayson's dream back there, whose dream are we in now?"

"Interesting question," said Henry, and at first I thought he was going to leave it at that. But then he added, "There are only two possibilities: Either this is my dream, in which case I'm dreaming about you. Or . . ." He fell silent again.

"Or it's my dream, and then I'm dreaming about you." It was a very nice dream at that. I smiled up at him. "You know something? I've never held hands with a boy before."

He stopped and raised an eyebrow incredulously. "Really not?"

"No." His voice had sounded so intrigued that I was quick to add, "But of course I've kissed and so on. Lots of times." At least in my dreams. Once—and I was ashamed of it to that day—once even with Justin Bieber. On the other hand, my experiences in real life could be counted on the fingers of one hand. Well, to be precise, on two of the fingers of one hand.

"Oh, well, that reassures me," said Henry ironically, but I had the impression that he was holding my hand a little more firmly as we strolled on.

"This feels different from a normal dream," I said. "It's like the other night in the cemetery. I know all the time that it's a dream. So I can say things that I'd never say otherwise."

"That kind of thing is called lucid dreaming. When you realize that you're dreaming . . ."

"I know, I read up on it on the Internet. But the Internet didn't say anything about other people being able to have the same dream at the same time."

"No, you won't find anything on the Internet about that."

"Where will I, then? And what does it all have to do with Grayson's sweater and these doors? Do you have one too?"

"Of course." Annoyingly, my last question was the only one he answered.

We went a little way farther in silence. Then he said, "I'll show you my door if you show me yours."

"I think that one could be my mother's." I pointed to the pale-gray shop door that I'd noticed earlier.

"Matthews's Moonshine Antiquarian Books? I've never seen that one before. Looks pretty."

"I'm sure it's Mom's. It even has her name on it. She went back to her maiden name of Matthews when she and my father divorced. And a bookshop like that suits her down to the ground, only if I went through that doorway, I wouldn't be in a bookshop, would I? I'd be in the dream that my mother is dreaming at this moment."

"If you could get through the doorway at all . . ."

I shook myself. "I bet she dreams of Ernest all night— yuck. Just remind me of that so I never happen to go in there by mistake!"

Even as I was saying that, I realized how absurd it was, but Henry only laughed.

"Yes, there are some dreams one really wouldn't want to share. Take Jasper, for instance. Most of the people in his dreams are stark naked. . . ." He suddenly stopped. "This door is mine, by the way."

"How funny. Right opposite mine," I said. "There was a red one there a little while ago."

"Yes, they keep changing places. I still haven't entirely worked out the system behind it."

His door, like mine, looked rather old, but it was taller and broader than mine, and painted black. There was a classical knocker shaped like a lion's head, and the words DREAM ON were carved into the lintel of the door, which made me smile. The only odd thing was that instead of a single keyhole, Henry's door had three of them, one above the other.

Meanwhile, Henry was scrutinizing my door. "Looks as if it led into a cottage in the Cotswolds," he said. "Except for the lizard. Does the lizard have some deeper meaning?"

"How would I know?" I shrugged my shoulders. "Why do you have so many locks on your door?"

He didn't answer at once. Then he said, "I just don't like having unexpected visitors."

I tried to think about that, but it was difficult to work it out clearly. Maybe because Henry was still holding my hand. "If these are the ways into our dreams, then why are we out here?" I asked. "And what's going on in there without us?"

"I've no idea. I suspect that without us nothing goes on in there, but of course we can't be sure. It's something like the light inside the refrigerator. . . ."

The sound of a door latching made us both jump. Jump away from each other, to be precise. But there wasn't anyone in sight. The corridor was empty.

"We'd better go home now and . . . er . . . get a bit of sleep." Henry gave me a crooked grin. He had let go of my hand and was taking three keys out of his jeans pocket.

"Why are you whispering? There isn't anyone here." I stared back the way the sound had come from.

"You never know." Henry turned the keys in their key-holes, one by one, and each time there was a loud, metallic click. "Sleep well, Liv. It was nice sharing a dream with you."

"Yes. I thought so too." Sighing, I turned to my lizard doorknob. A pity the dream was over. I still had so many questions. And after all . . . "Thanks for holding hands."

Henry was half into his doorway when he turned back to me again. "You're welcome. Oh, and Liv?"

"Hmm?"

"If I were you, I really wouldn't go to Arthur's party."

"Oh." I tried not to show that my feelings were hurt. First Grayson, now Henry.

"Unless you're really, really keen on something danger-ous with an uncertain outcome," he said, his eyes twinkling.

I felt rather as if I'd been caught out in something.

"Seriously, if you're clever, you'd better stay away from us. We'll just have to find someone else to take Anabel's place."

"Take her place doing what?" I asked, but the black door had already closed behind him, and I could hear him bolting it on the inside. Three times.

If you're clever . . . Well, I wasn't stupid, anyway. So I also knew that people who said things like *You'd better stay away from us* had something to hide. But that had been clear to me all along. There was more than one mystery to be revealed here. And it was in the nature of mysteries to be a little dangerous as well.

Maybe it was only my imagination that made me think it was suddenly turning cold. The light seemed to be paler, the shadows in the corridor deeper, and I was overcome by an unpleasant sense of not being alone. I quickly opened my green door, slipped inside, and let the latch click shut behind me. Not a second later, I heard knocking on the wood from the other side of the door, a very soft, gentle sound, hardly more than scraping or scratching. Something told me it would be better not to look and see what made that sound.

"There you are at last, Livvy," someone said behind me, and when I turned around, I saw Mia, Lottie, and Mom sitting in the Finchleys' brightly lit kitchen, with playing cards on the table.

"Did you hear that?" I asked.

"What?"

"Well, that strange scraping at the—" I hesitated, because when I turned again, the door had disappeared. Where it had been I now saw the kitchen window, framed by what were probably the most hideous tartan curtains in the world.

Somewhere or other, an alarm clock was going off.

15

"IS THAT FOR SCHOOL?" asked Lottie, pointing to my notebook.

"Yes," I said untruthfully, hoping she wouldn't read what I had just been writing.

TIME OF DAY: 2 a.m.
GRAYSON'S SWEATER: on
MEMORY OF A DREAM: yes
MEMORY OF GREEN DOOR IN THE DREAM: yes
DETAILED DESCRIPTION OF THE DREAM:
A flood. Lottie, Mia, Mom, and I are drifting through an unknown city on a raft. Buttercup is swimming along at the same time. I see the green door on one of the flooded houses. I know that for some reason it's important, but I don't feel like swimming over to it. The water looks cold. I'm sure there are crocodiles in it.

"Schoolwork on a Saturday, and before breakfast at that? Aren't you overdoing things a bit? I'm worried about those dark shadows under your eyes." Lottie stroked my hair. "If I didn't know better, I'd think you weren't getting enough sleep. But it can't be that. You've been in bed before ten every evening."

"Yes, so I have." For the last two days I'd hardly been able to wait until it was evening and I could go to bed. That was because I'd decided to investigate the dream phenomenon by deliberately experimenting on myself. Because what did Sherlock Holmes say? "It is a capital mistake to theorize before one has data. Insensibly one begins to twist facts to suit theories, instead of theories to suit facts."

So I had started a series of experiments. Dreams with Grayson's sweater on and dreams without it. I had set my alarm clock to go off on the hour, every hour, and kept careful records. Now I was reading through the notes I'd made again, so as to evaluate them scientifically.

TIME OF DAY: 3 a.m.
GRAYSON'S SWEATER: off
MEMORY OF A DREAM: yes
MEMORY OF GREEN DOOR IN THE DREAM: yes
DETAILED DESCRIPTION OF THE DREAM:
My kung fu teacher Mr. Wu and I are standing at Adliswil aerial cableway station in Switzerland with a lot of tourists, and Mr. Wu wants me to demonstrate the lift kick, using the strength of my neck, on a fat American woman tourist in a lilac T-shirt. When I ask him if he's gone right off his rocker, he says, "Confucius says the wise man forgets insults just as the ungrateful man forgets good deeds." The green door is part of the cableway, so it is hanging in midair. All the same, I go through it and find myself in the corridor.

It all looks peaceful and harmless. Not a trace of any sinister, scraping, or scrabbling creature. I look for Grayson's door and say Freddy's name three times backward. But the door is locked. I shake the handle hard. Frightful Freddy says I have no manners. I say the wise man forgets insults just as the ungrateful man forgets good deeds. Then I shake the handles of two more doors, just for fun, so to speak. They are all locked. An alarm clock rings loudly. My alarm clock. I curse it.

I suppressed a groan. All this read more like the notes of a lunatic than something that could be scientifically evaluated.

"My bet is iron deficiency, but she could have something else." Lottie had turned to Mom, who was just wandering across the living room half dressed. Family Meeting Number Two was planned for today, minus quails but plus Lottie, Buttercup, house-clearing operation, and choice of color for walls (also presumably plus more nervous breakdowns from Florence). There was still a good half an hour to go before we had to set out, but Mom's nerves were already shot to pieces. Buttercup was trotting after Mom, with her dog leash in her mouth.

"We ought to make an appointment for Liv to see the doctor," suggested Lottie.

"Hmm?" As usual, Mom had heard only the last thing anyone said. She seemed to be searching for something. "Aren't you feeling well, mousie? Today of all days, when you want to go to that party?"

"I'm feeling fine. Lottie's just worried about the rings under my eyes."

"Oh, you can borrow my concealer. Then no one will notice them. Has anyone seen the dog leash?"

"Woof," went Butter, but Mom paid no attention. Instead, she turned to Lottie. "Don't worry, I had much worse rings under my eyes at Liv's age."

"Because you were smoking pot, Mom."

"Nonsense. I never smoked pot until I went to college." Mom turned frantically around on her own axis. "Mia, do put that thing down and get dressed! I don't want us to be too late. Ernest's youngest brother is going to be there, and the painters, and where the hell is that . . ."

Lottie took the leash out of Buttercup's mouth and handed it to Mom.

"At the age of fifteen, anyway, I had rings under my eyes for entirely different reasons," said Mom, still following her own train of thought. She looked at the dog leash in surprise. "No, not what you may be thinking. I was sitting up at night writing poetry. I was unhappily in love."

"Poor you. What was his name?" asked Mia.

"Whose name?"

"The name of the boy you were writing poetry about when you were fifteen and unhappily in love."

"Oh, there were so many of them." Mom made a throwaway gesture, and Buttercup took the chance to retrieve her dog leash. "At that age you fall in love with someone else every three weeks."

"Maybe *you* did," said Mia. "Liv and I aren't so susceptible. Right, Livvy? We're not hormone-driven dimwits with brains made of pink candy floss."

I wasn't so sure of that any longer. I feared I was thinking

about Henry and the way he looked or smiled too often . . .
but, okay, I was still far from being a hormone-driven dim-
wit with a pink-candy-floss brain. There was no reason to be
that way either. When Henry had passed me in school yesterday morning, all he'd said was a friendly "Hi, cheese
girl," and nothing, absolutely nothing, about him had shown
that we'd been holding hands in a dream. My sound human
reason told me the same thing, but there was still that funny
feeling in the pit of my stomach, and I simply couldn't ignore
it. That was another reason why I'd begun my series of nocturnal experiments: one way or another, those dreams were
driving me nuts.

TIME OF DAY: 4 a.m.
GRAYSON'S SWEATER: on
MEMORY OF A DREAM: No. Oh God, I feel so tired.
Stupid experiment.
MEMORY OF GREEN DOOR IN THE DREAM: no
DETAILED DESCRIPTION OF THE DREAM: —

TIME OF DAY: 5 a.m.
GRAYSON'S SWEATER: on
MEMORY OF A DREAM: yes
MEMORY OF GREEN DOOR IN THE DREAM: yes
DETAILED DESCRIPTION OF THE DREAM:
I'm lying in a hammock in a beautiful garden, under cherry
trees in blossom, surrounded by high brick walls. I see the
green door in one of the walls, and I know I ought to go
through it so as to carry on with my empirical investigation.
But my eyelids are so heavy, and the hammock is so

comfortable, and the buzzing of the bees makes me all
sleepy...wonderful...Grrr!!! The darn alarm clock goes off.

TIME OF DAY: 6 a.m.
GRAYSON'S SWEATER: on
MEMORY OF A DREAM: yes
MEMORY OF GREEN DOOR IN THE DREAM: yes
DETAILED DESCRIPTION OF THE DREAM:
Right, so I may be tired to death. Guess I fell asleep only
about a minute before the alarm went off, so only a short
dream. Slipped through green door in corridor, went over
to Grayson's door, quick chat with Freddy, went through
Grayson's door, landed in a classroom. Grayson's English class,
every bit as boring as the real thing, horribly realistic. Was
woken before anything interesting could happen.

So what did that mean? Except that I'd been propping my
eyes open for two nights running just to check exactly when
I had gone through what door in my dreams? I felt like tearing my hair out.

"Woof." Buttercup was standing in front of me, her leash
in her mouth, her head to one side. Clever dog—fresh air
was exactly what I needed at this moment. I closed my ring-
bound notebook and stood up.

"I'll take Butter out for a little walk," I offered. "Then
you can get dressed in peace."

"Mind you don't get lost again," said Lottie anxiously,
and Mom backed her up. "Make sure you're here on the dot."

Their warning against getting lost, unfortunately, had
more sense in it than you might think, because here in London,

my usually reliable internal navigation system had let me down badly several times. It wasn't just that the streets in this part of town all looked to me just like each other, with their old-fashioned rows of brick houses, especially in the rain; I was also inclined to go the wrong way when I got off the bus, and I pointed confidently south when I really wanted to go north. Obviously my brain was having difficulty in adjusting to the Northern instead of the Southern Hemisphere.

But with Buttercup beside me, I was sure to find my way back. There was a Labrador retriever somewhere in her gene pool, and they were excellent tracker dogs.

She scampered happily off in the direction of Kenwood Park (or so I hoped, anyway). It was a bright September morning, and a fresh wind blew the hair away from my face and ruffled Buttercup's coat. We turned into a street called Well Walk. It really lived up to its pleasant name; there was a broad green central strip down the middle of the carriage-way, with tall trees and benches, and even two picturesque red telephone boxes looking as if they'd been put there specially for tourists. The houses on the right and left of the road all had beautiful doors that could equally well have turned up in my mysterious corridor.

Slowly, the chaos inside my head was sorting itself out a little. When I looked at the notes I'd made on the last two nights, they did allow me to draw a few general conclusions. First: The green door turned up in every dream sooner or later. It was sometimes quite a while before I actually noticed it, but when I did I also knew that I was dreaming, and then I could decide much of what happened next in the dream for myself. For instance, I could go through the door into the corridor. Second: If I was wearing Grayson's sweater, I could go through his door, but if I wasn't wearing it his door was locked. Third: In fact, all the doors along that corridor seemed to be locked. Fourth: I could clearly dream in great detail of people I'd never met in real life. I'd recognized the girl who had been sitting in the stands beside Florence in Grayson's basketball nightmare the next morning, from a photo in the Tittle-Tattle blog, and only half an hour later I'd seen her in person, standing in the schoolyard. With Grayson. She was Emily Clark, editor of the school magazine *reflexx*. So she was both Grayson's girlfriend and his boss, if Secrecy was to be believed. After this discovery, Mia had put Emily at the very top of her list of suspects for people who might be Secrecy. It made sense: first, as editor in chief of the magazine, Emily had access to all kinds of sources and a great deal of information; second, she wrote well; and third, she was very close to Florence and Grayson and was sure to hear all the latest news of the Spencer family.

And last night, Friday night, I had met Anabel Scott, Arthur's girlfriend (or ex-girlfriend, according to Secrecy), in another dream. Judging by my notes on my dreams, that had been between three and four in the morning, and it had been the most interesting dream of all. The trouble I'd taken was kind of worth it for that dream alone.

Once again, in the dream, I'd been on the aerial cableway with a philosophical Mr. Wu, so I'd been happy to go out of my green doorway into the corridor. After I'd dutifully made small talk with Frightful Freddy and shaken Grayson's locked door—I wasn't wearing his sweater—I walked aimlessly along the corridor, looking at the doors and wondering who they belonged to. Matthews's Moonshine Antiquarian Bookshop (closed) was of course the way into

Mom's dreams, and I could imagine that the door painted sky blue, overgrown with ivy, and decorated with carved owls on the lintel was Mia's, particularly as it had a pot of forget-me-nots outside it, and they were Mia's favorite flowers. I passed Henry's door again too, and when I pushed down the door handle—after all, this was part of my series of experiments—someone spoke behind me.

"He never forgets to lock it," said a girl's soft voice.

I spun around, one hand on my racing heart.

"Sorry, I didn't mean to startle you," said the girl. She was small and delicately built. Golden-blond, wavy hair framed her regular features and flowed over her slender shoulders almost down to her waist.

"You look like Botticelli's Venus!" I exclaimed.

"Yes, but only when I'm standing around in a seashell with no clothes on." The girl smiled and offered me her hand. "Hi. I'm Anabel Scott. Are you Henry's girlfriend?"

"Er . . . not exactly." I had to pull myself together if I was going to take my eyes off her. Anabel Scott was one of Secrecy's favorite subjects for a good gossip, and even I—to be honest—had already felt very curious about her. She was immaculate from head to foot. No wonder Arthur had fallen in love with her. Optically, at least, they were the perfect couple.

I returned her smile, took the hand that she was still holding out, and shook it, which made me feel very odd. But, hey, this was a polite sort of dream. For a moment I wondered what to say next. "Nice to meet you, even if it's only in a dream"? "Aren't you studying in Switzerland?" "Are you really lying in bed right now, fast asleep?" And "are the rumors about you and Arthur splitting up right?" Instead I said, "I'm Liv Silver. I'm . . . er . . . new here." In this corridor.

Anabel's green eyes widened. "Then you're the girl Arthur was talking about. . . . The girl who can help us."

"Help you with what?"

She looked cautiously around, and I wondered what she was expecting. Did she think Frightful Freddy was going to creep up behind us and pinch our bottoms?

"I'm not really supposed to tell you anything about it," she finally whispered, biting the perfect curve of her lower lip. "But it's my fault, after all. I got the boys into this situation."

There are some phrases that have an irresistible effect on me, whether in real life or in a dream. One of them, anyway, was "I'm not really supposed to tell you anything about it." It came right next to "You'd better keep away from us."

"You're right," I whispered back. "It's certainly safer for you not to talk about it."

Anabel hesitated. A tiny frown appeared on her perfect brow.

"Well, I'd better be going," I said casually. "It was nice getting to know you."

As I turned to walk away, she started talking nineteen to the dozen. My word, that had been really easy.

"I convinced the boys to do it at Halloween last year. You do understand that, don't you?" she exclaimed. "It was really meant to be just a game. How was I to guess that . . . ?" Once again she looked anxiously around. "You mustn't lie to him. He can see right into your soul, and he's pitiless if you don't follow his rules."

Who? What? What on earth are you talking about? Those were only a few of the questions on the tip of my tongue. I started with the first.

"Who?" For the sake of dramatic effect, I leaned forward and spoke in as mysterious a whisper as hers. "Who's pitiless?"

She shook her head and avoided answering my question. "I do love Arthur—you must believe me. I always thought all that stuff about the one great love of your life was nonsense—until I met Arthur. . . . It was like a tsunami rolling over us. I knew we were meant for each other, I knew he was the man I'd been waiting for all my life." She faltered and bit her lip.

Good heavens. You could hardly get more theatrical. Quite apart from the fact that I was always suspicious of anyone baring her heart about her great passion to a total stranger, hadn't there been something different about it in the Tittle-Tattle blog? Arthur was the one great love of her life? She had to be kidding. How about that ex-boyfriend Tom Something? And wasn't he dead?

She let out a sigh. "At least, I ought to have known that you can't lie to him."

"You mean Arthur?"

Anabel looked at me in surprise. "No! I'm talking about *him.*" Only now did I notice that the pupils of her eyes were enormous. Her words went wandering down the corridor and were thrown back from the walls as a whispering echo. "I mean the one we conjured up by playing the game."

I stared at her. "Conjured up? Who did you conjure up?" And why?

Anabel said nothing for a couple of seconds, and then she

whispered, "He has many names. Lord of the Winds. Keeper of the Shadows. Demon of the Night."

The corridor became noticeably darker. A cold draft of air touched my arms, and I felt the little hairs on the back of my neck standing on end. Not so much because of what Anabel was saying as because she was clearly frightened. I could see it in her eyes.

"He is lord over dreams. The Akkadians called him Lilu. In Sumerian his name is Lulila, in Persian mythology he is . . ."

"Lulila, Lord of the Winds?" The little hairs on the back of my neck lay down in their usual position, and I burst into a fit of the giggles. I really couldn't help it.

Anabel was staring at me, wide-eyed. "You shouldn't . . . No one makes fun of a Demon of the Night."

"I'm sorry . . ." I gasped, trying to control myself. "But if he doesn't want to be laughed at, maybe he ought to give himself a more terrifying name." Oh, this was useless. Another peal of laughter made its way out of me. "Really, I mean, Lulila! Sounds like something out of a lullaby for Teletubbies."

The fear in Anabel's face had given way to incredulous astonishment, along with something else that I couldn't identify because my vision was blurred by tears of mirth. *Lulila, Lord of the Winds . . .* There was no stopping my laughter—it was as if I'd never heard anything funnier in my life.

Anabel seemed to be frozen rigid with horror.

I knew myself that my reaction was totally inappropriate. Particularly as the light in the corridor had turned so atmospherically gloomy and the temperature had distinctly fallen lower. But before I could pull myself together and apologize to Anabel, the alarm clock went off.

And I found myself awake, still laughing.

Even now, out taking Buttercup for a walk, I couldn't help giggling so loudly that she turned her head and gave me an inquiring glance.

"It's all right, Butter," I told her. "Do your business, then we'll go back, and I'll give your coat a little brushing." I looked at the time. "Anyway, you're going to see your future home today. And your new patchwork family, along with the patchwork family cat. We want you to look cute, so that all of them will love you."

Buttercup stood still, put her head to one side, and looked so cute that even the most conservative tomcat in the world would take her into his patchwork heart. Even the Pope's cat, if he happened to have one.

Then she barked at a cyclist so suddenly that he almost collided with a lamppost.

I giggled again. That dog was a real little devil.

Speaking of which, it was quite difficult to bring Lulila up on the Internet (there were any number of children's-wear stores with that name), but I did finally find a list of Sumerian gods and demons. *Lulila, Sumerian demon of the night.* Unfortunately that was all. However, I was able to add another point to the scientific evaluation of my dreams on record. Fifth, I was obviously able to dream of things that I couldn't possibly know.

16

FOR VARIOUS REASONS, there was a little tension in the air when we arrived at Ernest's house. First, we really were twenty minutes late (but it wasn't my fault; it was because, led astray by Miss Seventy Percent Sure Mia, we'd boarded the wrong bus), and second, Mia and I had deep forebodings about Lottie and Florence and how they would get on.

"If she makes a single nasty remark . . . ," muttered Mia ominously to herself.

We hadn't told Lottie how furious Florence had been at the idea of giving up some of her space; even Mom hadn't dropped the faintest hint. Otherwise, we all knew Lottie either wouldn't have come with us or, considerably more likely, would have insisted on moving into the broom cupboard.

"Or if she has any kind of silly look on her face . . . ," Mia went on.

Myself, I stared at Frightful Freddy outside the Spencers' front door and could only just stop myself saying "Ydderf, Ydderf, Ydderf" instead of ringing the bell. Strange how familiar I'd become with that overweight stone statue over the last few nights. I almost expected it to wink at me.

Mia and I had run from the bus stop, shaking off Mom and Lottie, and only now did they round the corner, gasping for breath. At the same time, unfortunately, so did a tall man in corduroys and a roll-neck pullover, coming from the opposite direction and apparently in just as much of a hurry. He stumbled over the dog leash, which didn't amuse Butter at all. She began yapping and kicking up a fuss, and there was minor chaos. Mia and I tried to grab her collar, but that wasn't so easy; Buttercup twisted and turned like an eel. The extra-long leash wrapped itself around Lottie's feet and the man's legs, and they both fell over while Mom stood there watching and saying, "Bad dog!" about ten times in a row, not very helpfully.

At last I managed to drag Buttercup away by her collar, and Lottie and the man got to their feet. In doing that they banged their heads together, and when Lottie said, "Ouch!" Buttercup would happily have leaped to her defense. She barked reproachfully.

"Bad dog," said Mom faintly.

The man rubbed his forehead. "Are you all right?" he asked Lottie, and I really thought the better of him. Anyone else in his position would have threatened us with legal proceedings.

"I'm so sorry," said Lottie, rather breathlessly, putting a strand of brown hair back from her face. "I'm usually a very nice dog."

Mia put her hand in front of her mouth so as not to burst out laughing.

"Er, I mean she is," stammered Lottie, going red in the

face. The sight of the tall man seemed to have confused her terribly. "She's a dear, good dog. I . . . er . . . it's just that she doesn't like postmen."

"Well, I'm not a postman," the tall man assured her. "I'm the black sheep of the Spencer family, Ernest's brother Charles. And you must be the new additions to our family. I'm very glad to meet you all."

Now that we had time to take a closer look at him, we weren't really surprised by these revelations, because Charles was very like Ernest: the same broad shoulders, the same blue eyes, the same bald patch on the way, the same enormous elephant ears. Even his voice was very like Ernest's.

He shook hands with us one by one, and we told him our names and assured him that we were pleased to meet him, too. When it was Lottie's turn, she blushed even more and explained that she was the mindchilder.

"Or something like that, anyway," murmured Mom.

Mia and I exchanged glances of alarm. What on earth was the matter with Lottie? We could hardly believe our ears when our mindchilder went on to reveal her family secrets that even we had never known before.

"I used to be the black sheep of my own family," she said cheerfully. "But then my cousin Franziska fell in love with her cleaning lady, so that made her the black sheep instead. Until my cousin Basti converted his hotel into a swingers' club and—"

"Let's leave the details until later," Mom hastily interrupted her, firmly pressing the doorbell. "After all, there's no end of furniture to move. . . . Oh, hello, Ernest darling! I'm so sorry we're late, but it wasn't my fault."

"We boarded the bong wrus," explained Lottie with a

blissful smile, although it wasn't meant for Ernest. I was gradually getting the idea of what was going on.

"I think we've found a possible candidate for Operation Marrying Off Lottie," I whispered to Mia as we went indoors. "That black sheep with the beginnings of a bald patch somehow seems to be her type."

"Yup," agreed Mia. "I'll just sound him out."

And so she did, by asking a whole series of indiscreet questions while wearing her sweetest smile. The questions were addressed either to Charles himself or to his relations.

By the end of that day we'd made a good deal of progress. First, we had introduced Spot and Buttercup to each other, which, considering Butter's inauspicious first appearance, proved surprisingly simple. They began with a staring match, Spot looking down with a haughty expression from his place on the sofa, Buttercup snuffling anxiously as she kept close to Lottie's legs. Then they decided to ignore each other for the rest of the day. Spot was much better at that than Buttercup, who kept casting suspicious glances at the sofa but otherwise stayed with us as we went all around the house. We got a lot of exercise, because we had to move what felt like forty tons of furniture and boxes from right to left, from up to down. We basically cleared everything out and put it back in a different place.

Meanwhile, we'd looked at over fifty shades of white paint for the walls, picking the ones with the prettiest names ("Old Lace" for Lottie, "Snow White" for Mia, "Seashell" for me). Here, surprisingly, Florence turned out to be an adviser with a good sense of style, while Grayson was practically color-blind. ("Are you trying to be funny? They're all white, for heaven's sake!")

We had also put together an exhaustive file on Ernest's brother Charles. He was thirty-nine years old, childless, and had been on his own for two years. Getting divorced from his ex-wife, Eleanor, "the greedy dragon," had cost him a holiday home in the south of France, a Jaguar, and endless nervous stress. The vertical line between his eyebrows was also Eleanor's doing, or so Florence claimed. He played tennis, donated to the World Wildlife Fund, liked open-air classical music concerts in the park, and a band called Lambchop. Speaking of lambs, he was known as the black sheep of the family not because—for instance—he sprayed graffiti on the walls of tunnels or grew his own cannabis or did whatever else you might expect a black sheep to do, but just because, unlike his three older brothers, he hadn't studied law or gone into politics. Instead, he was a dentist with a practice in Islington. Mia and I were rather disappointed. A veterinarian would have been fine, but a dentist—well, that wasn't quite so toothsome, if you see what I mean. . . .

However, Charles wasn't the only one who had to undergo cross-examination; Lottie herself was bombarded with peculiar questions, because clearly Florence had a problem with Germans, so she wanted to know whether there had been any Nazis in Lottie's family and, if so, whether she felt guilty and what she was doing about it.

Mia would happily have come to blows with Florence over that question, but Lottie said that as far as she knew, any Nazis in the family had died in the Second World War, and Florence seemed happy with that for now. She appeared to have come to terms with the merger between our families, and the rearrangement of the Spencer household that was part of it. At least she wasn't complaining anymore and did not seem about to fall into hysterics. I was almost disappointed. I'd liked Florence better when she lost her self-control and let rip.

And of course Mom wasn't about to spare me embarrassing remarks. For practical reasons, she kept them until lunchtime, because then everyone would get the benefit of hearing them.

"It's sweet of you to take Liv to that party with you this evening," she said, beaming at Grayson. All I needed now was for her to pat his cheek. "I always say, young people don't spend Saturday evening at home unless they have a temperature of a hundred degrees. I'm so glad Liv won't be a wallflower here in London."

"Er . . ." Grayson was clearly at a loss for words. He glanced at me, and I couldn't resist a mischievous grin.

"Mom, I don't think you're up to date with the latest developments. You'll embarrass Grayson. You see, he'd rather I didn't go to the party this evening."

Ernest put his soup spoon down. "What did you say?"

Grayson put a piece of bread in his mouth and muttered something that no one could make out. I felt slightly sorry for him, but he'd been asking for it.

"Nonsense, mousie," said Mom. "Why, you have Grayson to thank for your invitation to the party in the first place. Isn't that so, Grayson?"

Grayson swallowed. "Yes, well, but it . . . I've . . . um . . . er." A quick glance at me, and then he seemed to pull himself together. He went on, without quite so much stammering, "These parties are rather wild. I mean, there's a lot of alcohol flowing, and what with Liv being only fifteen, I thought it would be better if she stayed at home and . . ."

Oh, really, this was too much. "I'm going to be sixteen in three weeks' time," I said, stung.

"Really? You don't look it."

"Grayson!" Ernest gave him a stern glance. So did I. What did he mean, I didn't look it?

"I can tell what he's thinking," said Mom. "He's a responsible boy—he only wants to protect Liv." She turned to her future stepson. "But there's really no need for you to worry, Grayson dear. You just have fun at the party—Liv can look after herself perfectly well." She leaned over to Ernest and whispered loud enough for everyone at the table to hear her. "Too well, I sometimes think. At her age I'd already done it all: my first hangover, my first joint, my first experience of sex. Liv is something of a late developer there. I'm rather afraid she may take after her father. He never did anything in his life without thinking it over first. Or no, I'm wrong about that; after all, he married me." She laughed.

Ernest joined in her laughter, although he looked slightly confused, like his brother Charles, who at least seemed to be relieved that he wasn't under attack this time.

"Hear that?" I said to Grayson. "The more dangerous your friends are, the better my mother will like it. Even if they go holding the Black Mass by night in cemeteries."

I could have been just imagining it, but I thought that Grayson turned a little pale. He tightened his lips, pushed his chair back, and stood up. "I'm going back to moving the furniture."

"If Grayson doesn't want to look after Liv, I can do it," Florence volunteered as Grayson left the room with a last, dark glance at me. "I'm going on to Arthur's party right after our meeting of the ball committee."

I had no chance to get indignant about that, because Mom pricked up her ears again the moment she heard the word *ball*. Her interest pleased Florence, who began describing the Autumn Ball and all the party dresses in glowing colors as the most romantic day in the year. An absolute must in the life of anyone at Frognal Academy, although—and at this point a brief and distinctly malicious smile flitted over Florence's face—although sad, very sad, to say, it was only for upper school students.

Mom looked as if she were going to burst into tears of disappointment right away.

"Younger students can go to the ball only as someone older's dancing partner." Florence's voice was positively dripping with regret. "And the stupid thing is, Grayson's already taking Emily."

Mom sighed.

"But with a little luck, I might be able to find Liv a part-ner . . . ," added Florence.

Yes, that was exactly what Persephone had predicted. And of course, Mom fell straight into Florence's trap.

"Really?" she said enthusiastically, and I could see that, in her mind's eye, she was already choosing my ball dress. "Liv, mousie, wouldn't that be great?"

"Hmm . . . Difficult, but I think Emily's brother Sam is still free." Florence frowned, as if working that out had really been a great strain. "Maybe I could persuade him to take Liv to the ball."

Sure, Sam. Or Pimply Sam, as Persephone had called him.

"But of course I can't promise anything."

This was getting better and better. Next I supposed we'd

have to go on our knees to Pimply Sam and beg him to go to the ball with me. Maybe even bribe him.

"It sounds like a truly horrific occasion," I said with emphasis. "Let me make one thing clear: I'd sooner have a root canal without anesthetic than go to that ball."

"Liv!" exclaimed Mom, and Florence, piqued, raised her eyebrows, muttering something about foxes and sour grapes.

"I once had a root canal without anesthetic," said Lottie, "and believe me, it's not something you'd ever want to do."

"Root canal without anesthetic?" repeated Charles incredulously, and Lottie nodded.

"My uncle Kurt is a dentist. A bad dentist, a mean old miser, and a sadist." With a sideways glance at Florence, Lottie made haste to add, "He's not a Nazi, all the same."

"Then I suppose you don't especially like dentists?" Charles's tone of voice was distinctly regretful. "I mean, if you've had such bad experiences."

Lottie blushed and launched into a peculiar speech about sadistic dentists, getting her words all mixed up again, until Buttercup nudged her with her nose and prevented the worst from happening. During lunch, she had been lying under the table looking anxiously at the sleeping cat. But now she obviously wanted to help Lottie out of a fix by reminding her that it was long past time for her usual midday walk. Lottie seized the chance to shut her mouth and pick up the dog leash. I felt sure she was in urgent need of some fresh air. A little cold water splashed in her face wouldn't have been a bad idea either.

Thoughtfully, Florence watched her go. "I think she has a funny accent, even for someone German," she said, but so quietly that (I hoped) Lottie couldn't hear her. "What breed is that dog of yours, by the way?"

I was opening my mouth to defend Lottie's accent (she didn't have one—she was just getting her words mixed up today) and to enumerate all the dog breeds that had, presumably, featured among Buttercup's forebears (it was a long list), when Mia interrupted me.

"Buttercup is an Entlebuch Biosphere dog," she explained, perfectly straight-faced. "It's a very rare and valuable breed of Swiss herd dogs."

Buttercup, who had trotted after Lottie, turned back at these words, looking as rare and valuable and cute as she could manage. So did Lottie, who was waiting for her in the doorway.

"Delightful dog," said Charles enthusiastically.

Mia bent over her plate and muttered, but luckily not at such high volume as Mom, "All the same, we like veterinarians better."

17

ARTHUR'S FATHER'S VILLA was exactly what I'd originally expected Ernest's house to be like—roller garage door on the street with a CCV camera over it, garden like a park, porch with pillars that might have played a leading part in *Gone with the Wind*, and—honestly!—a fountain in the front hall. It was hard to imagine anyone simply living here.

"Looks like a private clinic for the drug-addicted kids of millionaires," I whispered to Grayson.

"That's not so far from the truth," said Grayson. "Except that you can get plenty of drugs and alcohol around here."

"My mother would be really glad of that," I said.

"I'm sure she would." Grayson rubbed his forehead. "She's rather different from most mothers, right?"

"You noticed? I'm glad you're speaking to me again, incidentally." On the way here he'd simply stared grumpily ahead of him. When I got into the car, he managed a "hello," but apart from that, not a word had passed his lips.

He shrugged. "One way or another, I can't change it now. You're here, although I did warn you against it."

"Yes," I said, satisfied. In the car I'd been so tired, I'd been afraid I might simply fall asleep beside the silent Grayson. My empirical studies at night and the furniture moving had drained me. But now I was more or less awake and ready to solve a few mysteries.

A young man who looked badly stressed out had opened the door and sent us off down a side corridor with the words, "The young people's party is in the pool house." According to Grayson, the young man was the private secretary of Arthur's father, who was also throwing a little party tonight. (Arthur's father, I mean, not the secretary.) Although the word *little* was presumably to be taken relatively among the Hamiltons.

The pool, for instance, was at least fifteen yards long, and the pool house around it larger than anywhere I'd ever lived. All that glass was rather alarming. This would be no place to start throwing stones. At the near end of the room there was a bar so well equipped that it might have been in a pub. The lighting in the pool was beautiful, but although the water looked really inviting, no one was swimming. Maybe that would be for later. It was rather full in here, and several people were dancing so close to the edge of the pool that they'd probably fall in sooner or later, and then they'd *have* to swim.

Anyway, the mood was cheerful. At the sight of several girls in slinky dresses and high heels I wondered whether I ought to feel underdressed and develop a little inferiority complex, but then, thank goodness, I saw several others in jeans and T-shirts, and breathed a sigh of relief. My dark-blue shirt had a low neckline, and the new jeans that I'd bought in Zurich on one of Papa's generous days fitted perfectly. I was also wearing lip gloss, mascara, Mom's concealer, and a little silver butterfly barrette in my hair that Mia had given me because it was too kitschy for her.

"There's Arthur and Jasper," I said. I almost had to shout—the mixture of party music and all those voices talking at once was an acoustic disaster in a building with so much glass. "Why is Jasper doing a thumbs-up sign and grinning in that weird way?"

"Because he thinks I've worked a miracle and brought you here in spite of your mother's opposition," replied Grayson, while Arthur and Jasper made their way toward us through the dancers. "You can simply say no." He took hold of my arms and looked pleadingly at me. "Listen, Liv, do please simply say no."

"No to what?" I asked, but Arthur and Jasper had already reached us.

"Hey, it's little Liz! With her hair down and no glasses. Wow!" Jasper was beaming at me. "Good work, Grayson," he said, raising his hand for high fives with Grayson. Grayson, however, just grinned rather awkwardly. And his hand was still firmly around my forearm.

"I'm so glad it worked, Liv," said Arthur. He looked even better than usual, if possible, without his school uniform. A classical Michelangelo statue, except that he wasn't naked but in jeans and a close-fitting black polo shirt.

"But I . . . ," I began. However, Grayson interrupted me.

"It wasn't easy to convince her mother," he said, holding my arm a little more firmly. "I had to promise to drop her off home again at eleven."

"Oh . . ." I tried not to look at Grayson in consternation.

"Well, better than nothing," was all Arthur said. "Are you hungry? My father's having a party of his own this evening, celebrating some kind of business deal. I made sure catering would keep something for us. Sushi, dumplings, and raspberry tarts."

"And we almost winkled a redheaded waitress away from the main party," said Jasper. "But unfortunately Arthur's dad wanted to keep her for himself—hey, is that Henry over there?"

I took a deep breath, preparing to arm myself against whatever might happen. Even the mention of Henry's name made my heart miss half a beat. It didn't help that he looked as if he'd had his hair blow-dried in a tropical storm, wind force twelve. The way we'd held hands in a dream made me feel awkward, although his behavior gave me no reason at all to suppose he could have dreamed anything like the same thing. We'd studiously ignored each other in school. That's to say, he had ignored me and I'd pretended to ignore him.

"Hey, you were going to be here two hours ago," said Jasper.

"Yes, I know." Henry looked at Grayson's hand, which was still grasping my forearm. Grayson jumped and let go of my arm, as if he'd only just noticed that he'd been cutting off my blood supply all this time.

"Sorry," said Henry. There were dark shadows under his eyes. "I couldn't get away from home—the usual little family weekend crisis." He and Grayson performed their funny kindergarten ritual again, hooking fingers together, clapping hands, and for a moment Grayson's face relaxed slightly.

"Is everything okay now?" Arthur sympathetically asked Henry.

Henry nodded but seemed not to want to answer at any

length. "Hi, cheese girl," he said instead, smiling at me. "Here after all?"

"Yes, my terribly strict mother said I could go out this evening for once," I said, with a surreptitious glance at Grayson.

"But only until eleven," he said, unmoved.

"Oh, shit!" Jasper pointed to a redheaded girl in a blue, off-the-shoulder dress so short that it could have passed as a swimsuit. "Who invited Madison?"

So that was Jasper's ex. She was standing very close to a boy on one of the long sides of the shining, turquoise pool, laughing very loudly.

"Madison is here with Nathan," said Arthur. "You have to be strong now, Jasper. I'll just go over and say hi, okay? But I'll be right back."

"Huh," said Jasper, watching as Arthur joined the two beside the pool. "It's all the same to me. The way she acts as if *she* were the one who dumped *me* is annoying, that's all. When all the time it was the other way around, of course."

"Of course," murmured Grayson.

"I mean . . . *Nathan*! I ask you! Imagine Madison trying to make me jealous of that garden gnome, of all people! Me, Jasper Grant! When his nose . . . Just look at that huge nose of his, and then compare it with his tiny little—"

"Yes, calm down, Jasper. We're on your side," Henry interrupted.

Jasper, surprisingly, changed his tone of voice from injured to sweet as honey. "Wouldn't anyone feel sorry for Madison? Wouldn't *you*, little Lizzie?" Without taking his eyes off his ex-girlfriend, he put an arm around my shoulders. "First she chases me for months on end, writing me high-flown love letters, then as soon as I dump her, she throws herself at the next comer. Out of sheer desperation." He had come a little closer to me with every word he said, and now his lips were almost touching my ear. "Wow, you smell good, by the way."

"Leave her alone, Jasper," said Grayson, but Jasper ignored him.

"What's that perfume you're wearing?" he whispered in my ear. "It's driving me crazy!"

"Obviously. Particularly as I'm not wearing any perfume at all." I freed myself from his grasp, although much more gently than I'd normally have done, because Madison was still looking at us.

"Would you like something to drink?" Jasper asked me, and when I nodded, he beamed. "I'm going to create a new drink this evening just for you. I'll call it Sweet Liz in honor of the sweetest girl in the room."

Henry snorted, amused.

"Her name is Liv," said Grayson, irritated. "*L-I-V*. And she's only fifteen, Jas, so you're not going to fill her up with alcohol or use her to make Madison jealous. And what's more—"

Jasper interrupted him. "Go away, spoilsport. Talk to your Emily." He pointed to two girls who were just coming in through the wide-open doors at the near end of the pool building, Florence and a slender girl with shoulder-length brown hair. Emily Clark, editor in chief of the students' magazine.

Feeling curious, I stood on tiptoe to get a better view. Florence was looking lovely. Her shining hair fell to her casual leather jacket, which she'd combined with a short skirt and boots. Emily was at least a head taller, and with her severe haircut, black blazer, and black pants she looked like Florence's elder sister—or a college student who took her studies very seriously. Or like someone who wants to sell you insurance. Mia and I suspected that Emily was behind Secrecy and the Tittle-Tattle blog—a suspicion based largely on the fact that over the three years of its existence, the blog had never said anything mean about Emily, apart from a comment on the unattractive appearance of horse-riding helmets, and some minor digs at the good marks Emily always got in school. However, the term *pushy* used about her could be taken as a cleverly disguised compliment—or as talking herself up—and the photo of Emily in horse-riding gear was not at all unattractive. In fact, she was probably the only person in the world who didn't look silly with a hard hat on.

"Has Emancipated Emily actually been to the hairdresser?" asked Jasper. "And is that *lipstick* she's wearing?" He whistled softly through his teeth. "She's fallen for you in a big way, Grayson."

As if to prove his point, Emily smiled and waved to us, while Florence turned to a dark-haired boy with slumped shoulders whose facial-skin problem was obvious even from here, in spite of the dim light. Good heavens—that must be Pimply Sam, no doubt about it. His gaze was wandering around. Florence had probably just been offering him a hundred pounds to take me to the Autumn Ball, and now he wanted to see if the offer was large enough. I was fairly sure that Mom, too, would be ready to pay that and even more to see her daughter in a Victorian-style ball dress.

I got into cover behind Grayson.

"What with the gracious way Emily is smiling and waving,

you might think she was standing on the balcony of Buckingham Palace," said Henry. "I'd say she's waiting for her prince to turn up."

Grayson sighed deeply, and Jasper nudged him in the ribs. "Go on. We'll look after Liz."

"Liv!"

"That's what I said."

"Okay. I'll be right back," said Grayson to no one in particular. He turned and wandered over to Emily. Jasper, Henry, and I watched their meeting.

"Ordinary sort of noncommittal peck on both cheeks," commented Henry.

"Just the kind of kiss I give my aunt Gertrude when we see each other," I said. (And I held my breath too, because Aunt Gertrude always smelled of a not-very-nice mixture of wet dog and hairspray.)

However, Emily didn't seem satisfied with an Aunt Gertrude kiss. She glanced briefly our way, then put both arms around Grayson's neck and pulled his mouth down to hers. It was a tongue kiss worthy of Hollywood.

"Uh-huh," went Jasper.

And Henry said, "Too bad about the lipstick, then."

"I guess she just doesn't want anyone to think she might smell of wet dog, like my aunt Gertrude," I said.

"Between you and me, I think she always does smell of the stables a bit," whispered Arthur, who had come up behind us again, unnoticed. "Of hay and leather and horse droppings . . . but don't say so to Grayson. Especially since it looks like she's getting to feel more passionate about him than her horse."

"And her horse is called Conquest of Paradise," added

Henry. Without even looking, I knew what kind of face he was making. I tried not to giggle.

Emily and Grayson were still kissing, and it was getting kind of embarrassing to watch.

"Maybe they'd better look for a room somewhere," murmured Jasper. Henry and Arthur exchanged a brief glance.

Then Arthur suddenly asked, "Er, Liv, would you like to see our home cinema and the film archive?"

All at once I was wide awake and concentrating intently. Was something about to happen? Was I going to find out just why Grayson had tried so hard to keep me away from this party? Jasper, Henry, and Arthur seemed equally interested. They were looking at me expectantly. You could almost have said they were lying in wait for me.

Do please simply say no—I hadn't forgotten Grayson's words.

"Yes," I said firmly. "I'd love to."

18

ONLY IN THE CORRIDOR going back to the main house did I realize exactly how loud the party music had been. There was a squeaking in my ears, but we left the thumping basses behind, and finally only our footsteps echoed at unnaturally loud volume on the polished granite flagstones.

I turned around. "Where's Jasper?"

"He's mixing us a couple of drinks, then he'll follow. This way." We had reached the end of the corridor and turned into the front hall, where the fountain was peacefully playing. There was no one in sight, but you could hear muted voices and piano music.

"The cinema and the film archive are down on the lower floor," Arthur explained, opening a door.

Ahead of us, a flight of stairs led down. My feet stopped of their own accord.

"Maybe it's not the best idea to go down into a gloomy cellar with two guys you hardly know, eh, Liv?" Henry appeared next to me, looking at me sideways, his eyebrows ironically raised as usual.

Oddly enough, I'd been thinking exactly the same thing (and so, obviously, had my feet). Hadn't Mom said, only a few hours ago, that she was afraid I'd never do anything in my life without mulling it over first, just like my father? Who did she think she was kidding?

But as Mr. Wu always said, "He who thinks too long before taking the next step will spend his life standing on one leg."

I started moving again. What was there to be scared of, I asked myself with my sweetest, most innocent smile. (I could do the eyebrow-raising trick myself, too, and pretty well, but I was going to keep that for later. You want to go easy on imitating tricks like that, or the effect soon wears off.)

"The lower floor isn't a gloomy cellar, and we're not strangers." Arthur sounded slightly insulted, and sure enough the word *cellar* turned out to be unsuitable when we arrived in the home cinema. Thanks to a series of handsome ceiling and wall lights, it was bright as day, and the corridor—which, with all its doors, reminded me a little of the corridor in my dreams—was luxuriously carpeted.

"All the same, the walls here are really thick. No one would hear your screams." Henry didn't seem to know when to drop the subject.

I shrugged my shoulders casually, and this time I quoted out loud from Mr. Wu's wide range of proverbs: "But if the dragon wants to rise in the air, it must fly against the wind." *Also, I can do kung fu.*

Henry laughed, and Arthur opened a heavy door at the end of the corridor.

"Come in!" he said with an inviting gesture and stood aside for me.

Impressed, I stared at the rows of cinema seats upholstered in red velour and rising like a ramp, at least ten seats per row, framed by steps to left and right. The fitted carpet on the steps was soft and black. Crazy. These people really did have a genuine cinema in their cellar! When Arthur turned a switch near the door, the auditorium was gently illuminated by countless tiny lights shining like stars on the ceiling, which was lined with black fabric.

A sharp scream rang out. I looked instinctively at the loudspeakers, because the scream could easily have come from *Scary Movie*, but two heads emerged in one of the back rows of seats. One was the head of a man, gray haired and distinguished looking, the other the head of a woman with an expensive Bond Street hairstyle, although at this moment she seemed to be beside herself.

"Oh, Mrs. Kelly. And Sir Braxton. Sorry to disturb you," said Arthur politely, turning the switch farther until the starry sky consisted entirely of supernovas, and the cinema was bathed in bright, clear light. "My friends and I will be gone again in half an hour's time, or thereabouts."

"Bloody hell," muttered the man, and he began frantically adjusting his clothes. It took him only a few seconds, and then he came storming down the steps, his shirt still unbuttoned. I didn't get out of his way fast enough, and he promptly ran into my shoulder with the force of a suburban train coming into a station. If Henry hadn't caught me, I'd have fallen over.

"Lout," I said. Even though I understood why he was in such a hurry, he didn't have to use me as a buffer.

"Do you mean me?" Henry laughed quietly and stroked

the hair back from my forehead before he let me go. I tried to go on breathing normally. The last thing I wanted was for him to notice how confused he made me feel when I was near him.

It took the poor woman a little longer to get fully dressed again. When she finally came down the steps, red in the face, she kept her gaze fixed on the floor.

"How nice to see you again, Mrs. Kelly," said Arthur, sketching a bow as she raced past us. In spite of her high heels, her speed was worthy of the Olympic Games. "And give your husband my regards if he happens to be at the party too."

Mrs. Kelly hurried along the corridor as if she hadn't heard him.

"That was mean of you," said Henry.

"Sir Braxton could have waited for her," I said sympathetically.

"Ah, well." Arthur closed the door to the corridor and dimmed the light again. "Real gentlemen are nearly extinct these days, as my grandmother is always saying. Where were we? Oh, yes." He smiled at me. "Well, what do you think of our cinema?"

I was wide awake again at once, and on the ball. "It's great," I said cautiously, stroking the soft velour of an upholstered armrest. And why exactly were we here?

"I could find us a 1950s horror film from the archive next door," suggested Arthur. He was still standing beside the door, hands in his jeans pockets. "They're not a bit scary, but if my father's to be believed, they're amazingly valuable from the cinema enthusiast's point of view. What do you like best, Liv? Zombies, ghosts, vampires . . . ?"

"Or maybe demons?" added Henry.

Was that the cue? Were secrets finally about to be aired?

I assumed my innocent-little-lamb smile again. "But we can't watch a film right now—you have fifty guests up there."

"More like seventy by this time, I guess," said Arthur, shrugging his shoulders. "But they'll do fine without me. This is more important."

Something bumped into the door.

"Good, our drinks." Arthur opened the door, and Jasper stumbled in, laden with glasses, several bottles, a bucket of ice cubes, and two oranges that he had wedged between his ear and his shoulder, with his head tilted to one side. His face was half hidden by a bunch of mint that he'd stuck in his mouth. It fell out when he started talking. Henry was just in time to catch it before it fell to the floor.

"I couldn't find a tray, so I thought I'd just mix the drinks down here," explained Jasper, trying to put everything else carefully down on one of the seats. "Well? Have you asked her yet?"

"Asked her what?" I retrieved the oranges as they were rolling away over the black fitted carpet.

"Well, whether you'll . . . join in our game instead of Anabel," replied Jasper. "Only, of course it won't work unless you're still a virgin. So first of all we ought to ask, right away: *Are* you a virgin?"

What in heaven's name was that to do with him? What was the idea?

"Oh, keep your mouth shut, Jas," said Henry as the innocent-little-lamb smile disappeared from my face.

"What do you mean?" Baffled, Jasper frowned. "What's

the point of spending hours explaining what it's all about to her, and then maybe it turns out that she wouldn't be right for the part anyway? I read only the other day that, on average, girls first do it aged fifteen, and she's fifteen and hot stuff, or she would be if she didn't wear those funny glasses, so it's a perfectly reasonable question. Are you still a virgin, Liv, yes or no?"

I stared at them, thunderstruck. "You're involved in a game which only *virgins* can play?"

"Oh, brilliant, Jasper. Now she thinks we're out of our minds."

"I didn't mean to do that." Jasper looked repentant. "I just didn't want to waste time. How would you two have gone about it, then?"

Henry leaned against the wall and folded his arms. "Presumably we'd have begun by pointing out the advantages of the game before going on to the crazy part."

"Slowly and carefully." Arthur looked distinctly less amused than Henry.

"What kind of game, exactly, is it?" I quickly asked.

Arthur opened his mouth to tell me, but Jasper got in first. "Not a game you play with dice. And it's not about winning, either. It's more a kind of role-playing game—not that anyone is really playing a part. Basically it's not a *game* at all. If you feel confused now, so do I. I call it confusing too. Very confusing. So confusing that right now I'm going to mix us a drink before I go on." He had lined up the glasses on the armrest of the cinema seat and unscrewed the top of a bottle of gin.

Arthur was looking as if he'd like to grab Jasper and hold

his mouth closed, but after a glance at Henry, he contented himself with flashing his eyes furiously at Jasper instead. In his own turn, Jasper took no notice whatsoever of his friend's attempt to communicate wordlessly with him. "I'm ready to admit that I still don't really understand it," he chattered on. "Especially all that dream business—it's really way out. But with a little practice it worked for me, too, and wow, all that about the wishes bowled me over, and yup, it's cool, or anyway it was cool until . . . Oh, shit, I've gone and forgotten the chalice for saying the Mass."

This just could not be true! Now he was carrying on about the stupid chalice for saying Mass! "It was cool until what?" I asked, more impatiently than I meant.

"Until we broke the rules. Well, it was really only Anabel, but that makes no difference to him." Jasper had decided to stop complaining about the chalice. He poured lavish amounts of gin over the ice cubes. "It's like this: at least one of the players must have virgin blood, because the last seal can be broken only with virgin blood, and at Halloween last year, when we began playing the game, well, I still thought that just about qualified most of us, up to and including Anabel—sorry, Arthur. . . ."

"That's okay." Arthur had dropped into one of the cinema seats, burying his head in his hands. He'd clearly given up trying to make Jasper keep quiet.

I rubbed my arms inconspicuously, or so I hoped. They had come up in goose bumps, because only then did it dawn on me that what Jasper said made reasonably good sense, in light of the story Anabel had told me in my dream last night. About a game they had begun playing last Halloween . . . a game that had gotten out of control, and Anabel said it was her fault.

I glanced quickly at Henry, who was still leaning back against the wall. Like Arthur, he had stopped making any attempt to stop Jasper. Maybe because so far I hadn't run away screaming, or maybe simply because no one *could* have stopped Jasper at this point.

Jasper had put down the gin bottle and was now pouring vermouth into the glasses—plenty of it too. The mere smell was enough to make you tipsy.

"But then it turned out, surprisingly, that Grayson had a relationship with Maisie, and Henry is a stupid mystery-monger who never tells us anything, while Arthur had lost his virginity when he was fifteen to that really cute French trainee teacher, but unfortunately he'd forgotten to tell his best friend about it." Here Jasper favored Arthur with a reproachful glance. "So, in fact—and who'd have thought it?—at the beginning of the game, Anabel really was the only one of us who hadn't had sex yet. Basically, one of us would have been enough. But then Anabel went and, er, broke the rules of the game, exactly when and who with I don't know, but anyway it's a very complicated and dramatic story, and everything went wrong, and now we need a new Anabel, one who's guaranteed to be a virgin and stay a virgin until the end of the game. So how about it, Liv? Are you a virgin, yes or no?" As he'd come out with the last few sentences all in a rush, he was now gasping for air.

Arthur gave a hollow groan.

"Well, Liv, so now you're in the loop," said Henry sarcastically. "Are you well and truly scared?"

Unfortunately I wasn't. If anything, the opposite. I was burning to ask a few concrete questions, but I didn't yet want to admit how much I already knew. Particularly as most of what I did know came from some very dubious dreams.

"I think I'd like to know something about the advantages of the dreams," I said. "You mentioned those."

"Oh, there are plenty of *them*! Let's see . . ." Jasper frowned, thinking hard. "If you join the game, for instance, you'd have four potential partners for the Autumn Ball right away. Any girl at our school would be envious of you!"

Henry laughed briefly. "You're using the Autumn Ball as bait?"

"Why not? Other girls would commit murder for such a choice of partners. I should have mentioned that first, shouldn't I?"

"Oh, Jasper, you're a hopeless case." Arthur put his hand out. "Give me a glass of that."

"I haven't finished mixing the drinks yet," said Jasper, rapping him on the knuckles. "They still need Campari and a slice of orange. And a sprig of mint. We were going to get sozzled in style, remember?"

At that moment the door was opened, and bright light from the corridor fell into the home cinema.

"Hi, Grayson." Arthur fished up the gin bottle from Jasper's seat.

" 'Hi, Grayson,' is it?" repeated Grayson angrily. "Have you all lost your marbles? Simply going off with Liv when for once I don't keep an eye on you for a minute?"

"It was much more than a minute," murmured Henry.

"The drinks are ready now," said Jasper.

"You're the utter end, all of you!"

Arthur heaved a deep sigh. "Come on in and shut the door, Grayson."

But Grayson shook his head. "It's getting late. I must take Liv h—oh, for heaven's sake, Arthur, are you drinking gin straight from the bottle?"

"Get off your high horse, Grayson," said Henry. "Nothing's happened to Liv."

"Exactly." Arthur draped his legs over the armrest of the seat next to him and offered Grayson the bottle. "Have a swig of that and don't look at us as if we just robbed a bank. We were only trying to initiate Liv into our mystery."

"Oh yes? I hope you didn't leave anything out—Anabel's dog, for instance, and the nightmares, and what—oh, forget it!" Grayson looked as if he'd explode with fury any moment now. "Come along, Liv. We're leaving," he said through his teeth.

I didn't move from the spot. He was looking rather desperate, but I just couldn't leave yet, not when I was so close to finding out what was at the heart of the mystery.

"It's only ten fifteen, man. Relax," said Arthur, glancing at his watch. "Please," he added almost pleadingly.

Grayson closed the door. "I've told you a hundred times, we have to find another solution—but you just ignore me, of course. Why won't you listen, for once in your lives—oh, damn it! Whatever they've told you, Liv, you must simply forget it again!"

"I'd like to understand it first," I said.

"That's the trouble," said Arthur. "It's really hard to understand if you haven't experienced it."

"And I explained it very well," said Jasper, offended. "Particularly considering that I don't understand it myself."

Grayson was going to say something, but I got in first. "So you were playing a game last Halloween—a game that isn't a real game, and at least one of the players still has to be a virgin," I said hastily. "Right?"

"Right!" Jasper cast a triumphant look around the rest of the company. "There, you see? She *does* get the idea!"

The others didn't react. Grayson rubbed his forehead with the back of his hand, Arthur took another swig from the gin bottle, Henry picked separate leaves off the bunch of mint and rubbed them to pieces in his fingers.

"But *why*?" I asked.

Henry looked up. "Why are we playing the game, or why do the rules of the game say that at least one of the players must be a virgin?"

"Both," I said.

The silence went on for some time. Even Jasper didn't answer me but took a pocketknife out of his jeans and tried slicing one of the oranges with it. He wasn't very successful.

"Well, let's put it this way." It was Arthur's voice, slightly metallic and hollow, that finally broke the silence. "It was Halloween, and there was a power cut all over North London, so our party ended earlier than expected. We were all wound up and in love and ready to do something crazy."

"You were in love," Henry corrected him. "The rest of us were just drunk."

"True." Grayson, resigned, leaned back against the door.

"Anyway, we were in a really good mood," Arthur went on. "It was the middle of the night, we were on our own in Anabel's house, and the red wine from her father's cellar was good stuff. . . ."

"And don't forget to tell her it was really scary Halloween

weather outside, dark and misty and so on." Jasper was taking center stage again, although he was still slaughtering the orange. "Anabel had lit a lot of candles, and when she brought out that mysterious book and suggested trying something quite different for a change, it kind of felt, well . . . the right thing to do. Conjuring up a demon on Halloween—I mean, sounds perfect, doesn't it? It was fun, too, at first, and it seemed to me as harmless as . . . as telling your fortune by reading the tea leaves. No one expects the tea leaves to develop an independent life of their own and come tormenting you in your dreams by night. Or go about murdering dogs . . ."

Ah, we were coming to the point at long last.

"So that's your game? Conjuring up demons?" And what did the dog have to do with it?

Jasper nodded. "I know it sounds totally idiotic."

"It *is* totally idiotic," said Grayson.

"It was only meant to be a joke. None of us expected it to work." Jasper sighed. "We simply repeated the words after Anabel, added a few drops of our blood to the red wine we were drinking, drew a funny sort of penta-thingy on the floor—"

"Pentagram, Jas, for about the thousandth time," said Henry.

"Whatever you say." Jasper rolled his eyes. "Then we made our wishes. No one could have guessed that the whole thing would turn out so . . . so *real*."

It sounded to me like they needed an exorcist more than a virgin. "You mean conjuring up this demon really worked?" I was making such an effort to banish any doubt or mockery from my voice that I sounded like a psychotherapist in a bad

TV film, doing her level best to understand. A psychotherapist whose voice shows how crazy she thinks her patients
are. "Exactly how do I picture this scene to myself?"

No one told me. Henry, apparently lost in thought, was
letting scraps of green mint leaves drop to the floor, a frowning Arthur was watching the ice cubes in Jasper's glasses
melt, Grayson was biting his lower lip, and Jasper was still
murdering the orange.

I was beginning to feel tired of working so hard to winkle
their secrets out of them, especially since an answer always
gave rise to another ten questions. "So on Halloween last
year you conjured up a demon, for fun," I said, summing up
the results to date. "According to a game that you found in
an old book, with instructions saying one of the players must
be a virgin. But because your virgin turned out not to be a
virgin anymore, you need a substitute player. And for some
reason or other, that's why you picked me."

But I knew the reason: it was because I'd landed right in
front of them during that dream on Monday night.

"Assuming you *are* still a virgin," confirmed Jasper.

"Yes, I get that bit. What I don't get, apart from just
how the game works, is why you don't stop playing it.
Simple."

"No, it's not simple at all. That's why." Jasper leaned forward and went on, lowering his voice, "We did try, but you
see, you can't make a pact with a demon and then just wriggle
out of it."

"I see. Of course you can't," I replied in my best psychotherapist's voice, looking inquiringly at Henry. For a
moment I felt as if I were back in Highgate Cemetery. Henry

suspected that they hadn't been dreaming *of me*, they'd been dreaming *with me*, I was fairly sure of that—but the way it looked, he hadn't shared his suspicions with the others. Apart, maybe, from Grayson, who kept on asking for his sweater back.

I tried to phrase my next question in such a way that they'd be forced to give me more information. "But what, exactly, did this demon do to you? Looks like you really believe in it, right?"

Once again, all I got was silence. Silly mistake. I ought to have refrained from asking that second question. I sighed. I wasn't about to get any further this way.

"Okay," I said, to cut the whole thing short.

"Okay?" Jasper wasn't the only one to give me an inquiring glance.

I took a deep breath and looked all around at them. "Okay, I'll do it. I'll take over for Anabel in your game, but only if you answer all my questions, and believe me, I have a whole lot of them."

The moment I'd said that, the atmosphere in the room was entirely different. They suddenly all began talking at once.

"Do you mean you really are still a virgin?" cried Jasper. "I knew it! An ugly pair of glasses like that must be good for something!"

Arthur put the gin bottle down, stood up, and said solemnly, "Liv Silver, you've saved our lives! And I promise to answer all your questions as well as I can." He laughed. "Oh, I'd just love to give you a hug—only, if I do that, I bet Grayson will land a punch on me."

Grayson did indeed look as if he'd like to hit Arthur. "You don't know what you're doing," he said, adding something else, but it was lost in all the noise his friends were making.

Only Henry said nothing. He just looked at me and shook his head almost imperceptibly. Then he smiled.

19

"I'LL TAKE YOU UP," said Grayson after he had managed, as if by magic, to maneuver Ernest's wide Mercedes into a tiny little parking space. "So you won't be in trouble for staying out so late."

"Are you crazy?" I slammed the passenger door much harder than necessary. "It's ten past eleven, and we're here only because you made up that fairy tale about my strict mother and I didn't want to show you up in front of your friends." And I'd have liked so much to stay there. In the time I had left to me, I hadn't been able to ask even a fraction of the questions whirring around in my head. On the short drive back Grayson had said nothing to help in clarifying the situation; he had just told me off, saying "damn it all" and "downright stupid" with above-average frequency.

Even so, however, I'd been given a few answers that I needed to think over thoroughly. To be honest, I couldn't wait to open my notebook and write it all down—this time maybe with the help of clearly organized graphs.

Grayson had climbed out of the car too. "We're in London. Do you know how high the crime rate in this city is?"

"Yes, sure, it's hardly safe to walk a step in this run-down area." I pointed to the nostalgically old-fashioned streetlights ahead of us in the sleeping street, which looked like an advertising brochure for idyllic town living. "Street gangs indulging in shoot-outs the whole time, sex fiends lurking in front gardens, and isn't that Jack the Ripper just coming around the corner—oh, shit!"

It wasn't Jack the Ripper, it was Mom, who'd been taking Buttercup for her evening walk, just coming around the corner. But that was about as bad.

"If I were you, I'd get right back in that car and drive away, Grayson!" I hissed.

"Don't make such a damn fuss. I only want to take you to the damn door, because that's damn well the right thing to do!" Grayson wasted his last chance of flight by shooting furious glances at me from his caramel-colored eyes.

And by then Mom had seen us. "Yoo-hoo," she called, letting Buttercup off the leash so that she could run on ahead and jump up at us.

I was able to relish the surprised expression on Grayson's face for two seconds. "Your own fault, if you ask me," I said sweetly. "Now you can explain why we're back at only just after eleven."

"Because her daughter always says yes when she ought to say no?" Grayson bent down to pat Buttercup and imitated my voice. "What? You're doing something forbidden and dangerous that I don't understand, and in addition I've been expressly warned against it? Yes, sure, I'd just love to join in!"

"You are such a . . ." As I was searching for the right word, Mom reached us.

"Hello, you two! Back already? Wasn't it a good party?"

"Yes, it was great." I smiled as maliciously as possible. "But Grayson wanted to get rid of me."

"I only wanted to keep you from having to go to Accident and Emergency with alcohol poisoning after your first party in London," Grayson retorted. "One of Jasper's drinks would have been quite enough for that."

I wasn't smiling anymore, certainly not maliciously. "I beg your pardon? I didn't even have a sip."

"No, because I brought you home in good time. If they'd offered you one, you'd have been unable to say no, because it's such a difficult word for you to understand."

"Oh, my dears!" Mom looked positively moved. "You're behaving just like a real brother and sister! I must call Ernest and tell him."

I rolled my eyes. Typical! She saw only what she wanted to see. I climbed the steps to the front door of the apartment block, shaking my head. Buttercup followed me. "See you sometime," I said as haughtily as possible.

But Grayson wasn't through with me yet. "I'd like to come in with you," I heard him saying. "If I may."

"Of course you may, dear," said Mom before I could spin around and strike Grayson dead with a look. She fished the front door key out of her pocket and unlocked the door. "Lottie's been baking blueberry muffins. Baking soothes her nerves, so she had to bake three trays of muffins today. . . . I'm afraid meeting Charles has turned her ideas upside down."

My own ideas were turned upside down as well.

"What are you looking like that for?" Grayson pushed his way past me at the door and ran upstairs ahead of me. Buttercup followed him, flapping her ears happily. I didn't catch up with the two of them until just before the door of our apartment.

"What's the idea?" I hissed at Grayson. My hair had fallen over my face, and when I pushed it back I realized that my butterfly barrette had gone missing. I must have lost it somewhere.

"What do you mean?" Grayson crouched down to tickle Buttercup's tummy. The treacherous dog had rolled over on her back in front of him. "I suppose I'm allowed to eat a few blueberry muffins with my new family."

"Of course you are," said Mom, who had made it to the fourth floor too, without ruining her hairstyle and almost without getting breathless. "We're very glad to see you."

That was not entirely true. Only Mom was glad to see him. Lottie and Mia didn't look glad so much as embarrassed to see Grayson when they set eyes on him. They were in their bathrobes and had covered their faces with greenish-gray face masks, which made them look a little like zombies.

"Nice apartment," said Grayson politely while Lottie and Mia took refuge in the bathroom.

I laughed out loud. "You're such a hypocrite!"

Mom looked sternly at me. "I have no idea why you two have quarreled, but I hope you'll make up again soon." She put her head to one side. "Muffins?"

"Yes, please," said Grayson. "Can Liv and I maybe eat them in her room? So that we can make up the quarrel at our leisure?"

What in the world did he mean?

"Of course." Deeply moved, Mom put a hand to her breast. "You know, Liv has always wanted a big brother. Oh, this is all so . . . I really must call Ernest." And with one last, emotional sigh, she disappeared into her bedroom. I stared after her, left speechless.

Grayson was strolling down the corridor. "Which is your room?" he asked. "This one?"

"Yes, but . . . can you please tell me what all this is in aid of? Isn't Emily waiting for you back at the party?"

"Presumably." He was getting his iPhone out of his jeans with one hand and already opening the door of my room with the other. "Are you going to get us those muffins?"

I was taken by surprise, and I almost switched on too late. But then I felt boiling hot as I thought of my dream reports. They were lying on the chest of drawers in my room, and I definitely didn't want Grayson seeing them. So I pushed them aside and put the notebook and any loose sheets of paper together before he could get a look. However, that wasn't his idea at all. He was making purposefully for my bed—or, to be exact, the foot of my bed. I had put his hooded sweater there, carefully folded, so that Lottie wouldn't think of washing it until I'd finished my empirical investigations. He picked it up with a satisfied smile.

I saw it all at once. "Oh, so *that's* why you're carrying on like this!" I said. "You want your silly sweater back."

Bloody hell. I really had underestimated him. I'd never have expected him to be so cunning.

Grayson was checking his iPhone. "That's right," he said casually, looking at the display. "I kind of had an idea you weren't going to give it back of your own accord. . . . Hey, there's a lot going on at the party. Looks like Jasper is just trying to drown poor Nathan in the pool. I'd better get straight back. Don't want to miss this! Sweet dreams, Liv."

The self-satisfied grin on his face was more than I could stand. Ditto the feeling that I'd been hoodwinked.

"Not so fast!" I threw myself against the door, barring his way out. "We haven't made up yet!"

He obviously hadn't expected that. He stared at me in surprise, looking more like his usual self already.

I gave him one of my sugary-sweet smiles. "Want me to fetch Mom to help us do it? She's really good at that kind of thing."

"Very funny. I really do have to get back there now," said Grayson, and I was pleased to see that he didn't seem so casual anymore.

I didn't move from the spot. "You ought to have thought of that before. I mean, before you started on about the crime rate in London. Does Emily know you meet your friends in cemeteries at night to conjure up demons?"

"We don't meet to—no. No, she doesn't know." He began pacing restlessly up and down the room. He clearly realized that he wasn't going to get past me without the use of violence. "And she must never know. Emily is the most rational person I've ever met. She wouldn't understand how anyone can get mixed up with something like this. She'd simply say I was out of my mind. Emily doesn't even believe her horoscope."

"Nor do I, to be honest. Any more than I believe in demons."

"I suppose you think I believed in that sort of thing,

do you?" he asked, heatedly. "Even now I don't really believe in it. It's just that . . . well, a few odd and really bad things happened, and I simply don't have a logical explanation for all that."

I was still feeling pretty cross, but unfortunately I understood exactly what he meant. "If you eliminate all the logical solutions to a problem, then the illogical solution—even though it's impossible—has to be the right one," I said, and he smiled.

"Sherlock Holmes, right?"

Surprised, I nodded.

For a moment there was silence between us. Grayson sat down on the edge of my bed and looked at me as if he were expecting something.

I hesitated for a moment. Then I asked, "Will you tell me about it? I mean, so that I have a chance of understanding it all?"

"I don't know. . . ." Doubtfully, Grayson pushed his hair back from his forehead. "I'm still angry with you for not listening to me."

"But don't you think it would be better to explain than go on bawling me out? After all, I've promised to help you and your friends."

"You could still change your mind." A glimmer of hope came into his face.

I just shook my head and dropped onto the bed beside him. "Start with the dreams," I said.

He didn't start with the dreams—he went even farther back. But at least he started. He told me about Jasper, Arthur, Henry, and himself, how they'd been friends ever since elementary school; he told me about the heights and depths of their friendship, and all the silly things they'd seen and done together over the years. Finally he came to that strange night at Halloween last year. The way he told the story, it sounded just as ridiculous as Jasper's version, and I made a great effort to keep as straight a face as I could, in case he jumped up again and ran for it. I have to admit, that was a real challenge (keeping a straight face, I mean), especially when Grayson finally and reluctantly went into detail.

Anabel had shown them a dusty old book with sealed pages that had apparently been in her family's possession for generations. If you followed the rituals in this book, Anabel claimed, you could conjure up an ancient demon from the underworld—a demon that could help you to gain immeasurable power and grant your dearest wishes.

I only just managed to bite back the words, "Yup, and I expect immortality was on offer too?" Extraordinary. Surely they couldn't have been as drunk as that. Although they obviously had been, because after they'd performed the gruesome ritual of initiation, if I was to believe what Grayson said, they'd really gone all out for the rest of it. After breaking the first seal, they drew magic symbols on the floor in chalk, scribbled mysterious words on each other's skin, and recited the spells and oaths that Anabel read out to them— half of them in Latin. They promised, in high-flown terms, to keep the rules laid down in the book all the way to the end and free the demon from the underworld if he, in return, granted their secret wishes, which they wrote down on paper and then solemnly burned. They sealed the whole agreement in their blood, letting drops of it fall into a chalice, mixing it with red wine, and drank from the chalice in turn.

In short, they behaved like kids in nursery school. Well, like kids in vampire nursery school.

I wasn't in the least surprised when, at this point in his story, Grayson gave vent to an ashamed kind of sound, like a mixture of a groan and a howl.

"So did your demon appear?" I could finally forget about keeping a straight face. "Or did you just wake with frightful hangovers the next day?"

Grayson glowered at me. "Okay, I know how ridiculous it sounds. And I'd have forgotten the whole thing again right away—so would the others. But those dreams began the very next night. . . ." He shuddered. "In my dream, the demon reminded me of the promise we'd given him in exchange for granting our wishes."

"That's only logical. Your unconscious mind had to process that idiotic stuff somehow or other," I said.

"Could be." Grayson rubbed his forehead. Suddenly his expression was just like Mom's when she's desperately searching for something she put down somewhere. "But then how would you explain the fact that we all dreamed exactly the same thing that night? All of us without exception. The demon insisted that we must break the second seal and go on to the next ritual—"

There was a beep somewhere in Grayson's jeans pocket, clearly his cell phone announcing a text message coming in. He didn't take the phone out, but I was glad of the short diversion, because for a moment I really had felt rather queasy in the pit of my stomach.

"So you all dreamed of a demon?" I wanted to know more of the details. "What did he look like?"

Grayson made a vague gesture. "I think he took visible shape only in Jasper's dreams—he swears to this day that the demon looked like Saruman the White, except with horns and a black cloak. For the rest of us he was only a shadow, a whispering voice, a bodiless presence, although that wasn't as frightening as it sounds, it was more—I don't know how to put it—more *seductive*." He sighed. "An extraordinary coincidence? We weren't sure. We opened the second seal in Anabel's book."

I'd probably have done exactly the same.

"This time I was stone-cold sober, so the ritual seemed to me a bit more ridiculous than before, if anything, but we went through with it."

"Then what?" I realized that by now I was listening to Grayson intently. Maybe rather *too* intently.

"Nothing much at first. Except that our dreams got more and more lifelike and vivid. We dreamed of the demon and each other, of doors and corridors, and the next day we could remember exactly what we'd said to one another in those dreams." He bit his lower lip. "As if we really had met. That was . . . was frightening. Well, to me and Anabel, anyway. Henry thought it was interesting, Arthur thought it was exhilarating, and Jasper—oh, I think Jasper just thought it was funny."

I sensed that we were coming to the point of the story, and I had that queasy feeling in the pit of my stomach again. "So you could dream together," I summed it up. "And not having any logical explanation for that, you started believing in the demon's existence."

He managed to shake his head and nod at the same time. "Let's say we were getting more and more inclined to believe that he did exist outside our imagination. So we went on and broke the next seals, one after another. Several rituals from the book were carried out only in our dreams, on a night of the new moon, and the fascinating thing was that we could do it anywhere we liked. In places where you wouldn't normally go at night."

Like Highgate Cemetery, I almost said. But I still wasn't sure whether Grayson really knew that I'd been with them during the cemetery dream, or whether he was only considering the possibility because of his sweater.

"Arthur, Henry, and Anabel were fascinated by the dreams and the possibilities they opened up—they got positively addicted to trying out all sorts of things, and visiting other people's dreams."

I could understand that. "How about you and Jasper?"

He shrugged. "Jasper thought it was all too confusing and too much of a strain, I guess, and in time I somehow . . . I came to feel it wasn't right. Apart from the fact that I'm not particularly interested in what other people dream."

"You *really aren't*? You're not interested in anyone else's dreams?" That had just slipped out before I could stop myself.

"The exception proves the rule." A fleeting smile passed over Grayson's face. "One way or another, it doesn't seem fair to spy on people in their dreams," he said, and I couldn't help feeling a little bit ashamed of myself. His voice turned serious again. "But that way, the demon had already fulfilled part of our pact. Because if you can get into other people's dreams, knowing their most secret fears and longings means nothing less than—"

"Immeasurable power," I whispered, trying to ignore the goose bumps crawling up my arms. To take my mind off them, I went over to the window and stared at the outline of a maple tree growing in the backyard of the building. I had to concentrate. "Right. So far we don't have any logical explanation for those dreams," I said in a firm voice. "But then again, if we're going to be objective about it, there's no well-founded evidence that a demon of any kind really exists. Yours appeared, if at all, only in your dreams."

"Right," Grayson admitted. "And I was clinging to that idea myself. Until . . ." And here he paused for a moment. "Until our wishes began coming true. First Jasper's, then mine, then Arthur's. . . ."

I turned around and looked at him incredulously. "The most secret wishes of your hearts?"

He nodded. "Yes. What we'd written on those pieces of paper at Halloween actually happened."

"And you simply told each other those wishes? I mean, they were secret, weren't they?"

"That's right, but when you've known each other as well and as long as we have, you also know what your friends really want, what they long for. . . ." For a moment he couldn't go on; then he seemed to pull himself together. "Well, and you know Jasper a bit by now yourself. He's not the type to keep his own secrets very long. He lasted exactly a day before telling us his wish. Sure enough, the Frognal Flames did win the schools' basketball championship, even though we were still way down in the rankings on Halloween, so that when we won, it really did seem like a miracle."

I felt a liberating urge to laugh rise in me, and it simply couldn't be stopped. Admittedly, I'd let myself be carried away a little too far by the story over the last few minutes, especially all that about the dreams, but now my mind was perfectly clear again. The schools' basketball championship? *Hello?* "I guess it couldn't get much more demonic than that," I said, still laughing. "Couldn't it be just that your team played well?"

Grayson didn't join in my laughter. "It wasn't just that one wish that came true," he said quietly when at last I was in control of myself again.

The sound of his voice sobered me up at once. "What did you wish for, then?" I asked, sitting back down beside Grayson.

Grayson's hands were stroking the hooded sweater. "That's not important. What matters is that it came true."

There was a knock on the door, and Mom looked around it. She beamed radiantly when she saw us sitting side by side on my bed. "Oh, I'm so glad you've made up," she said. "But, Grayson, didn't you want to get back to the party? I'm sure your girlfriend is expecting you!"

"Er . . . yes, that's right," said Grayson, getting to his feet. "I ought to have been back ages ago."

I wondered whether to snatch the hooded sweater away from him again and lock myself in the bathroom with it, or to shout something like, "Hey, wait, that wasn't all!" But in front of Mom's watchful eyes that wasn't really going to work. So I had no option but to follow Grayson out into the corridor. Losing the sweater was a nuisance, but in a few days' time we'd be living under the same roof and I was too tired this evening anyway to continue my empirical investigations. I was going to brush my teeth quickly and then go to sleep, all at once. Everything else could wait until tomorrow.

Mom kissed Grayson good-bye on both cheeks and gave

him a box of blueberry muffins. "For the party—after midnight is when parties usually get going," she said.

"I'll go down to the front door of the building with you." I made my way past Mom. "It's supposed to be locked on the inside after ten in the evening. Can't be too careful in this part of London. Positively teeming with criminals . . ."

Grayson grinned, but he didn't protest. We went downstairs together, and I cast him surreptitious glances. It was a pity he had to go, now that he'd been so free with his information.

"Did your wish have anything to do with Emily?" I couldn't help asking.

"No. Why?"

I thought it over and decided to try again from another angle. "How high was the probability of your wish coming true anyway?"

"Less than thirty percent," he replied promptly.

Thirty percent. The chances of a white Christmas in these latitudes were even less. But if it snowed on December 24, did we always assume it was the work of a demon? I wondered whether to put my graphic comparison to Grayson, but we'd already reached the front door. Feeling the cold night air on my bare forearms, I shivered.

Grayson took the car key out of his jeans pocket. "I wouldn't have thought it, but somehow it did me good to talk to you about all this." He leaned forward and dropped a light kiss on my cheek. "Thanks for not laughing at me all the time."

Embarrassed, I cleared my throat. "This is a difficult case, Dr. Watson," I said in my best Sherlock Holmes voice. "With an exceptionally mysterious component. But I'm sure that there'll turn out to be a logical explanation for everything in the end."

"I'd have liked to keep you out of it." Grayson smiled faintly. "But somehow or other it looks like we're both involved now."

Yes, and to be honest I didn't really mind that too much.

"See you." Grayson turned to go, and I watched him thoughtfully as he walked away. He wasn't so bad after all, really.

Halfway to Ernest's Mercedes he stopped and turned around again. "It was Huntington's disease," he said suddenly.

"What?"

"My wish." His fingers were playing nervously with the car key.

I missed a breath.

"My mother died of Huntington's. And my grandfather and one of my uncles before her." His voice had changed. It sounded perfectly flat, and he wasn't looking at me, but kept his head bent. "There was a probability factor of over seventy percent that Florence and I had inherited the Huntington's mutation as well."

I could only look at him, shocked.

"For years, Dad refused to let us take the gene test," he went on hastily. "But Florence and I couldn't live with the uncertainty, and finally we applied to be tested for it." He paused for a moment. "*That* was my wish. That Florence and I wouldn't die of the disease."

"So you're both healthy?" When he nodded, I let out a deep breath. I'd have liked to say something nice, something comforting, but I felt terribly helpless. I'd known that his mother died when he and Florence were still very small, but the reason was news to me. "And now you're wondering whether the result of the test would have been the same if you hadn't entered into a pact with a demon?"

"Yes" was all he said. "In weak moments I think our health could be the work of the demon. That's sick, isn't it?" At last he raised his head and looked me in the eyes. "And then—then I wonder what he'll take away from me if I break his rules."

ABOUT ME:
My name is Secrecy—I'm right here among
you, and I know *all* your secrets.

9 September, 3 a.m.

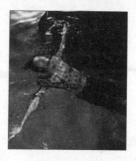

Arthur Hamilton's start-of-the-
season party really lived up to the
Hamiltons' reputation for wild
parties. The photo shows Nathan
Woods of the Frognal Flames
chilling out in the pool after five
cocktails. Such a shame he forgot
to take off his shoes and his clothes
first, and remove his cell phone from his pocket. Ah, well,
these things happen. . . . There's a version of the story going
the rounds that says Nathan didn't jump, he was pushed, and
pushed by Madison's ex, Jasper, who is terribly jealous of
Nathan and regrets splitting up with Madison. But then, this
version goes back to Madison herself, and she also claims that
her hair is naturally red. As if no one could remember that until
four years ago she was still a nondescript mongrel blonde.

Will Nathan still be taking Madison to the Autumn Ball?
I'll let you know. As it happens, I've already received a

nomination for her as Ball Queen. From her little sister's e-mail account. Oops!

By the way, one of the few middle-school girls at the party was Liv Silver, accompanied by her future stepbrother. I'm pretty sure we'll also be seeing Liv at the Autumn Ball—the question is, who with?

This is where you'll find out first, that's for sure—and very soon, unless I'm much mistaken.

See you soon!

Love from Secrecy

PS—To get you in the mood for the ball, here's a link to Johann Strauss's waltz *Homage to Queen Victoria*. Remember how Hazel Pritchard stumbled while dancing last year and brought half the others on the floor down with her?

20

"SO WHAT ARE WE GOING TO DO with you, you ugly little toad?" Lindsay tapped her long fake fingernails against each other. "You deserve a lesson, don't you agree?"

Since that was a purely rhetorical question, I said nothing. I knew exactly what was coming next. I could see gleeful anticipation in Lindsay's baby-blue eyes. And nothing I said, no amount of begging and pleading, was going to stop her.

"We haven't squished anyone's hand in the door for a long time," said Samantha, who had twisted my arm behind my back and was holding me in a firm grip. Samantha, tall and rather fat, was considered the most dangerous of the gang, because she was the one who usually carried out the punishment. Audrey helped her beat people up by holding the victim in place, and Lindsay generally just watched, but she was the one who decided what kind of torture it was going to be. Least dangerous was probably Abigail, who just kept watch. Like now.

"Wow, yes, let's squish her hand in the door." Audrey

clapped her hands enthusiastically. Samantha twisted my arm a notch higher, and I had difficulty in suppressing a cry of pain. I'd never felt so helpless in my life.

"Okay," said Lindsay. "But let's baptize her first, know what I mean?"

"Wow, yes," rejoiced Audrey again. "First we'll dunk her head in the toilet, then we'll squish her hand in the door. . . . Are you left-handed or right-handed?"

Samantha laughed out loud. "Makes no difference. It hurts the same on both sides." She pushed me forward, and Audrey helped her by grabbing my ponytail in one hand and dragging me into the toilet cubicle. As I stumbled past the mirror, I caught a glimpse of my wide, frightened eyes in a face as white as a sheet. I also saw Audrey's heavily made-up face and Lindsay's grin of pleasure. And a green door in the tiled wall. Samantha kicked me in the calves so that I fell on my knees right in front of the toilet bowl. Audrey pulled my head back by the hair and giggled. "She's lucky—the cleaning lady's just been in here."

"Depends which is unhealthier, dirt or disinfectant. Any last words before you take a drink?" asked Lindsay.

Samantha kicked me encouragingly in the back, but I said nothing. A sarcastic remark would be a sheer waste of time; Lindsay and her gang didn't understand sarcasm. They didn't even know how to spell the word, and to be honest I couldn't think of anything sarcastic right at that moment. I only wanted to call for my mom. And cry, but I wasn't going to give them the satisfaction. I tried resisting with all my might one last time, and Samantha kicked me, so hard this time that against my will I screamed.

I didn't have a chance.

Samantha's fat hand was around my neck, pitilessly forcing my head down into the toilet bowl, while her other hand was still twisting my arm.

Suddenly Lindsay stopped laughing, and instead I heard her give a frightened gasp. Someone said, in a cold, angry voice, "Let go of her at once, you beast!" and extraordinarily Samantha did let go of me and stagger back. The blood shot painfully back into my arm as I struggled up.

A tall boy with untidy hair had come to my aid. Henry. He had pushed Lindsay aside and hauled Samantha roughly out of the toilet by her arm. Audrey had fled to the washbasins and was gawping at Henry in confusion. I felt confused too.

There was something wrong about this.

"Where did you spring from all of a sudden?" asked Audrey, and Lindsay said, "This is a girls' toilet, idiot." However, they all looked worried, almost afraid. Even Samantha, who'd never usually have let anyone call her a beast with impunity. Beside Henry, she suddenly didn't look so tall and strong. She was rubbing the arm that he had held and muttering something offensive.

"You really are the end!" Henry's gray eyes were flashing with anger. "Four against one, and she's much smaller than any of you. Get out, before I dunk your own ugly mugs in the toilet bowl."

They didn't wait for a second warning but turned around and ran for it. I heard them slagging Abigail off outside the door; she was supposed to make sure no one came in. Abigail didn't seem to know what they were talking about, and said at least seven times, "What guy do you mean?" Then their voices retreated, and all was quiet.

I was leaning against the cubicle wall, still breathing

much too fast. Henry stroked my hair back from my forehead, which didn't exactly help to calm me down.

He was looking at me with concern. "Hey, it's all right, Liv."

"But at this point they always dunk my head in the toilet," I tried to explain. "And you don't belong here."

"I know, but I couldn't stand by and watch what they were doing." His fingertips ran carefully over my cheek. "My God, what kind of monsters were those?"

"Junior high school monsters," I said.

"*Junior* high school? But they were enormous."

"From overeating, because I guess they were already confiscating the other kids' lunch boxes in elementary school. And since they're not very bright, they probably had to repeat a year there more than once." I'd slowly realized how he came to be here. "This is a dream, isn't it? Because we're in Berkeley, and I didn't know you yet in Berkeley." My knees were giving way with relief. Only a dream, thank goodness. "Of course—the green door! I caught a glimpse of it in the mirror, and I wondered . . ."

"Why on earth would you dream something like that, Liv?" Henry was still stroking me.

"Because that's exactly what happened. Three years ago, in Berkeley. Only, no one came to my rescue then." Instead I'd spent quarter of an hour throwing up my guts. At least that had spared me the door-squishing torture. They'd tried it out a few weeks later on a girl called Erin. I still felt sick when I remembered Erin's hand.

"So that's why you look so . . . young." Henry smiled. "Cute. The braces on your teeth!"

I ran my tongue over my teeth. I remembered all that

metal in my mouth only too well. All the same, I didn't want to look thirteen in front of Henry.

He whistled through his teeth as my body came closer to its present self. His protective instinct seemed to be dying down, the concern vanished from his face, and he stopped stroking me. With a broad grin, he leaned back on the opposite cubicle wall and folded his arms. "You've really grown in the last three years."

"Yes, and unfortunately so has my nose." I looked past him at the mirror, ran my hand over the bridge of my nose, and checked my restyling to see if it had worked. To keep things simple, I'd opted for the same outfit as last time: jeans, sneakers, and the ninja T-shirt. I wondered whether to give my hair a little more volume, but that would have felt like cheating.

"I like your nose," said Henry.

"Maybe because your own nose is too long." I smiled up at him. I'd grown, yes, but I was still much shorter than him. It had been sweet, the way he'd defended me just now. He was always so nice to me in dreams, much nicer than in real life. On the other hand . . . "What are you doing here? This is my own personal nightmare, *and* it's the girls' toilet! You've no business being here."

He ignored my questions and looked in the mirror too. "My nose is not too long. It's just right. After all, a nose has to fit the rest of the face." His reflection winked at me. "Maybe we could go somewhere else? It's kind of unromantic here."

"Yes, and linked to so many unpleasant memories." I sighed. "To be honest, I had no idea I still kept dreaming of the same one. And that I remembered their faces and voices so precisely."

Henry turned serious again at once. "I hope they were at least expelled from the school?"

I shook my head. I'd never been able to tell a teacher what happened. I hadn't told Mom, either; she'd have been terribly upset. Only Lottie noticed something wrong with me and made me tell her. She had turned white as a sheet, and then she took me off to Mr. Wu so that I could learn to defend myself. The next morning she had gone to school with me and made me point out Audrey, Samantha, Lindsay, and Abigail to her. I don't know what she did then, but they never bothered me again. After a few weeks of Mr. Wu's lessons, I was so good at kung fu that I almost wished they had.

"We could go after them and beat them up properly," Henry suggested. "Now that you know you're only dreaming."

I waved the idea away. "No. I guess if I saw them today, I'd only feel sorry for them. Come on, Henry, what are you doing here? Tell me."

"I simply wanted to visit you. I wasn't to know I'd land in a girls' toilet at the worst moment of your life." He held out his hand. "Come along. Let's go somewhere nicer."

"That wasn't the worst moment of my life." I took his hand as if it were the most normal and natural thing in the world and let him lead me out of the cubicle and over to the green door, which looked out of place among the tiles with graffiti scrawled over them. To be honest, I didn't feel that it was at all natural to be holding Henry's hand. Nor, obviously, did my heart, because it began beating faster again.

Henry put his free hand on the lizard and seemed about to open the door.

"No," I said, because an idea had just occurred to me. I drew him away from the door. "Not yet."

"But . . ."

I didn't let him finish. "Since you're here, we could stay a little while. There are some nice places in Berkeley. Come this way." I pushed the door to the girls' toilets open and was glad to find nothing on the other side of the broad, bleak school corridor but sunlight and a fresh breeze. Yes, this kind of dreaming was fun. And I was good at it too, because everything looked exactly as I remembered it. We were standing high up in Berkeley Hills. You could see half the city and the bay from here. The evening sunlight bathed everything in a soft, golden glow.

I led Henry over to a bench under a huge tree. It had once been my favorite place, and I used to sit there for hours, playing the guitar and looking out to sea. I couldn't keep back a triumphant smile. If this wasn't a romantic spot, what was?

"We used to live only a little way up the road here."

"Not bad," said Henry, impressed, and I didn't know if he meant my ability to stage an elegant change of scene, moving straight from a disgusting school toilet to a place with such a breathtaking view, or the fact that we had once lived there. And the house really hadn't been bad—it even had a pool. But we had to share it with a grumpy philosophy lecturer and her mother, who cleaned house obsessively, so we never felt really at home there, more like guests in a boardinghouse.

"This is Indian Rock Park," I explained, hoping he wouldn't spot the notice a few yards away that had just reminded me of the park's name. "Butter once caught a squirrel here."

"Who's Butter?" Henry sat down on the bench, and I joined him, so that I could go on holding his hand.

"Our dog, Princess Buttercup. My father gave her to us when he and Mom divorced. As a kind of consolation, I think."

"Oh, I know about *that* kind of thing. Whenever we're given a new pet, we call it after Dad's latest girlfriend, to make things easier." He gave me a wry smile. "We generally use her stage name because it's likely to sound better. The rabbits are Candy Love, Tyra Sprinkle, Daisy Doll, and Bambi Lamour, and then there are a couple of ponies who go by the names of Moira Mystery and Nikki Baby."

I glanced incredulously at him. How frightful. I'd never complain of my family again. "You have a lot of . . . of pets." I cautiously squeezed his hand, and his smile deepened. Oh God, he had such nice eyes. As for his nose, it was just the right length. And his hair . . .

He cleared his throat. "Er . . . that was meant to be funny," he said. "But you're welcome to go on looking at me sympathetically."

Sympathetically? I looked awkwardly away. Damn. It was far harder to work out how much time was passing in a dream while you looked deeply into someone's eyes. Too deeply, in this case.

My eye fell on something else. It was leaning against the tree beside the bench.

"My guitar," I said, feeling moved. My unconscious mind was working overtime on the romantic effects.

"How nice," said Henry ironically. "Would you like to play me something?"

"Over my dead body," I said, feeling the blood rush into my face. My thoughts had in fact been racing forward, entirely out of control, and I'd already imagined Henry warbling something by Taylor Swift while the sun sank slowly, the sky over the sea turned red, and a pod of whales swam past down in the bay. . . . Oh my God! And had I really just thought his hair looked like spun gold in this light? It was enough to make you want to throw up! I must have lost my marbles. A little more of this, and I'd be one of those hormone-driven dimwits that Mia despised so much.

I abruptly let go of his hand.

Henry looked at me inquiringly, and I could hardly stand up to his gaze. What would he think of me? First he had to rescue me from a violent girl gang, then I dragged him off to a sunset scene in the hills with a guitar at the ready. . . .

I tried to strike a matter-of-fact note. "You still haven't answered my question: What are you doing in my dream?"

Henry leaned back and folded his arms.

"And how did you get through my door? I thought it would work only if . . ." I fell silent again.

"If what? If someone was wearing Grayson's sweater?" With a little laugh, Henry took something glittery out of his jeans pocket and held it up in the air. It was my butterfly barrette.

I swallowed. Oh, so *that* was it.

"Strictly speaking, you only need something that belongs to the other person," Henry went on. "And then of course you have to find the right door and overcome the barriers."

He looked around, intrigued. "Where has that mist suddenly come from?"

"Even here the sun doesn't always shine," I said tartly. "In fact, these parts are well known for sudden atmospheric changes." That wasn't true: I'd just wanted to tone down the romantically warm and rosy sunset a little. Mist had been the first thing to occur to me. Unfortunately swaths of mist rising majestically up the hills from the sea still looked romantic. However, at least we were rid of that kitschy soft-focus light that made it impossible for me to think clearly.

"What kind of barriers do you mean?" I looked around for my door. Where had it gone? Oh, over there, embedded in one of the huge rocks that gave the park its name.

Henry shrugged. "Most people protect their doors unconsciously. More or less strongly, as the case may be. Like Grayson with his Frightful Freddy. But I could simply walk through yours. No barrier at all, nothing in the way at all."

"I see," I said slowly, trying to look as if I really did. "So anyone who happens to have stolen, let's say, a hair clip from me can just walk in?"

"Looks like it. Obviously you're a very trusting person."

I tried not to let his smile take my mind off the subject. "But you aren't. Your unconscious mind has installed no less than three locks on your door."

Henry shook his head. "No, Liv. That wasn't my unconscious mind. That was *me*." He rubbed his bare arms, shivering. "Can't you make the sun shine again? That would be much nicer. I mean, considering that we're in California?"

I thoughtfully chewed my lower lip. "So I could protect my own door against unwanted visitors?"

"Yes, and you should." Henry's tone of voice had changed. He didn't sound amused anymore; he sounded deadly earnest. "There could well be other people interested in your dreams. It's in dreams more than anywhere else that you get to know people best—along with all their weaknesses and their secrets."

"I see. . . ." Or rather, I thought, *I don't entirely see yet*. I looked at the door again. It was weird to think that anyone in possession of some personal item of mine could simply break into my dreams. Much worse than the idea of someone reading my dream diary. I suddenly felt an urgent need to nail boards over the door, fit padlocks, and organize myself an enormous guard dog.

"Then why didn't Grayson protect his door better?" I asked. "I mean, any idiot can say 'Freddy' backward."

"Grayson is the most honest, openhearted person I know," replied Henry. "I don't think he has much to hide even in his dreams. Also, he's much too modest and doesn't think that anyone would be interested in them." He shrugged his shoulders. "And he doesn't really want to bother about all this; it's too uncanny for his liking."

"But not for yours?"

With a sigh, Henry leaned forward and reached for my guitar. "Oh yes, it's too uncanny for my liking too. But that's just what makes it so interesting."

I nodded. "Exactly. The most interesting things are always the most dangerous," I said quietly. "But all the same you want to explore them."

"Or, alternatively, it's for that very reason you want to explore them." Abruptly, Henry looked away and began tuning the guitar.

"Oh, please say you can't play the guitar!" It just slipped out.

He raised an eyebrow. "Because . . . ?"

"Because . . ." *Because that would make you just too perfect!* It was quite enough for him to have nice eyes and be able to recite Victorian poetry and for me to get a warm feeling inside when he smiled. Maybe, however, he played very badly, and then there'd at least be something about him that I could think was stupid. I looked at him challengingly. "Can you play it or are you just pretending?"

He plucked the strings and gave me a superior smile. "This is a dream, Liv, and if I wanted to, I could play the guitar like Carlos Santana. Or Paul Galbraith. It's up to you which."

"Oh." Who was Paul Galbraith? I'd have to Google him tomorrow morning.

Henry began playing, very softly. Bach. And he played well. I stared at his fingers. You surely couldn't just dream a technique like that. Or could you? You could fly in a dream, after all, without actually knowing how flying worked.

All the same . . . wow.

"Carried away, are you?" asked Henry mockingly, and I pulled myself together. He was still wearing that superior smile.

"Dream on," I said, with as much scorn as possible in my voice. "That prelude is so easy, I could play it when I was eight."

"Yes, sure." He put the guitar down and stood up. "I'll be

off. Before the alarm sounds and brings this nice dream to an end." His smile was outrageous. "And thanks for those interesting insights into your psyche."

"You're welcome." I suppressed an urge to grind my teeth. "You can keep the barrette. Although you might just as well give it back to me, because you certainly won't be coming through that door again."

"I hope not," he replied, suddenly perfectly serious again. He took the barrette out of his pocket, put it on the palm of his hand, and stared at it. The silver butterfly quivered, began beating its wings, and rose in the air. Openmouthed, I watched it go.

"Remember, they must be really effective barriers," said Henry. "And it's not only human beings they must keep out."

"But also . . . ?" Reluctantly, I tore myself away from the sight of the butterfly on its way. "The Lord of Shadows and Darkness? The mysterious Master of the Winds? Wouldn't he have to steal some personal possession of mine, or doesn't he need cheap tricks like that?"

He sighed. "Maybe you ought to take all this a little more seriously."

"Sorry, I can't. Without firm evidence, I don't believe in demons who haunt you in your dreams and can grant wishes." I looked him in the eye. "Do you?"

He held my gaze without moving a muscle. "Maybe what happened is really just coincidence. But maybe it isn't. How do you explain this?" He made a sweeping gesture. "How do you explain our dream?"

I hadn't gone as far as that yet in my thoughts. Being so tired when Grayson left, I'd gone to sleep before I could work it all out. "I . . . er . . . psychology?" I said a little defiantly.

"Psychology?" He snorted with amusement.

"A still-unexplored field of psychology. I think with a little practice anyone could dream like that—even without any pact with the dev—with a demon. I found the way through my own green door all by myself, without any demonic help."

"Are you quite sure of that?"

Well . . .

"Yes," I said firmly. "Because demons don't exist. Okay, so your team won the basketball championship, and Grayson and Florence didn't inherit that gene—but where's the connection? It's simple: as long as I don't see any demon standing right in front of me in person, I won't believe he exists. An apparition in a dream doesn't count—that would be purely psychological."

"And suppose *your* dearest wish were granted?" Henry looked down at the ground and pushed some pebbles back and forth with the toe of his shoe.

"That would depend on the wish," I said. "Only if I'd wished for something absolutely impossible like . . . like talking to animals, traveling in time, or marrying Lottie off to Prince Harry. Then, maybe, my belief might waver. Although come to think of it, Lottie and Prince Harry wouldn't really be unlikely enough to make me believe in demons. What did you wish for?"

Henry didn't reply. His eyes wandered very slowly from the pebbles to my feet, up my legs, and over my ninja T-shirt to my face, and I felt myself blushing. Again. When he reached my eyes, he repeated, "I must be going, like I said. But it was very nice dreaming with you, Liv."

Typical. He always had to go when things got too personal. "Did it come true?" I asked as he turned away.

Silence.

He had already reached the green door among the rocks when he turned around again, his hand on the lizard door handle. "I knew that you'd want to join in. You were far too inquisitive to say no. And somehow I'd have been disappointed if you had."

"I wasn't just being inquisitive—I . . . I . . ." Stammering, I was searching for the right words.

"Go on. So it was the prospect of partners for the Autumn Ball that convinced you?"

"Ha-ha."

"What was it, then?" he asked.

"I thought you and your friends needed my help," I said firmly. "Against that dangerous demon you're so scared of."

"And there was I, thinking you didn't believe in demons."

"I don't! That's why I'm the right person for the job. Honestly, Henry, do you believe in this demon? Really and truly, I mean?"

"Really and truly?" He had opened the door, and I could see the faint light from the corridor beyond it. But now he let go of the lizard door handle and was beside me again with a couple of steps. Before I could react, he had bent down to me and kissed me on the mouth. It wasn't a very long kiss, not much more than a gentle touch of his lips. All the same, I closed my eyes. It was a reflex action and I couldn't help it.

When I opened my eyes again, just the beat of a butterfly wing later, Henry was back in the doorway. Far away from me.

"It's difficult to say what's real and what isn't in this situation," he said. "And yes—I do think there's something strange about all this. But that doesn't necessarily mean it has to be sinister." With that, he let the door latch gently behind him, and then he was out of sight.

21

"THE BUFFET WILL OFFER a cross section of specialties from all the British colonies of Victorian times, and there'll be autumn-leaf confetti falling from the ceiling onto the dance floor." Persephone drank some of her mineral water to moisten her throat. And she needed it, because for a quarter of an hour she had been talking enthusiastically about the strictly secret surprises that the Autumn Ball would have in store for its guests. So far, however, there'd been nothing really surprising about them. All the same, the two girls sitting with us in the cafeteria were hanging on Persephone's every word. I'd forgotten their names, and it was possible that they had never told me what they were called, so for the sake of simplicity I thought of them as Itsy and Bitsy from the nursery rhyme about the spider.

"It's amazing to think you're going for the second time," said Itsy to Persephone. "You're so lucky."

"Luck has nothing to do with it." Persephone gave me a conspiratorial smile. "Does it, Liv?" She looked across to where Florence and Emily were sitting, two tables away from us. With them there was also the spotty boy, whom I had correctly identified as Emily's brother because of his likeness to her, and who according to Persephone was my ticket to Paradise. So I kept trying to hide behind Bitsy's broad back, in case they saw me and it occurred to Florence to introduce us. I very much hoped they'd finish eating before we did, because we'd have to pass their table to hand in our trays.

"You can't just wait for your prince to ride up on his white horse—you have to make use of your connections," Persephone went on. "And you mustn't on any account be too picky about your partner for the ball. For instance, last year I went with Ben Ryan—"

"Isn't he gay?"

"Yes, but you mustn't mind that sort of thing if you want to go to the ball when you're in the middle school. My partner this year isn't my first choice either, you know. Gabriel bites his fingernails, and he has hands the size of toilet lids, but anyway he's better than no partner at all. You have to look at these things pragmatically, not romantically, understand? Which doesn't mean you can't aspire to higher things—anyone can dream."

Itsy and Bitsy nodded reverently. "But not everyone has a sister on the ball committee," said Itsy.

"And no one's going to ask us." Bitsy sadly stirred her tiramisu.

"Well, probably not," Persephone agreed. "But I'll tell you all about it. And show you photos. This year couples are being photographed against a real Victorian stage setting, and the prints will be in sepia. People in the pictures will look like authentic characters out of an Oscar Wilde novel like *Jane Eyre*."

"Oh, how incredibly romantic," breathed Itsy. "Considered pragmatically, I mean."

"*Jane Eyre* isn't by Oscar Wilde. But *The Canterville Ghost* is," I murmured. "And it's *very* romantic, too."

Persephone was about to say something. She took a deep breath and pointed her spoon at me, but then she froze and opened her eyes very wide, a sure sign that Jasper was in sight. I'd have liked to have a good laugh about that, but I was definitely the last person who could do so. Because wherever Jasper turned up, Henry usually wasn't far away, and the mere sight of him made my heart beat faster.

I turned around. And sure enough, Jasper, Arthur, Henry, and Grayson had just come into the cafeteria, and as usual all eyes were drawn to them. It must be awful to have people staring at you like that. But then, why did they always go about together, walking in time with each other? Or stand, like now, in the sunniest place in the room and look around, apparently in search of someone, so that their hair shone in every shade of blond? And so that any idiot was bound to notice how good looking they were?

Their eyes passed over me as fleetingly as over everyone else in the room; I wasn't even sure if they noticed me at all in this sea of school uniforms and heads. As if nothing linked us together. As if that conversation in the Hamiltons' home cinema had never taken place. As if I'd only dreamed it.

Mom, Mia, Lottie, Ernest, and I had spent all Sunday sightseeing, like any ordinary bunch of tourists in London. Big Ben, the Tower, St. Paul's, Hyde Park, Buckingham

Palace, the Millennium Bridge, and the London Eye—Ernest had us going all over the place and took what felt like two million photos of us. Grayson and Florence hadn't joined our party, understandably, since they'd lived in London all their lives. However, in the evening Florence had come with us to the performance of *Hamlet* at the Globe Theatre that finished our day of tourism, and she had spoiled the whole performance for me by sitting next to me and murmuring the text along with the actors under her breath when the play got really exciting. It turned out that she had played Ophelia in the last school performance. The most beautiful Ophelia of all time, of course. But I couldn't bring myself to hate her anymore, not now that I knew her mother had died of Huntington's disease. It must have been terrible not to know whether she and Grayson carried the gene. When Hamlet said, *"There are more things in heaven and earth, Horatio, than are dreamt of in your philosophy,"* I couldn't help nodding. How true, how very true.

All things considered, it had been a lovely day, even if I'd rather have looked around Highgate or wandered about Notting Hill. I could always make up for that later—without Ernest. The hours had flown by, and I'd hardly had time to think about demons, wishes, dreams, and kisses, let alone work out graphs and diagrams. I was worn out at the end of *Hamlet* ("The rest is silence"), and I had fallen into bed and slept all night—not entirely dreamlessly, but long and deeply, in the certainty that no one could come through my green door now if I didn't want them to. Not even Henry, whose hair was shining like liquid woodland honey in the sun over there.

Oh no, had I really just thought that? Liquid woodland

honey—*hello?* Ashamed of myself, I bit my lower lip and was grateful, yet again, that no one could read my thoughts.

At least I was breathing to some extent normally, which was more than could be said of Persephone. Only when my friends who went in for conjuring up demons were sitting down at Florence and Emily's table did Persephone relax. She took a deep breath. "Like I said—anyone can dream," she repeated, as if nothing had happened. "But you still have to be realistic."

Itsy sighed soulfully. "That Arthur Hamilton is so incredibly handsome! I get goose bumps whenever I set eyes on him. But Henry Harper is totally sweet too. And sexy."

"He'd be even sweeter if he did something about his hair," said Persephone. "Like Jasper—his is always perfectly styled. I think Jasper is the most virile-looking of those four. Kind of grown-up."

"And doesn't he just behave that way too," I muttered.

"I think Grayson is the most handsome," said Bitsy. "Next-most handsome after Arthur, I mean. He always has a nice look in his eyes, and they're such a lovely brown."

"Yes, right. Like dark caramel," I said. But then I pulled myself together. Oh God, I had to get out of here—this silly gossip was infectious. I abruptly pushed back my chair and stood up. "I forgot that my sister has something important to . . . Er, would one of you be kind enough to hand back my tray for me when you've finished? Thanks a million." And without waiting for an answer, I made my escape, going a long way around the table where Henry and the others were sitting.

Mia was astonished when I turned up in the lower school

cafeteria and dropped into a chair at her table. Not without some pride, she introduced me to her neighbor, Daisy Dawn.

Daisy Dawn was delighted to meet me, what with my being Mia's sister and getting mentioned so often in the Tittle-Tattle blog.

"We were just talking about the Autumn Ball," she told me, her eyes shining. "Lacey says she heard from Hannah that Anabel Scott is coming back from Switzerland specially to go to the ball. So that Arthur won't have to go with anyone else. I can't wait to see what dress she'll wear this year. Last year it was velvet, dark red, gorgeous."

I groaned. This just could not be true! The epidemic of idiocy was spreading like wildfire.

"Okay, I'd better be on my way. Very nice to meet you, Daisy Dawn."

Still in the lower school cafeteria, with Mia's baffled gaze on my back, I walked faster, and in the corridor I broke into a run. Rather breathless, I finally reached my locker and tapped in the four-digit code that opened the lock. The short sprint had done me good; all that pink candy floss had removed itself from my brain.

"Four, three, two, one. Not what I'd call a particularly secure combination." I spun around. Henry! Hadn't he been in the cafeteria just now?

"Go on, then, rob me!" I said quickly, before I could blush scarlet or think up anything soppily stupid about gray eyes or hair the color of woodland honey. "You'd be able to lay hands on an amazingly valuable math textbook about functions and equations, a pair of sneakers size seven, and a genuine antique cell phone fit to go into a museum. I've been wishing for years that someone would steal it from me."

When Henry laughed, my stomach had that odd feeling again. The corners of his mouth crinkled so cutely, and he had very good teeth, and I couldn't imagine why I'd ever thought his nose too long. And those incredibly fascinating eyes . . .

"Are you all right?" he asked seriously.

"I'm fine," I said, calling myself to order.

"And what's not certain?"

Aha! "Wouldn't you like to know?" Henry must have tried going through my green door into my dreams last night—that would also explain the dark shadows under his eyes. I grinned gleefully. *What's not certain?* That question was part of the barriers I'd used to secure my door. And a much more imaginative one than Henry's boring locks and keys, as well as obviously being more difficult than Grayson's. Only someone who knew the right answer would be able to get in.

Henry smiled. "Yes, I really would like to know. But I'm glad you took my advice. A very effective barrier. For me, anyway."

"Not just you," I said confidently.

"Is it from a poem? Shakespeare, maybe?"

"No," I said. "Much more difficult than that. Any old demon could Google 'Shakespeare.'"

"Hmm." Henry frowned. "I love a good puzzle."

Just like me.

We said nothing for a moment. Then Henry said, "By the way, I'm supposed to be telling you that we'll all meet at Jasper's house on Saturday to go through your admission to the circle. Jasper's parents will be away for the weekend."

As soon as Saturday? "I thought it would be at the time of the new moon." I bit back the other questions that were trying to pass my lips at the same time. (Does it hurt? Is it a bad thing that I can't stand the sight of blood? *Am I right out of my mind?*)

"No, Saturday's a good day. Unless you've thought better of the whole idea."

I slowly shook my head and quoted one of Mr. Wu's proverbs. "Ships are not made to lie in harbor."

"Excellent," said Henry. "Then we'll see each other on Saturday."

"Yes, *that's* certain," I replied, to provoke him.

"Oh, how mean of you. Can't you at least give me a little hint?"

At that moment the bell rang for the end of break. Even more students crowded into the corridor, the voices grew louder, locker doors were opened and slammed shut again.

"A hint? Okay." I had to admit that this was fun. "Let's see . . . the answer has to be in German. Does that get you anywhere?"

"No, not really." Henry thoughtfully bit his lower lip. "German, then. Hence that dirndl. . . . Oh, hi, Florence, Emily. And Sam. Again."

Oh no, I must get out of here. Even if, at close quarters, Sam wasn't quite as spotty as I'd thought.

Florence conjured up a smile on her face. I was amazed by her professional maneuvering. "Hello, Liv. Nice to see you here. Meet Sam and Emily."

"I'm Sam's sister," Emily explained. "And Grayson's girlfriend. Glad to meet you. We somehow never got around to it at the party last Saturday."

Very true: First you were busy smooching like there was no tomorrow, then I was promising your boyfriend and *his* friends to help them liberate a demon from the underworld.

Sam didn't say anything. He just looked uncomfortable. Henry, on the other hand, gave the impression of being extremely amused.

"Sam is sixteen. And very clever," said Florence.

"Yes, his IQ is fifteen points above mine. And I've been ranked as highly gifted," said Emily.

Oh, shit.

"He jumped two classes and will be doing his A levels next summer." His mother couldn't have sounded prouder than Florence. "And after that—where are you going to study, Sam?"

"Harvard," said Sam, looking even more uncomfortable.

"Oh, what a coincidence!" cooed Florence. "You see, Liv is half American, and as far as I know her family comes from the Boston area, don't they?"

"Well, yes. My grandparents and my aunt Gertrude live there." I closed my locker door. "I'm afraid I'm in a hurry. I have to get up to the second floor."

"Oh, that's good—we're on our way there too," said Florence.

Bloody hell. I stood where I was as if rooted to the ground. My eyes went briefly to Henry, who was standing with his back to the locker, listening with interest. Should I try my luck with the toilets? Surely they wouldn't follow me there. Or, at least, not all of them.

Florence took my arm. "On the way up, Sam can ask you something too. Go on, ask her, Sam."

Oh no, this was all speeding up much too quickly for me. Maybe I ought to tear myself away and run for it? Spotty

Sam might be clever, but he didn't seem to be especially athletic. He'd never catch up with me.

On the other hand, I felt a little sorry for him. It must be awful to be bossed about by his sister and her best friend and made to ask a girl who was a perfect stranger to go to some rotten ball with him. The girls in his class were all older than him, and therefore presumably not so keen on being his dancing partner. And then there was the skin problem. . . . Poor Sam.

I tried a small smile at him. Maybe he just wanted to ask me something perfectly harmless, for instance whether I liked the school lunches, or if I enjoyed spelling bees, or what my favorite—

"Would you like to come to the ball with me?" asked Sam.

No! No, no, no, no, no.

Experimentally, I tried closing my eyes for a moment, but it didn't help. The poor boy was still standing in front of me, looking as if he'd sink into the ground at any moment. What would he do if I said no? Cry? Run away? Get a rope? What on earth do you say in such a situation?

"Er. That is really very . . . nice of you. . . ." I stammered, desperately searching for more words, while Florence and Emily looked at me expectantly. I had no idea what Henry was doing, but I suspected he was grinning.

I *hated* Florence. This was all her fault. I mean, I'd made it perfectly clear what I thought of the ball. I'd sooner have a root canal without anesthetic. That's what I'd said, hadn't I?

"I know," said Sam.

I know? I beg your pardon? "What do you know?"

"I know it's nice of me to ask you," said Sam. "You're in

the middle school. I could ask any girl I liked in the middle school, but Florence thought the two of us would be a good idea, kind of a family thing. So will you come to the ball with me?"

I opened my mouth (or rather, I didn't have to, because it was already wide open), but before I could say anything, Henry had intervened.

"Although that really was a wildly romantic and totally irresistible invitation, I'm afraid Liv will have to refuse it," he said.

That was certainly more elegant than the abrupt "No!" that had been on the tip of my tongue.

"Henry!" Florence let go of me and darted a furious glance at him. "You keep out of this. Of course Liv is going to the ball with Sam. We've already fixed—"

"The whole thing. Yes, I'm sure you have." Henry came over to me. "But Liv can't go to the ball with Sam because she's already going with me." He winked at me. "Isn't that right, Liv?"

All eyes were resting on me again.

"Yes," I said. "That's right."

"I don't believe it," said Florence. "You two hardly know each other."

"Well, Sam's only this minute met Liv himself," said Henry.

"You hate occasions like that, Henry. You didn't go last year either."

"Then it's high time I did," said Henry. "After all, this is my last year at the Frognal Academy. My last chance to wear the wonderful get-up of white tie and tails, and dance waltzes lifting my partner in the air—"

"But . . ." Florence turned to me. "Why didn't you say anything about this yesterday evening, Liv?"

I tried to hold her gimlet glance. "I wasn't to know you were making plans like that. . . . I'm very sorry."

"Hmm." Florence still seemed to be suspicious, but Emily looked as if she'd like to throttle someone. With her bare hands. Sam, on the other hand, appeared to be composed to the point of indifference. I wondered whether to recommend other partners for him, two really nice girls who certainly wouldn't say no, but he probably wouldn't get far with the names Itsy and Bitsy.

"We're off," said Emily, pulling Sam away by his sleeve. "I said right away this was a stupid idea."

Florence followed the two of them, after giving us a last inquiring look. "No you didn't!" we heard her say.

I breathed a sigh of relief. "That was a close thing," I said, looking into Henry's laughing gray eyes. "Thank you!"

"You're welcome, cheese girl. Now will you tell me what's not certain?"

"No! But you were so nice just now that I'll give you another little hint," I added, lowering my voice to a mysterious whisper. "It's about someone called Hans."

And then I had to run again so as not to be late for the geography lesson.

ON THE FOLLOWING SATURDAY, we moved out of the Finchleys' apartment and into the Spencers' house. To be honest, it was no big deal. Ernest had originally set aside three days for the move. He had bought a new power screwdriver and a new drill, he had made sure that Mrs. Dimbleby would be available to provide meals and his brother Charles for "the heavy lifting," he had hired a van and organized everything as if the general staff of an army would be involved. Only when Mom showed him our entire stored possessions did he realize that two trips back and forth in Charles's station wagon would do the job and that we had no paintings or furniture calling for the power screwdriver or the drill to put them in place—indeed, nothing else that justified having a military general at work on the operation. I wondered what he'd expected. We'd always lived in furnished accommodations and had learned not to want things any larger than a book. (Apart from my guitar and a teddy bear called Mr. Twinkle.)

In addition, we were extremely experienced in moving

house, and unpacking crates was mere routine. By lunchtime all our possessions were in their proper places, the house had been cleaned up after the move, and Mom said, as she always did after filling the bookshelves, "Home is where your books are."

Rather confused, Ernest viewed it all from the laundry room. According to his military plan of action, after we had fortified ourselves at lunch with Mrs. Dimbleby's shepherd's pie, the real work of moving house was due to begin. Instead, everyone knocked off work for the day. Except for Grayson, who had to be in school because the Frognal Flames were defending their championship in the opening game of the season. Mom suggested that we might go to the sports hall and spend our free afternoon cheering Grayson and his team on. She'd been a cheerleader in her youth and would have loved Mia and me to follow in her footsteps. When she heard that there weren't any cheerleaders at Frognal Academy, she was horrified, muttered something about "unemotional Brits," and didn't pursue her plan any further. Instead, she joined Mrs. Dimbleby in the kitchen to winkle the shepherd's pie recipe out of her. Not that Mom was much good at cooking, but she liked to give the impression that she was. And the shepherd's pie really had been good—so good that Mia let us know her vegetarian phase was now over.

Mrs. Dimbleby was around sixty, had hair tinted pale pink (a mistake at the hair salon, as she assured me), and was slightly overweight. I took her into my heart at once because of her hearty laugh and the way she fed Buttercup tender morsels of meat in the kitchen.

I was also very pleased with my new room. Yes, it was the smallest of the five bedrooms on the second floor, but it was about 175 square feet, making it bigger than many rooms that Mia and I had shared over the last few years, and I felt comfortable in it at once. I loved the wood floor, the built-in bookshelves, and the walls painted in a soft color. The best thing, however, was the broad, comfortably upholstered window seat with a view of the garden. The only disadvantage was that my room was right next to Ernest and Mom's master bedroom. I could only hope the walls were thick enough for me to be able to forget that at night. I also hoped very much that Ernest wasn't in the habit of going around the house in his underpants, because I didn't know whether my nerves were strong enough for that. But of course the master bedroom had a bathroom of its own. Florence, Grayson, Mia, and I had to share the bathroom at the top of the stairs. Although it had two washbasins, a shower, and a tub, Florence wanted us to draw up a timetable so as to avoid traffic jams in the morning, as she put it. Since there were plenty of toilets in the house and Lottie had a bathroom to herself up in the attic, I wasn't worried about traffic jams. I had enough worries already. Up to and including the fact that this evening I was going to conjure up a demon for the first time in my life.

I had told Mom that Grayson and a couple of his friends had organized a games evening and invited me to come. That wasn't so far from the truth, and I didn't even have to tell a lie, so long as Mom refrained from asking what kind of game we were going to play ("Oh, one of those with demons and buckets of blood"). Of course Mom had immediately given me permission to go. She never tired of saying how glad she was that my days as a social wallflower were over.

The week had passed incredibly quickly. On Tuesday the

Tittle-Tattle blog had headlined the news that I was going to the ball with Henry. "What does she have that other girls don't? Has Henry Harper really fallen victim to her charms, or did Grayson Spencer make him ask her?" There was no mention of Sam's previous invitation to me. Another reason to suspect Emily of being behind Secrecy. Naturally she wasn't about to write anything that showed her brother in a poor light.

The publicity given to the news was one thing; it was almost outweighed, however, by the fact that Florence had told Mom about it. As might have been expected, Mom could hardly contain her delight and immediately got Florence to give her the names of two shops that apparently sold enchantingly beautiful ball dresses. So now I had a double problem. On Thursday afternoon Mom managed to drag me off to one of those shops, and sure enough, the ball dresses really were enchanting. Particularly when you looked at the price tags. But Mom had shed tears of joy when I stood in front of her in a smoky blue tulle confection with a huge skirt, and I didn't have the heart to explain that the invitation to the ball was a fake, because Henry had only wanted to rescue me from Spotty Sam. And now I couldn't think how to tell Henry that my Mom had spent three hundred pounds on a ball dress for me. . . . How that could have happened I had no idea myself.

And another puzzle was how on earth I was going to keep any secrets at all, living under the same roof as Grayson and that tattletale Florence, with information flowing freely in both directions.

However, some good things had also happened that week: I'd joined the White Crane Kung Fu Club in West

Hampstead, signing on for an advanced class. The first training session yesterday had been great fun. The instructor, Mr. Arden, wasn't as good at kung fu itself as Mr. Wu, but he was generous with his praise and didn't get on my nerves by quoting Chinese proverbs. Also, he thought more highly of the self-defense aspect of martial arts than the integration of mind and body that Mr. Wu was always going on about, and the self-defense aspect was exactly what I needed.

In spite of all these diversions, I'd begun feeling slightly more scared with every passing day—first and foremost because I didn't know just what I'd be facing that evening. Remembering the cemetery dream, my main fear was that I wouldn't be able to keep a straight face if I had to recite high-flown invocations or draw diagrams on the ground. I wasn't sure whether it had really been such a good idea to agree to go along with acting as Anabel's replacement. Not because by now I was genuinely scared of a demon, seeing that there were no such things, but because people who went in for such rituals weren't the best of company to keep.

I had deliberately kept away from the dream corridor in my sleep. Since going to see *Hamlet*, I had certainly dreamed silly theatrical dreams every night, dreams in which Florence played the part of Ophelia. All the same, in the certain knowledge that no one could overcome my dream barriers and pay me a surprise visit, I had always slept very well.

When Grayson came home early in the evening and in a very good mood after his basketball game, Florence was out at a meeting of the ball committee, and Mom and Ernest were taking Buttercup for a walk in the park. Lottie, Mia, and I were taking advantage of Buttercup's absence to make friends with Spot, the ginger cat. Following Mrs. Dimbleby's example, we fed him tender morsels of meat, and we were very pleased when he let us stroke him, purring so loudly that the whole sofa seemed to vibrate.

Mia beamed at Grayson. "He likes us," she said proudly.

"He likes everyone, even my grandma," Grayson said as he passed us.

I followed him into the kitchen. "Well, did you win?" I asked.

"Yes. Of course." Grayson unscrewed the cap from a bottle of water and drank half of it in a single draft. "A hundred and four to sixty-two. We *annihilated* them."

"Oh yes, I quite forgot you'd win every game because you made a pact with a demon. A very sensible thing to do," I said, watching the water gurgle its way out of the bottle and into Grayson. What was he—a camel? "Er, about this evening . . ."

Grayson put down the bottle. "You've changed your mind," he said in relief.

"No, I haven't. I just wanted to know what I ought to wear."

"What?" He rolled his eyes. "What you're already wearing will be fine."

"You can't be serious!" I looked down at my clothes, which were filthy after the house moving. In addition, my FREAK OUT AND CALL MOM T-shirt was at least a size too small for me.

"It doesn't matter one bit what you wear," said Grayson. "Since when have you been so *girly*? Choosing clothes is the least of our problems."

He was right there, of course. All the same, I spent a lot of time getting ready for the evening. If I had a date with a demon, then I wanted to look my best, okay? Apart from other people present, and I didn't mind going to a bit of trouble for them. The trick, however, was for no one to think I'd really made any particular effort. I was already wearing contact lenses instead of glasses today, so I wiped off my lip gloss again. I didn't want to go giving Henry any ideas.

The closer the evening came, the more excited I felt, and I couldn't really work out why. Because of Henry? Or because all my questions were going to be answered at last? By the time Grayson parked Ernest's Mercedes outside Jasper's parents' pretty terraced house in Pilgrim's Lane, I realized, to my own horror, that part of me—and not such a small part at that—had begun looking forward to the evening.

It was also, presumably, the crazy part of me.

23

THE BOOK DIDN'T LOOK nearly as old as I'd expected. It wasn't much more than a notebook worn shabby at the corners, and with yellowing pages. Whoever had written down the instructions for liberating the demon from the underworld hadn't done it in the Dark Ages with a quill pen made from a sharpened crow's feather, but very much later. It was maybe even written with a ballpoint, but I couldn't tell for sure because of the candlelight. However, the seal holding the last pages of the book together did look pretty old. And appropriately enough, it was blood red, like the remains of the seals that had already been broken and were still clinging to the pages.

"It's a copy made in the 1970s," said Arthur, as if he had read my thoughts.

"Ah," I replied. "And it was just standing around on the bookshelves of Anabel's family home?"

"Of course not," said Arthur. "She found it in an old desk. It was an heirloom."

"Of course," I replied, echoing him. In an old desk,

surprise, surprise. No doubt in a secret compartment, along with a magic ring and a letter from Santa Claus.

"And . . . have you thought of your wish, Liv?"

The dearest wish of my heart, hmm, yes. I had to admit that this little detail of the whole conjuring-up-demons business was the part that I found really tricky. Over the last few days I'd tried to forget the story of Grayson's wish about Huntington's disease. But every time I saw Grayson himself, I remembered what he had told me, and then I always got goose bumps. Even if there was an absolutely watertight, logical explanation in the form of the calculation of probability, I still couldn't . . .

"Liv?"

I hastily nodded. "Yes. I know what I'm going to wish for."

As usual, Henry was leaning back against a bookcase with his arms folded. Jasper's mother seemed to have a weakness for romance novels with pastel covers, and it intrigued me to read their titles right next to Henry's head. Titles like *Kiss Me, Rebel!* and *Let Me Die in Your Strong Arms*. I'd better not go on looking at them.

The Grants' living room was very tastefully furnished (apart from those books), at least when you imagined the furniture and rugs in their proper places—they had been moved over to one wall so that someone—Arthur?—could draw a huge pentagram on the dark wood floor. The mysterious and somehow angular sign framing the pentagram was nothing that I'd ever seen before.

The room was lit by candles standing on two chests of drawers, the sideboard, and the window seats, some of them rather too close to the curtains for my liking. Jasper and Grayson were busy lighting more candles and arranging them on the tables. However, it didn't make the atmosphere sinister, although that could also have been because of all the framed photographs of a beaming Jasper and his also-beaming big brother as babies and toddlers. My word, they'd been so cuddly. . . .

"Think very carefully about the wording of your wish," said Arthur, his eyes bent on the book. "Because it will be granted exactly as you put it. And the more complicated it is, the longer it will take. Maybe you ought to know that, too."

"How long did it take for your wish to be granted?" Although I'd asked the question quite casually, I had the impression that all present in the room held their breath for a moment to look at Arthur.

However, he didn't seem to notice. "We preserve silence on the subject of our wishes," he said without looking up from the book. Ah, so he'd already switched into pompous, high-flown mode. Maybe someone ought to tell him that while he looked gorgeous in the candlelight, that tone of voice was absolutely not sexy. "It is solely an agreement between you and the Prince of Shadows."

"I get it." My glance wandered to Henry, but I had to look away again at once, because as his head was tipped to one side, I could read the pink letters spelling out *Wild Desire*. How I hated Mrs. Grant's taste in literature! Why couldn't she collect thrillers?

"The words you have to say are mostly in Latin," Arthur went on. "We ought to go through their meaning, so that you don't have to ask about it during the ceremony." He lightly ran his hand over the cover of the book. "There's not much of it. In essence, you swear loyalty to the Lord of Shadows until the last seal is broken, and you swear it by your blood."

"In essence," I repeated.

"By your virgin blood," Arthur specified. "You confirm that you are a virgin and will be a virgin until the last seal is broken."

"And when exactly will that be? I mean, the bit about the last seal?"

"The Commander of the Night will let us know at the right time."

I raised my eyebrows. "Can't he be a little more precise? I wouldn't want to end up like my aunt Gertrude."

I could have sworn I heard Henry chuckle, but when I glanced at him he was staring intently at his hands.

"I mean, it's not that I'm in any hurry," I was quick to say. "I just want to be on the safe side."

"We think the last seal will be broken at Halloween," Grayson replied in Arthur's place. "On the day when it all began . . ." Oh, wonderful, now *he* was adopting that pompous tone of voice too. "Listen, Liv." He reached for my arm. "If you take the oath, you're promising to keep the rules and play the game to the end."

Yes, sure, I was going to say, but his gravity and the look in his eyes held me back.

"I'd like to be sure you really understand." He looked across at Arthur. "Arthur has forgotten this tiny detail, but if you don't keep the rules and play to the end, you offer the de—well, the Lord of Shadows—a forfeit. You promise him the dearest and most precious thing you have, the thing on which your heart's blood depends." He looked at me as if expecting me to throw it all up at this stage and run for the front door.

"I didn't forget," Arthur defended himself. For the first time since I'd known him, he looked a little nervous. "I was just coming to that."

Suddenly I was overcome by pity. That's why they were all still here. Because they were really and truly afraid that the demon could ask for his forfeit if they simply walked away from the rituals.

"The dearest and most precious thing you have," Grayson repeated. "So if you want to change your mind . . ."

I shook my head. I realized that Grayson wanted to frighten me, and he meant well, but if I backed out now, what good would that do anyone? Apart from the fact that then I'd never find out what was behind all this.

And as for the forfeit: Well, it wasn't as surprising and despicable as all that. How else was the demon going to hold people to their word? After all, in return he offered to grant their dearest wishes and give them immeasurable power, and he was a *demon*, for goodness' sake, not an angel—what did they expect? I'd have liked to say so out loud, but maybe that was going a bit too far. I wasn't about to start defending a demon I didn't believe in.

"Anything else I ought to know?" I asked instead. There were no such things as demons—that was the thought I had to bear in mind. Because demons didn't exist, they couldn't take anything away from you either, never mind what you promised them. So there.

Resigned, Grayson shook his head and let go of my arm.

"Then let's begin. Everything is ready," said Arthur

unctuously, pointing to the little table in the middle of the pentagram. On it, neatly arranged, stood a chalice, paper, a pen, and a knife.

Rather a large knife, I thought.

Grayson, whose eyes had been following mine, said, "It's Arthur's father's hunting knife. Handmade."

"Three hundred and fifty layers of Damascus steel," added Jasper who had so far kept surprisingly quiet. He hadn't even mixed any drinks. "Sharp as a scalpel."

I swallowed.

"The sharper the knife, the less it hurts," said Henry.

I supposed that was meant to encourage me. "Did I ever tell you that I can't stand the sight of blood?" I asked.

"Nor can I." Jasper blew out the match he'd been using to light the last candle. "I always just shut my eyes. You'd better do the same."

"Form a circle, brothers and sisters," demanded Arthur.

I bit my lip. The last time I'd formed a circle was in nursery school. *Ring-around-the-rosy, a pocket full of posies* . . . But then I looked at the knife again, and the laughter that had been threatening to burst out of me died down.

"Five have broken the seal, five have taken the oath, and five will open the gate, as it is written," said Arthur. "We have come together today to make the circle complete again and renew our oath."

And then a funny thing happened. If anyone had described all this to me beforehand, I'd have sworn that I'd be rolling about the floor in fits of laughter. But it wasn't like that. I didn't know whether it was because of all those candles, or because it was all so solemn and serious, or maybe because of Grayson's warning just now after all, but somehow or other I had a lump in my throat when I repeated what Arthur read out to me. I didn't even try to translate what I was saying, I only knew that *sanguis* meant blood, and it was easily the word most frequently used, in all forms of its declension. Now and then the others also had to repeat something, in voices that sounded rather flat as they muttered it, quite unlike Arthur, who was intoning his part as clearly and with as much feeling as if he were onstage.

Finally I had to go up to the table and write my wish on the sheet of paper. Although I took rather a long time—I wanted to be quite sure of what I was saying—the others waited patiently until I had finished. *I wish for demons not to exist, so that they can't hurt anyone either.* So maybe that wasn't brilliant, but in the circumstances I thought it was quite clever. Because it was a paradox, in the unlikely case that the demon really did exist. And you could always outwit supernatural powers that wished you ill with paradoxes. I knew that from all I'd ever read on the subject.

Arthur held the folded piece of paper in the flame of a candle and read out a Latin phrase from the book while the paper burned and fell to the floor in ashes.

Then it was over, and much sooner than I'd expected we got to the uncomfortable part of the evening.

"So we swear our loyalty to you who bear a thousand names and make your home in the night," said Arthur, solemnly handing me the dagger. "And we seal the oath with our blood."

I held the knife uncertainly up in the air. *Is this a dagger which I see before me . . . ?* Why did I think of Macbeth and all the nasty crimes he went on to commit at this point?

"Where, exactly?" I asked.

"The palm of your hand is best," said Henry. "It heals up faster than a fingertip. But don't press too hard; that blade really is infernally sharp. I'll help you if you like."

"No, it's all right. I can do it." I took a deep breath and pressed the point of the knife against the ball of my thumb. Blood immediately came out. Ouch. "Now what?"

"In here." Grayson held out the chalice; it was already half full of wine. Yuck. I watched, queasily, as a little trickle of blood ran from the cut over my hand and dripped into the chalice: one drop, two, three . . .

"That's enough," said Grayson, and Henry gave me a handkerchief that I could press down on the wound. It stung slightly, but it wasn't too bad. Not without pride, I handed the knife on to Grayson.

After they had all let their blood drip into the chalice—Jasper, as he had said, with his eyes closed—came the worst bit: Arthur swung the chalice around in the air for a while so that it would all be well mixed, and then everyone had to drink a mouthful and say *sed omnes una manet nox*, whatever that might mean. ("But all have a hand at night?" "By night all hands are one?" My Latin really was terrible.)

I was very careful to swallow the stuff without tasting it. I almost shivered when it had gone down. If that was red wine, I was never going to like it, even without an extra flavoring of blood. But at least it didn't make me retch.

The others were obviously cooler than me; you could see they took all this as routine. And Jasper even had two mouthfuls, probably telling himself it would act as a disinfectant after the cut.

"Now the circle is complete again, O Lord of Shadows and Darkness," said Arthur, looking satisfied. "We await your instructions for breaking the last seal and keeping our promise."

"But don't worry, you can take your time." Of course it was Jasper who had to ruin the solemn conclusion of the ceremony. He began blowing out the candles. "What's the matter with you all? It's true. He might as well wait until we've won the qualifying games."

24

"ARE YOU FAIR?" asked Hamlet, and Florence, a fragile apparition in a plain gown, her brown locks tied up on top of her head with ribbons, asked him back, in confusion, *"What means your lordship?"*

"Isn't that great? She's the perfect Ophelia," Lottie whispered, without taking her eyes off the stage, although she was right there sitting beside me. Not that Florence was as perfect as all that; to Hamlet's annoyance, she went straight on with his own lines: *"That if you be honest and fair, your honesty should admit no discourse to your beauty."*

"Er, yes, exactly, Ophelia," said Hamlet. "Just as I was about to say myself."

Florence gave him a nicely judged smile. *"Could beauty, my lord, have better commerce than with honesty?"*

Hamlet frowned. "Now that you mention it . . ."

He got no farther, because Florence was stealing his lines again. *"For the power of beauty will sooner transform honesty from what it is to a bawd!"*

"You take the very words out of my mouth," said Hamlet.

"I did love you once, but now you're nothing but a stupid cow stealing all my best lines."

"It's a very . . . very modern production," whispered Lottie enthusiastically. "And the setting is avant-garde too, such a lovely mixture of steampunk, folklore, and minimalism—incredibly extravagant."

"You don't mean it," I whispered back. The stage setting was terrible. Nothing matched anything else, and it certainly didn't suit Hamlet. He was now furious with Florence, because she was putting one hand to her breast and declaiming, with malicious glee, *"To be, or not to be: that is the question. . . ."*

"This is too much! I never should have stabbed poor old Polonius. I should have stabbed you!" shouted Hamlet, seizing Florence by the throat and forcing her back against a bright-green door in the backdrop onstage. "Who needs a dagger? I'll throttle you with my bare hands."

"Now he's importing a touch of *Othello*," said Lottie, impressed. "Hey, where are you going, Liv? And when did you learn to fly?"

"I can only do it in my dreams," I assured her, making straight through the air for my green door without even beating my wings, because I didn't really have any.

When I landed on the stage, Lottie applauded loudly, and Florence, her throat still in the clutches of the furious Hamlet, croaked, "I am *not* of ladies most deject and wretched, you bastard, woe to you, not me!" And she rammed her knee into Hamlet's stomach.

I could have sworn that tonight I'd be dreaming of Damascus steel blades dripping blood or, alternatively, beings with horns rising from strange chalk diagrams to demand the most precious thing I had, but no, instead I found myself back in the endless loop of silly dreams about *Hamlet* that had plagued me all this week. I thought I'd rather not know what that said about my state of mind.

I had to get out of here. Pushing Florence and Hamlet aside, I turned the lizard doorknob to get out into the corridor. When I closed the door behind me, I found myself in welcome silence.

Cautiously, I looked all around. There was no one else here, at least so far as I could see. Henry's black door was opposite mine again, and right next to Grayson's door. Frightful Freddy majestically lowered his beak when I waved to him. I could have visited Grayson in his dreams anytime I liked, because I was now in possession of a personal item of his again. That afternoon I had fished a blue T-shirt of his out of the laundry basket in the bathroom, one of the dark-blue shirts that were part of the school uniform. He must have had a dozen of them, so he'd never notice that one was missing. However, I didn't think Grayson's dreams would get me any farther tonight.

I wandered undecidedly a few steps up and down without really knowing what or who I was waiting for. I had no idea how long I'd been asleep. Grayson and I had come home just before midnight and gone to bed at once. *Home*—that was a funny feeling. I hadn't really accustomed myself to the idea yet. It still felt as if I were a guest visiting the Spencers.

There was nothing moving yet in the dream corridor. Next to the sky-blue door with carved owls that I thought was the way into Mia's dreams, I saw a pine door adorned with Christmas decorations. A garland of spruce with red velvet bows surrounded the door frame, and even before I deciphered the wording on the door itself, I knew whose it was. LOTTIE'S LOVE BAKERY said the notice. DELIVERIES PLEASE USE THE BACK DOOR. I sighed, touched. Lottie was such a darling! I was just about to sit down on her doorstep, under a sprig of mistletoe—very useful in case Henry needed an excuse to kiss me again (I loved these Christmas customs!), when I heard footsteps approaching.

But they weren't Henry's footsteps, as I had secretly hoped. They were Anabel's.

"I was looking for you," she said in her attractive voice.

I'd have gone looking for her, too, if I'd only known where, because our last meeting had left me feeling very anxious to know more about her.

She looked stunning, the same as before. With her jeans and flat ballerina shoes, she was wearing a low-necked sweater the same color as her eyes, a deep turquoise green.

"I'm sorry I didn't take things quite seriously enough last time we met," I said. That wasn't entirely true, but it was certainly a good idea for me to be on friendly terms with her. I just hoped fervently that she wouldn't come out with the name Lulila again, or I couldn't be guaranteed to keep a straight face.

"That's all right." Anabel sketched a smile, but she looked tense. "Listen, we don't have much time. I know you took the oath this evening." She glanced briefly around. "That's why I wanted to see you. I think that's . . . really brave of you."

"Well . . ." Somehow or other so did I.

"Brave and unselfish! It can all end well now, because of you. So long as you don't make the same mistake as I did. Come along. I want to show you something."

I looked at Henry's door on the other side of the corridor. "Where are we going, then?" I asked suspiciously.

"It's not far." Anabel had already gone a little way ahead. I followed her along the corridor, around a corner, into another corridor, and over to a double door that, with its heavy gold fittings and Gothic arch, looked like a church porch. Outwardly it didn't look quite right for Anabel. I'd have expected her to have something more delicate. But she pushed one wing of the door open as if it were to be taken for granted, then turned to me. "What are you waiting for?"

"Is this the door to your dreams? But I thought . . . I mean, I don't own anything of yours."

"You don't need it if I invite you in myself and ask you through the doorway."

"Oh. Same as with vampires?"

Anabel looked puzzled. She obviously wasn't very familiar with the habits of vampires. Well, demons were her special subject. "Come on. This will interest you. And help you to understand a few of the things involved in all this."

If so, there was nothing I'd rather do than understand them. I went through the doorway and into a sunny garden: trees, bushes, and colorful flower beds surrounded a large lawn, emerald green, not a weed in sight, and perfectly mown, a typically English expanse of turf. I could see a house farther away.

A little white dog came running out of the bushes and raced toward us. He had a ball in his mouth and dropped it expectantly at Anabel's feet before jumping up at her, wagging his tail.

"Stop it, Lancelot, you little rascal!" Anabel ruffled up his coat and laughed. Only now did I realize that so far I'd seen her only when she was tense and anxious. Laughter suited her. She picked up the ball that the dog had dropped and threw it into a flower bed. The little dog almost turned head over heels in his haste to catch up with his toy, a whirling bundle of fur on the green lawn.

I looked around the garden. "What did you want to show me?"

The radiance drained out of Anabel's face. "Him." She pointed to Lancelot, who had picked up the ball and was chasing back to us full speed ahead. "He was my very best friend. But now—see for yourself!"

At that moment Lancelot uttered a howl and collapsed as he ran. He lay on the lawn, twitching.

"Oh God, what's the matter with him?" I was going to help the dog, but Anabel caught my arm and held it.

"He's dying."

"What?" I asked, horrified.

"It's my fault. *He* took him away from me, do you understand? Because I broke the rules of the game. I'm showing you this so that you don't make the same mistake."

By *he* she must mean the demon. At that moment I wouldn't have laughed even if she'd called him by that comical name. "But what . . . How can he . . . Why?" I stammered helplessly as the little dog lay on the ground in convulsions. He twitched once or twice more, then stretched out his legs and did not move again.

"In real life it took much longer," said Anabel in a hollow voice. "He was lying outside my door trembling when I woke. He was in terrible pain, and he lay in my arms all the time looking at me, as if he wanted . . ." Her voice faltered.

"The veterinarian says it was internal bleeding—he bled to death."

"That's . . . Oh, I'm so sorry," I whispered. "But I don't understand. You think the demon killed your dog?"

"Lancelot was my forfeit." Anabel wiped a tear away from her cheek. "He was what I exchanged for my heart's desire. So when I broke the rules, he took Lancelot away from me."

I couldn't take my eyes off the limp little body on the grass. The dog was the dearest, most precious thing that Anabel had? I mean, I loved Buttercup so much, I really did, but I loved Mia, Mom, and Lottie even more (if not necessarily in that order). And Papa, too, when I came to think of it. But even if Anabel didn't have such a great relationship with her family, how about Arthur? When we first met, hadn't she called him her one great love?

I tried to concentrate. "What exactly happened?" I asked, secretly promising myself to scream, loud and long, if she went on with her usual hints and half explanations that she never ended properly.

But Anabel surprised me. "I had sex," she said, looking me in the eyes. "I'd sworn to keep my virginity until the end of the game, but . . . I didn't think it was so important. And also I was convinced that no one would ever know. But you can't keep any secrets from *him*. He was so angry, he threw me out of the circle. . . ."

"And murdered your dog," I said, finishing the sentence for her. All just because she wasn't a virgin anymore? That seemed to me a really stern reaction. Since when were demons so puritanical? It was unfair, too. I mean, it takes two to have sex, right? "Why wasn't the de—er, *he* angry with Arthur, then?"

"Arthur," breathed Anabel, and again tears came into her eyes. "That was the worst of it. To think that I hurt Arthur. I'll never forget the way he looked at me."

"The way Arthur . . . ?" Confused, I stared at her. Then, suddenly, I understood. "It wasn't with Arthur at all!" I said. "You slept with someone else!" Now all her evasions made sense at last, and it was so simple: Anabel had secretly had sex, and the demon had found out and told on her. The only question was who she had slept with. And why, if Arthur had been—how had she put it?—the tsunami of her life?

So there probably had been something in the rumors, as reported by the Tittle-Tattle blog, about the sparks still flying between her and her dead ex-boyfriend.

Anabel was looking hard at me. "Like I said, I wanted you to know. I owe you that. Because after all, I'm the one who got the boys into all this, and now you as well."

Well, yes. I certainly understood that by now. And in any case, *this is all my fault* seemed to be one of Anabel's favorite sayings.

But it obviously did her good to talk about it. She seemed strangely refreshed. With a gesture, she made the dead dog disappear from the lawn, conjured up a picnic rug out of nowhere, and spread it on the grass. A picnic basket and a few cushions completed the ensemble.

"What . . . ?" I murmured.

"Believe me, if I could somehow make it not have happened, I would," said Anabel, placing a little vase of flowers on the picnic rug. "I regret it every day. Arthur and I are like those pairs of lovers in great literature, destined for each other even beyond death. Romeo and Juliet. Tristan and Isolde . . ."

She'd certainly have made a good Ophelia; she had exactly the right amount of drama in her voice. Since her mind was on other things just now, it seemed to me that the right time for a catch question had come. I asked the first to occur to me.

"The book found in the cellar of your house—where does it actually come from?"

Anabel raised her head. "Oh, the book! Arthur knew at once that we'd found a real treasure. That the book would change our lives."

Okay. I'd have to come back to that later. But first there was another detail that I wanted to clear up.

"Your ex-boyfriend Tom . . . ," I began.

"Oh, *Tom*?" Anabel looked surprised. Then she nodded. "I see. You must have been reading the Tittle-Tattle blog, and now you think . . ." She paused for a moment. "Everyone thinks so, of course. Even Arthur."

What now? Did that mean she hadn't slept with Tom at all? Who was it, then? And in addition . . .

"Arthur was always terribly jealous of Tom. He hated him," said Anabel. "Because he was the first boy who kissed me."

"And now Tom is *dead*?" As I said that, goose bumps crept over my arms.

"Yes," Anabel confirmed quietly. "He died in a car accident in June. It wasn't his fault. A drunk truck driver knocked him down."

The goose bumps spread all over my body. Leaving aside all the other incidents, this seemed to me one remarkable coincidence too many.

Anabel straightened the picnic cushions. "As I said, I'm so sorry for what I did," she said. "And ever since, I've done all I can to make sure things are the same between Arthur and me as before. He does say he's forgiven me, but sometimes when I look into his eyes . . ." She wound her arms around herself. "I can still see the pain I gave him in them. And a chill that's like a knife going into my heart." Obviously she and Arthur shared a liking for emotional figures of speech. I was sorry for her, all the same. She really did seem deeply unhappy. "And then I'm afraid he will never see me the same way he did before," she whispered. "I—oh, look, here he comes!"

I turned around. Yes, it was Arthur just coming through the door and onto the lawn, carrying a bottle of wine. The sunlight made his hair shine like pure gold. And somehow I suddenly felt an urge to run away.

"Please don't tell him what we were talking about." With a nervous laugh, Anabel brushed a lock of hair back from her face.

"Is that the real Arthur, or are you just dreaming of him?"

She laughed. "The *real* Arthur is lying in bed in Hampstead, I hope."

"On his own, at that!" Arthur assured her.

Anabel went three steps toward him and flung her arms around his neck. Then she said, "Look who's here," and pointed to me. "I wanted to thank her."

"Hi, Liv." Was I imagining it, or was there a flash of something like triumph in his eyes? "How does it feel to be the heroine of the hour?" Arthur had put the wine bottle down and was embracing Anabel from behind, both hands around her waist. He tenderly pushed her heavy hair away from the nape of her neck and began covering it with kisses. "I've missed you so much, sweetie."

I looked away, feeling moved and embarrassed.

"Excuse us, Liv," said Anabel. "It's just that . . . I've been living in Switzerland for the last three weeks, over a thousand kilometers away. We can meet only in our dreams."

"Yes, but that's so much better than Skyping." With a laugh, Arthur drew Anabel even closer to him. "Would you like to share our picnic?"

"Er, no, I really don't want to be in the way." I did still have any number of open questions, but I also had plenty to think about for now.

Arthur drew Anabel down on the picnic rug. "A very sensible attitude," he said, and Anabel added, "See you soon, Liv." Neither of them watched as I opened the door and went out through Anabel's porch and into the corridor again.

25

EVEN FROM A DISTANCE, I could see Henry outside the green door, discussing something with Lottie, who was standing in the doorway and apparently didn't want to let him in. She had her hands on her hips and was wearing her best dirndl, the one with the black taffeta apron.

"The presence of the gods?" asked Henry.

Lottie shook her head. "Very pretty, but no. Not so elegiac. Right, what's not certain?"

Henry sighed. "Is it something by Goethe?"

"No." Lottie put her head to one side and plucked flirtatiously at the enormous taffeta bow at her waist. "Neither Goethe nor Schiller."

"You're only supposed to ask the question, Lottie, not give him hints," I told her. Henry spun around to me. "There you are at last," he said.

"Oh, but I like talking to him," said Lottie. "Such a polite boy." She beamed at me. "And he comes here every night. That sly lizard doorknob bit his finger, so it needed treatment, and we made friends."

"Yes, that really is a malicious touch to your barriers," Henry told me. "Since when do lizards have teeth?"

"Since they've had to keep unauthorized visitors out of my dreams," I replied. "It's a vampire lizard. A killer vampire lizard. And obviously a more reliable doorkeeper than my au pair."

"Did you know that Henry likes baking?" Lottie gave Henry a smile full of maternal pride. "He was very interested in my all-the-year-round vanilla crescents, and in return he gave me the recipe for making his walnut cake. And he asked if I could dance waltzes and whether I would teach him how. Wasn't that sweet?"

For a second I was left speechless. Now was the moment to raise my eyebrows and dart scornful looks at Henry.

He awkwardly scratched his nose. "The things one will do to solve a riddle," he murmured.

"Don't give up, young man. You must think of literature less, or let's say of folklore more," said Lottie encouragingly. "Go on, then, try again. What's not certain?"

Indignantly, I gasped for breath. "You're not the real Lottie, you're only a dream Lottie, and I appointed you my doorkeeper. If you don't do your job properly, I'm going to fire you and appoint Mr. Wu. He not only knows the tiger's claw technique, he won't be taken in so easily. Walnut cake! Huh!"

Lottie was offended. "I thought I'd brought you up to show more courtesy and respect," she said. "Do you want to come in? It's rather drafty out here."

"No, I'll stay outside for a while. Close the door," I told her sternly. "And don't let anyone in, understand?"

"The gratitude of the Germans?" Henry asked quickly before Lottie could go in and shut the door.

Regretfully, she shook her head. "Think more along folklore lines, I told you."

"Lottie!"

"All right! See you soon, Henry." Very slowly, and with many sighs of protest, she closed the door.

"The gratitude of the Germans?" I repeated, when we were finally alone.

Henry waved that away. "I found it on the Internet in some manifesto or other. Churchill was saying that the ingratitude of the Germans was certain."

"So you turned it on its head to say that the gratitude of the Germans was *not* certain?" I giggled. "Imagine thinking that up. But what does it have to do with Hans?"

"Oh, hell, this is a really difficult puzzle. I've looked up 'Hans' and 'not certain' hundreds of times on search engines, but . . . oh!" Something seemed to have occurred to him, because his eyes began to shine.

"What?"

"But I didn't look it up in German!" He slapped his forehead with his hand. "To think that didn't strike me before!"

"So what are you going to do now? Wake up and turn on your computer? Or take your dream cell phone out of your pocket and look it up here and now?" I laughed, and Henry laughed as well.

"You're in a good mood for someone who's just joined the club of lost souls," he commented.

"And you're pretty pessimistic if you've given yourself up as a lost soul," I retorted. "Although . . ." Suddenly I remembered exactly what I had just heard from Anabel, and my laughter died away. "Did you know Anabel's ex-boyfriend Tom?"

"Tom Holland? Yes, of course. He was one class above me. Why?"

"Well, because . . ." Because Arthur hated him, and now he's dead. No, I couldn't possibly say that. Unable to make up my mind, I bit my lower lip.

"Why don't we go somewhere more comfortable?" Henry gave me an inquiring glance. "For instance, through this green door?"

"Nice try," I said.

"Then at least let's go for a little walk." Henry smiled and held out his hand. I hesitated for only a second before putting my own hand into it. It was simply too nice a feeling for me to resist.

We slowly strolled down the corridor. As we came to the corner down which I had turned with Anabel recently, I asked, "What do you think will happen when the last seal is broken?"

Henry shrugged his shoulders. "You heard it for yourself today: the Lord of Shadows will break his chains, rise from the blood that has been shed, and show his gratitude to those who have kept faith with him."

When was I supposed to have heard that, then?

"That part seems to have escaped me," I said.

"Oh, yes, you don't know any Latin. At least, *cruor* means blood—but unlike *sanguis*, it means blood shed by violence. . . ."

"Don't you think that could be just metaphorical? Like the breaking-his-chains bit—I mean—*what was that?*" I'd heard a sound like the quiet squeal of a door hinge.

"No idea," said Henry, letting go of my hand and looking over my shoulder. "But maybe we'd better go somewhere we can talk undisturbed. To your place, for instance."

I turned around. Doors as far as the eye could see. But I couldn't see movement anywhere. So why did I suddenly feel I was under observation all the same?

"Come along!" Henry took my arm, a little too roughly, I thought, and led me on in the direction of our own doors. Normally I'd have protested, but right now I was very ready to follow him.

"There isn't anyone else here, is there?"

"You can never tell," he replied, and for the first time since I'd known him, his voice sounded a little grim. "If you have enough imagination and you can concentrate well, then you can take any shape you like in a dream."

"I know." After all, I'd been a barn owl. My imagination was strong enough; it was just my powers of concentration that left something to be desired. But all the same, the corridor was entirely empty.

The only question was why, in that case, Henry kept quickening his pace. And why was he whispering? That didn't exactly do anything to reassure me.

He looked over his shoulder once more. "If you're good enough at it, you can turn into someone else, or into a tiger, a gnat, a ceiling light, a tree, a breath of air. . . . For example, I could look just like Henry while I was really someone completely different."

Oh God. That was really the worst possible thing he could say to make me feel better. As we walked along I looked closely at him, examining the contours of his face, the gray eyes with their thick eyelashes, the straight nose, the delicate curve of his lips, the way they crinkled at the corners.

No, this was Henry sure enough.

"Shh." He stopped.

I had heard it too. A kind of rustling. Like a curtain being drawn aside. I clung to Henry's arm. There it was again. Yes, it sounded like fabric. Or as if someone was taking a deep breath through clenched teeth. Difficult to say where it came from. But never mind that, it was far too close anyway.

Henry kept leading me on, and I was very glad of that, because my knees were threatening to give way. That was typical: whenever someone was pursuing me in a dream, my knees tended to fail me. And the ground underfoot was suddenly like sand or deep snow, and I could move only in slow motion. I hated dreams like that.

That curious rustling sound again. What was that Henry had said just now about a breath of air? Could you be pursued by a breath of air—a rustling breath of air? With teeth?

"Don't you think it's somehow darker than before, Henry?"

Henry didn't answer. We'd reached our own doors again, but he didn't stop. He led me a little farther on, to a wooden door painted pink with flowers in many different colors all over it. Even the doorknob was shaped like a flower.

"And it's colder, too." I realized that I was beginning to sound a little hysterical. "Or am I just imagining it? Please say I'm just imagining it."

"I can do better than that: you're just dreaming all this." Henry ran his fingers over a yellow flower. It looked as if he were tickling it; at least, I heard a giggle. The bolt of the door shot back, and Henry pushed the door handle down.

I hesitated for a moment.

"Come on. You'll like it here." Henry drew me through the doorway, and the door latched softly after us, shutting out the corridor and whatever might be in it.

I sighed with relief. But my relief lasted only about a second.

Something damp plopped into my face, and I let out a small shriek of alarm.

Then I saw the soap bubbles. Hundreds of them! They were hovering in the air over a grass-covered, hilly landscape, with the bluest sky I'd ever seen above it. All the colors here were as intense as if someone had turned the color regulator of the TV set up to maximum. There were flowers everywhere, the leaves of the trees weren't just green, but sometimes yellow and pink, and in the distance I could see the towers of a palace. Golden towers.

Only a few yards away a carousel was going around to the soft music-box tune of the Disney song "It's a Small World." A fair-haired little girl was riding one of the brightly painted carousel horses, smiling to herself as she went around and around in circles. In spite of my shriek of alarm, she didn't seem to have noticed us.

"Where are we, in the Land of Oz?" I asked, wiping the dampness left by the soap bubble off my cheek. "But how come Shaun the Sheep is grazing over there? And look—a balloon tree!"

"I said you'd like it." Henry laughed. "Welcome to Amy's pink world of dreams. Isn't it wonderful?" He steered me away from the carousel into the shade of a tall apple tree bearing both blossoms and red-cheeked apples. And a few oranges as well, I noticed.

"Who's Amy?"

"My little sister." He pointed proudly to the carousel. "She's four, and she has the most relaxing dreams in the world, as you can see. I sometimes come here when it all gets too much for me, or I have a feeling that the world is a bad place. It's always in order here, anyway. Nothing at all happens. Have an apple?"

I shook my head. "You can't taste things in a dream."

"That depends on your powers of imagination." Henry grinned. "But I'm not much good at tasting and smelling in dreams either," he admitted. Suddenly he bent down and buried his nose in my hair. "Which is a pity, really."

I felt the blood rise to my face and sighed. "What was that thing outside?"

"Nothing good, presumably." Shrugging his shoulders, he sat down on a soft cushion of moss under the tree.

"And how was I able to get through that door? I don't know your sister, and I don't have anything personal belonging to her."

"What a good thing you were with me, then." A large soap bubble settled on Henry's hair without bursting. "Or you might still be wandering around out there, desperately shaking doorknobs and getting scared."

"Don't laugh. It was *really* creepy." I sat down beside Henry and wrapped my arms around my knees. "Do you think it's waiting for us outside the door? And if it is, how are we going to get home?"

"Who says we have to go out through the door again? We can simply stay here until we're awake."

The soap bubble was still there.

"*There is just one moon and one golden sun,*" sang Amy up on her carousel. "*And a smile means friendship to everyone.*"

"She's really sweet," I said.

"You're really sweet too," said Henry, with his eyes turned to my face. "Sometimes I can hardly believe just *how* sweet."

My heat began beating faster. And not very steadily.

"Even when I first saw you, at the airport with your cheese, I thought you were sweet."

Oh great, now I was finding it difficult to breathe steadily too. And when he leaned forward to me, I stopped breathing entirely. The idea that had just come into my head dissolved into its separate parts. Something about airports . . . Zurich . . . wasn't Anabel's school very close to Zurich? And . . . my God, Henry had lovely eyes. If he was going to kiss me now . . . maybe first I should . . . My hand went out quickly, and I touched the soap bubble on his hair with my forefinger.

His eyes widened in surprise.

"Sorry, but it looked funny, like a fruit dish upended on your head," I murmured, and sighed with disappointment as he sat up straight again. As if he'd never been going to kiss me.

And maybe he hadn't.

Also, what was it I'd just been thinking? It had been important in some way.

I heard hoofbeats behind us, and the next moment two ponies galloped past, one of them brown and white, the other pure white. At the sight of their flowing manes, Amy broke into peals of laughter as wholeheartedly as only small children can.

My breathing calmed down a little, but scraps of ideas were still whirling wildly around in my head. Suddenly it was all too much for me. All these secrets—there seemed to be more and more of them every day. Dreams that eluded any kind of logic. Henry, who turned my brain into pink candy floss as soon as he came close to me. Anabel and her strange confession. Arthur, who looked like an angel but also, for some reason, frightened me. And that . . . *something* outside in the corridor.

I rubbed my eyes. All at once I felt terribly tired, even though I was already asleep.

"Is everything all right?" asked Henry.

I took a deep breath. Then I instinctively reached for one of those scraps of ideas whirling through my head and dragged it into the light of day.

"Tom Holland," I said. "Is it true that Arthur hated him?"

Henry raised an eyebrow. "That's what I call an elegant way of changing the subject," he said. "Hated? I don't know that I'd go as far as that. But he couldn't stand him, that's true enough. To be honest, Tom wasn't exactly a sympathetic soul himself, more of an arrogant bastard. Arthur was jealous of him because he'd been in a relationship with Anabel before him. Tom used that fact to provoke Arthur whenever he could. Once they had such a violent fight that, when we intervened to separate them, Grayson got a black eye. When it comes to Anabel, Arthur's not entirely responsible for his own actions. He genuinely idolizes her."

"Hmm," I said. "Still? Anabel has told me how she . . . er . . . broke the rules of the game. Do you think he's forgiven her? For being unfaithful to him, I mean."

Frowning, Henry looked at me. "Liv—Arthur is one of my best friends. I'm not going to discuss him with you, certainly not when something so intimate's involved. And by the way, where did you meet Anabel?"

No, no, no—no counterquestions! I'd asked my question first. And I was very glad that, for a change, I could think clearly again. "But . . . don't you think it's strange that Tom Holland is dead?" I persisted.

Henry looked away. "Apparently the truck driver was drunk. That's terrible, but these things do happen."

"I know. But couldn't it be a fact that Arthur's dearest wish was granted when that car accident happened?"

His hesitation told me that this idea was not by any means new to him. Then he slowly shook his head, "Arthur couldn't stand Tom, that's true enough, but actually wishing him dead—no. That wouldn't be like Arthur."

At that moment there was a loud noise, and a shrill female voice drowned out the music-box tune of the carousel. "Which of you damn kids left those damn Lego bricks lying around here?"

I looked around for whoever had said that, or rather shouted it. But there was no one in sight.

"Do you want me to break my neck? That would suit your father nicely!" bawled the voice. It seemed to come from all sides at once. "Then he'd be rid of me forever—he could live happily ever after with that floozy of his!"

The carousel had stopped going round, and Amy was no longer looking serene, but rather worried.

"What's . . . ?" I began, but when I turned to Henry I saw that he had disappeared. I jumped up. Where the hell was he? Not a trace of him anywhere.

"Henry? *Henry?*" I cried, with panic rising in me. "Please come back! This isn't funny!"

But there was no sign of him.

"Go away! Just bloody leave me alone to lie here and die!" shouted the woman's voice, and Amy gave a start where she was sitting on the carousel. "No one's going to miss me anyway. No one!"

And then, as if someone had turned off the electricity, all around me went dark. The ground gave way under my feet, and I fell into the depths.

TITTLE-TATTLE BLOG

The Frognal Academy Tittle-Tattle Blog, with all the latest gossip, the best rumors, and the hottest scandals from our school.

ABOUT ME:

My name is Secrecy—I'm right here among you, and I know *all* your secrets.

18 September, 10:30 p.m.

Florence Spencer is going to the Autumn Ball with Callum Caspers. And if you just asked, "Callum WHO?" I know just how you feel. I had to look Callum up to see if he goes to this school at all. And in fact, he does. He's been here for six years. Oops.

I've found you a photo from the yearbook, showing last year's members of the Math Club— Callum is second from the left.

So all you nice, nondescript boys with uncool hobbies and funny hairstyles, don't worry: There's hope for you yet. One of these days the prettiest, most popular girl in the school could ask you whether you'd like to go to the ball with her. And then you must just brush the silly fringe off your forehead and say yes. Because that's what Callum Caspers did (let's call him C.C.—wouldn't that be better?), and the fringe hasn't slipped back over his face to this day. In fact, with Florence beside him, Callum doesn't look so nondescript and uncool after all.

But I still don't understand it. I mean, Florence really could have had ANYONE. Well, except for one . . . and maybe that's the nub of the matter. Has Florence lost her heart to Arthur Hamilton? Has she worked out the chances of replacing Anabel as Ball Queen at Arthur's side? And did she, on a short-circuit impulse, simply ask the first comer if he'd like to go to the ball with her when she found out that Anabel will be coming back from Switzerland specially for the occasion?

In that case, our friend C.C. just struck lucky.

Apart from that, I stick to my theory about long-distance relationships in general and this one in particular: Arthur and Anabel may get together once more for the ball, but sooner or later that will be the end of it all the same. Remember what I say: long before Christmas they'll both change their relationship status on Facebook to single—and then the race is wide open again. Until then, enjoy your luck, C.C. And chin up, Florence.

See you soon!

Love from Secrecy

PS—After a tough battle with the firefighting services, the ball committee now has the green light for onstage fireworks and ground-level mist-making machines—I have a good feeling about that, everyone! As soon as the official part of the evening is over and Mrs. Cook and Mrs. Beckett and their waltzes have finished, we start rocking! This is going to be the greatest ball night that Frognal Academy has ever known.

PPS—And below you will find a list of all the upper school boys who haven't chosen partners for the ball yet. Among the cream slices and other choice morsels is Jasper Grant. My advice, girls, is tallyho and get after him with a hue and cry. (It's a fact that he's a disaster as a dancer, but who's going to bother about that?)

26

I SAT UP WITH MY HEART THUDDING wildly. Thank God I was awake. I caught the echo of a scream in the air. Moonlight fell into my new room, and I was really glad to feel a soft mattress under me—so much nicer than falling into a bottomless abyss, surrounded by a black void.

But I had only a split second to enjoy my relief, because then I heard loud footsteps in the corridor, my door was flung open, and Mom rushed over to my bed. "What happened, mousie? Have you hurt yourself?"

"What?" I blinked at the light, confused.

Only a few seconds later, Mia, Buttercup, Grayson, and Florence arrived, and finally Ernest came running in.

"A burglar?" cried Mia.

"Did you see a ghost?" asked Florence at the same time. "Did Spot jump on your bed?"

"A bat, I expect?" Ernest was tying the belt of his bathrobe around his waist. (Good, so he didn't wander around the house half naked at night.) "Nothing to panic about.

They do sometimes lose their way and come into the house at this time of year—oh, but your window is closed."

The only one apart from Buttercup who didn't ask questions was Grayson. He just looked at me as if he knew exactly what had happened.

It took me some time to pull myself together and get my breathing reasonably well under control. Having everyone stare at me wide-eyed and bombard me with questions didn't really help. What were they all doing here?

"You screamed," Mia explained.

It must have been a frightful scream to be heard two rooms away. Only Lottie, on the floor above, evidently hadn't been woken.

"I had a silly dream, that's all," I muttered, avoiding Grayson's eyes. Butter licked my hand comfortingly.

"What of? Being skinned alive?" Florence looked at me as if she'd never seen anything more pathetic in her life— and she was right. With my hair untidy and drenched with sweat, and my worn-out old nightshirt, I was certainly no sight for sore eyes. "Uh-oh, don't they say that what you dream on your first night in a new house comes true?"

They said that, did they? What a delightful prospect.

"How unfortunate." Mia gave Florence an annihilating glance. "Especially if Liv dreamed of an ax murderer coming to slaughter you in your bed."

"My poor mousie. Please dream something nice from now on, will you?" Mom yawned and stroked my hair.

"And if you don't, then at least be quiet about it," added Florence huffily. "I nearly had a heart attack."

"It's only three thirty. I suggest we all go back to bed and try to get some more sleep," said Ernest. "But maybe you'd better leave your bedside light on, Liv."

You bet I would. I pulled the quilt up to my chin, because I suddenly felt icy cold.

"I'm sorry," I said wearily. "I really didn't mean to wake you all. Good night."

One by one they started leaving my room. Only Grayson turned back in the doorway again and looked at me.

"What's the matter?" I hissed, when he still hadn't said anything after about ten seconds. He was wearing only his pajama bottoms, and although (or perhaps because) I was feeling right off the wall, I couldn't help noticing how fit his upper body looked.

"I'm sorry," he said. "I shouldn't have dragged you into it." And before I could answer, he closed the door.

Wearily, I dropped back against the pillows. He wasn't to blame; it was all my own fault. I'd thought I was in control of events. I wasn't.

And it wasn't fun anymore either.

In rapid succession I remembered the fear in Anabel's voice, the dog dying on the lawn, the triumphant gleam in Arthur's eyes, and the invisible Something that had followed Henry and me along the corridor. Was it going to be like that every night now?

The story of Tom Holland had given me a lot to think about, and it badly shook my conviction that demons didn't exist. Suppose Henry was wrong and Arthur had wished Tom dead last year at Halloween after all—then how great was the probability that, young and healthy as he'd been, he really would die within the next nine months? Less than one percent, I'd guess. Far less than one percent. It would explain why Arthur took the whole thing so seriously—so deadly seriously, you might say: He felt sure that Tom's accident was the work of the demon. And I could even understand that.

I turned over on my other side and closed my eyes, exhausted. I'd simply have to ignore the green door as well as I could over the next few days, or I'd go right out of my mind. I'd sooner dream of Hamlet every night than of invisible pursuers, or falling into a void. Or of boys with gray eyes who simply vanished when things began to get romantic. It was about time to let my sound human reason take charge of this story again.

In fact, Henry did seem to have vanished, and not just from the dream. He didn't come to school on Monday, never mind how much I looked out for him. First I was just uneasy, but when he still didn't turn up on Tuesday, my uneasiness turned to mild hysteria. What did I know about these dreams and the laws governing them? Maybe that rustling thing had caught Henry, and . . . Or he was simply sick and I was in the process of going off my rocker. Because I was seriously considering the possibility of catching a cold in dream corridors. So much for sound human reason.

And when there was still no sign of Henry on Wednesday morning, although I lingered at my locker for an extra-long time, I suddenly realized how much I missed him. I also realized that I couldn't stand the uncertainty any longer. I'd have to swallow my pride and ask Grayson.

At that moment I heard Henry's voice.

"Has your locker hypnotized you, cheese girl? You've been staring at the same spot for a full minute."

I was so relieved to see him that my legs almost gave way beneath me. Of course, I couldn't come up with a smart answer right away.

"Henry!" In fact, I could only just suppress a deep sigh of relief.

He smiled. "I've missed you, too," he said. His eyes were bright, but you couldn't help seeing the dark shadows under them.

"Where've you been?" I managed to ask.

He opened his locker and took out a few books. "I had to see about something at home." Rather hesitantly, he added, "My mother had one of her bad turns. But it's all right again now."

Had it been his mother's voice breaking into Amy's colorful little-girl dream? *Which of you damn kids . . . ?* Not exactly what you'd want to hear your mother saying.

"You suddenly just disappeared, and then everything turned black," I murmured, suppressing the impulse to touch him just to make sure he was really there. I crossed my arms, to be on the safe side.

The bell rang for class.

"I'm sorry—I was woken, and then so was Amy." He closed his locker a little more forcefully than necessary. "I'd have liked to explain, but you haven't been in the dream corridor these last few nights."

"You could simply have phoned," I said. "In the daytime, I mean."

He looked at me thoughtfully. "Yes, I expect I could," he said. "I must go—I have a biology test. Active and passive transport mechanisms in the biomembrane. Cross your fingers for me."

Then he had disappeared into the crowd, and I began missing him all over again. If Persephone hadn't turned up to hold her cell phone under my nose, showing a picture of herself in a reed-green ball dress, I might even have run after him. For the first time, I was grateful to Persephone for her presence.

Over the following nights, however, there was no one to save me from thinking about Henry and myself. It took me forever to get to sleep, and when I did finally manage it, at least I didn't have nightmares (and I only once had to put up with Florence playing both leading parts in *Hamlet*), but the green door turned up all over the place. Again and again I was on the point of opening it, only to decide against the idea.

No, I wasn't about to make it so easy for him! If Henry wanted to talk to me, he could do it by day. He knew where to find me. Apart from which, you never knew whom or what else you might meet in that corridor.

But Henry seemed to be avoiding me. I met Arthur and Jasper now and then, but because I was always with Persephone, they just smiled and cast me meaningful glances. Maybe that did bring Persephone to the verge of a heart attack every time, but it cheered me up a bit. The dreams were one thing, but when I thought of the ritual in Jasper's living room, I couldn't help laughing.

My nights seemed to go on forever, while my days passed at surprising speed, not least because living with the Spencers was so strange and new for us all. But it worked out better than I'd expected. Maybe that was because Mom and Ernest were so obviously happy together. To be honest, I'd never seen Mom happier. In the circumstances, it was harder and harder for Mia and me to act as if we were always going to detest Ernest. We still avoided speaking to him directly, but if we weren't careful, an "Ernest" sometimes slipped out, instead of "Mr. Spencer." And a smile.

It was easy to get used to Grayson as well. He might have a few bad habits, like forgetting to put the milk back in the fridge, or leaving large blobs of toothpaste in the washbasin, but otherwise it was nice sharing a house with him. Buttercup in particular loved him to bits, because he played in the garden with her every day and praised her ability to fetch even when she bit his basketball in half. He didn't seem to spend much time with Emily during the week, but you knew at once when she was on the phone, because then his voice changed and he disappeared into his room as soon as he could. (We were all thankful for that; having Mom and Ernest going lovey-dovey the whole time was quite enough.)

Every morning on his way to work, Ernest first dropped Florence, Mia, and me off at school, then he took Mom to the rail station. Grayson cycled to school. He liked it, and anyway there wasn't any room left for him in the car.

Lottie enjoyed mothering three more people than before, plus a cat. She did all the food shopping, made supper, and saw to keeping the whole house neat and tidy and full of delicious cooking smells, and as usual her good temper spread to everyone.

By the end of the first week, even Spot and Buttercup were lying peacefully side by side on the sofa.

In fact, if Florence and I hadn't been getting on each other's nerves so badly, there'd have been an almost suspiciously harmonious atmosphere in the house and the enlarged family. But she could be relied on to spoil that. On the pretext of "just wanting to help," she meddled with every-thing: homework, dog training, a bathroom schedule—and plans for my sixteenth birthday.

Not that there had to be any real plans. We'd never made a big fuss about birthdays. A few presents, a cake, the essential phone call from Papa, and we usually went to the cinema in the evening—the perfect day! Florence, Grayson, and Ernest were welcome to a piece of my birthday cake, but apart from that I saw no reason for my birthday to be any different from usual this year.

However, I'd been reckoning without Florence.

On Friday afternoon I came home from school in a towering fury, ready to strangle Florence with my own hands. I found her sitting with Mom, Mia, and Lottie in the kitchen, teaching them all to play bridge. That idyllic sight was the last straw! I swept the cards off the table, leaned both hands on it, and faced Florence.

"How come Persephone Porter-Peregrin is going about claiming to have been invited to my birthday party?" I felt like shouting, but what came out of my mouth wasn't much more than a concentrated hiss.

For the first time since I'd known her, Florence looked taken aback. For about a second.

"But, mousie," said Mom, "I asked Florence to invite a few of your new friends."

"And it's obvious that you spend more time with Perse-phone than anyone else at school," said Florence, "so I thought—"

"Are you crazy?" I was getting closer to a shout now. "Persephone is driving me out of my mind! She follows me everywhere, talking to me the whole darn time! I mean, if at least she talked about something interesting! But oh no, she describes all the ball dresses she *didn't* buy, in detail! It's more than anyone could stand. I'd like a rest from it on my birthday, at least!"

"Mousie," said Mom again, "you're only sixteen once, as Florence said, and she's right. So we thought it would be nice to celebrate the day with a little more than just a birthday cake."

"Of course there'll be a birthday cake as well," said Lottie. "And balloons!"

"We're going to have a picnic," said Mom proudly. "A genuine English picnic in the park, with the family and all your new friends! We've thought of all kinds of nice games and things to do. Emily is going to bring a croquet set——"

"*Emily?*" I gasped for air.

"Well, as Grayson's girlfriend, of course she's invited. She's practically one of the family."

"And I have to bring Daisy Dawn along, too," said Mia, winking at me. "I mean, of course, I'm *allowed* to bring Daisy Dawn along."

"It will be great!" Mom was beaming at me. "Henry has said he'll come as well, and if we have a barbecue, maybe Charles will——"

"*Henry?*"

"Yes, mousie, the boy you're going to the ball with. I'm looking forward so much to meeting him." Mom frowned. "Oh, please don't say that he's another one driving you out of your mind."

"No!" Yes. No. Only a little. I was breathing with difficulty. Who else had Florence invited? Her dancing partner, the one she'd fished up from the anonymous depths of the

Math Club? Emily's disturbed brother Sam? Itsy and Bitsy? Jasper and Arthur? The London Symphony Orchestra? And maybe Secrecy to take birthday photographs as a memento?

"We only wanted to do something nice for you," said Mom. She could sense that my anger was beginning to die down and laid her hand on mine. "Now, please tell me why you're so upset. It will be a splendid day, and you deserve one!"

"But . . . but . . . you can't simply . . . I mean to say . . . ," I stammered.

"I know. I'd be overwhelmed myself in your place." Florence gave me a modest smile. "But there's no need to thank me. I was really happy to fix it all."

"You're only sixteen once," Mom repeated.

And Lottie said, "We're all looking forward to it so much!"

I gave up. They'd won. With a little luck, it would rain on my birthday and the picnic would be a washout. After all, we were in England, and this was fall.

"I'll just go and get my things for kung fu," I said, resigned.

27

IN SPITE OF ALL MY HOPES, September 30, my birthday, dawned as a clear day with a bright blue sky. A fine day straight out of a picture book. After midday, the sun steadily raised the air temperature to over seventy-five degrees, and we weren't the only ones to have thought of having a picnic in the park. But because Lottie, Florence, Ernest, and Mom, with extra help from Charles, had been busy since early morning moving half the contents of the house to the park, we'd been able to reserve one of the best places, with an impressive view downhill to the city. I wasn't allowed to arrive until everything was ready, and after I'd wriggled out of Persephone's warm embrace (her birthday present was a bracelet with the words BEST FRIENDS FOREVER on it; she had the exact counterpart), I had to admit that all that trouble had been worthwhile. The scenario would have done credit to any glossy lifestyle magazine, with a lavish supply of rugs and cushions, helium balloons, and delicious things to eat, skillfully arranged by Lottie on a garden table covered with a white cloth. There was even a matching string of white pennants with letters on them, spelling out SWEET SIXTEEN and waving in the wind between two trees.

Well, maybe they'd overdone a few things.

"Good heavens," I heard Emily ask Grayson, "are those by any chance your family's silver candlesticks?"

Yup, they were, and the huge flower arrangement was in a genuine crystal vase. We ate off the Spencers' good Wedgwood china, and there was champagne standing ready in a silver cooler, to be drunk out of proper champagne flutes, of course.

Grayson rubbed his hand over his forehead. Then he explained, "You're only sixteen once." He'd obviously taken Florence's mantra to heart. Emily sniffed dismissively.

"I don't like her," Mia whispered to me, extracting a cucumber and creamed salmon sandwich. "But I'm going to feed her a few bits of false information—and if any of them come up in the Tittle-Tattle blog over the next few days, then we'll know that she's Secrecy."

I was going to say something agreeing with her, but at that moment I saw Charles coming up the slope with a sun umbrella under his arm. Behind him came the tall figure of Henry, and my stomach turned a somersault.

I swallowed. "Would you think it very bad of me not to be immune to boys anymore, Mia?" It was pointless to go on denying it.

Mia gave me a surreptitious glance and sighed. "Is it a good feeling, at least?"

Hard to say. For the moment, yes. Just because Henry was coming straight toward me, over the grass and in the sunshine, and no one else in the whole world had a smile like his. And because . . .

"Liv, stop it!" hissed Mia. "You look like a lovelorn sheep!"

I gave a start. "As bad as that? Oh, that's terrible." I added—and I was to regret it in the course of the day—"If you see me looking like that again, give me a nudge or throw something at me. Promise?"

"With pleasure," said Mia, and three hours later, because she always kept her promises, I was black and blue around the ribs and had been hit by assorted flying objects: several chestnuts, a spoon, and a blueberry muffin. Or a mooberry bluffin, as Lottie put it when Charles was listening.

And whenever I looked at Lottie, I knew exactly what Mia had meant about the lovelorn sheep.

Apart from that, I caught myself beginning to enjoy the picnic party. The food was fantastic, particularly the scones and the Indian curried chicken morsels that Lottie had conjured up. Thanks to some skillful rearrangement of the seating plan (after all, I was the birthday girl) I had even managed to put Persephone between Mom and Henry as a buffer. That way Mom couldn't ask Henry any embarrassing questions—or even worse, tell him the gory details of my birth. But anyway, Henry was totally fascinated by Lottie, probably because she was the image of the dream Lottie guarding my green door. When we played a celebrity guessing game, we laughed a lot at Ernest, who thought he was Winston Churchill, although he was really meant to be Britney Spears, and Grayson mimed Frodo surprisingly well. We were all splitting our sides with laughter, except for Emily. But as it turned out, she didn't know *The Lord of the Rings*, because she thought fantasy was a sheer waste of time. By now Mia Silver, Private Investigator, had come to the conclusion that Emily didn't have the charm and lightness of heart that would have made her right for the role of Secrecy. However, maybe that was just a rather stiff and humorless but clever bit of camouflage.

When everyone finally sang "Happy Birthday" for me, and even the people sitting near us with their own picnic joined in, I had to admit that, all things considered, it had been a really successful birthday party. I knew I mustn't forget to say thank you to Florence later. Although she was overdoing it again now, making everyone get up and start playing croquet.

I decided not to, and instead I helped Charles and Lottie to clear away the dirty plates and pack them in crates, while Mom and Ernest took Buttercup for a walk around the park and Mia and Daisy fed bits of apple to some greedy squirrels.

Charles was pensively examining a half-eaten blueberry muffin. "I can't say I ever heard of mooberries before, but I definitely like them."

"Mooberries?" Lottie gave him a puzzled look. "What are they?"

I decided to leave the two of them to work it out together while I collected the empty glasses.

"Can I help?" asked a voice behind me, and I almost dropped a champagne glass with shock. Where on earth had Henry learned to creep up on people like that?

He smiled at me. "It's not much fun over there playing croquet. Florence isn't playing very well, Emily is complaining that Grayson holds his mallet the wrong way, and Persephone has just been describing your ball dress to me. In every detail."

I felt the blood shoot into my cheeks. I hadn't talked to him about the misunderstanding over the ball yet. . . .

"Amazing all the stuff that goes into a ball dress. Taffeta, tulle, beads, ruffles, roses, four different shades of smoky blue . . ." He looked inquiringly at me. "And what the hell is a duchess line?"

"Look, just because I have a ball dress doesn't mean I really have to go to that ball," I said hastily. When he raised one eyebrow I added, even more hastily, "It's just that . . . because Florence told Mom that you'd invited me . . . and all of a sudden I somehow had this dress . . . and I haven't the faintest idea myself what a duchess line is." I took a deep breath. No, this wasn't working. "Anyway," I said, trying to conclude with dignity, "I just wanted you to know it doesn't mean a thing. I couldn't care less about the ball."

"That's a pity," said Henry, "because I've already hunted down the medal that my great-grandfather was given for conspicuous gallantry in the face of the enemy. Grayson is terribly envious of me for having such a genuine, stylish accessory to my white tie and tails. The man from the evening-dress rental company and I tried to persuade him to carry a top hat, so that he'd stand out from the common herd as well, but we got nowhere."

I could only stare at him. A piece of apple promptly flew at my head.

"Sorry!" called Mia.

"How about a walk?" Henry held out his hand, and I took it before Mia could throw another piece of apple. Henry's hand felt strangely familiar and unfamiliar at the same time. In dreams his physical closeness didn't make me feel half so self-conscious.

We walked side by side in silence for a while, and I tried to get my breathing under control. Then we turned off along a sandy path leading through the trees. The sun fell through the changing leaves and cast splashes of gold on the ground.

"I've missed this," said Henry suddenly, and cleared his throat. "I've missed *you*."

If one of Mia's missiles had hit me at that moment, I wouldn't even have felt it. I stopped in the middle of the path. Henry turned to me and pushed back a strand of hair from my face.

"Dreaming somehow wasn't any fun without you," he said. And then he leaned forward and kissed me carefully on the mouth.

For a few seconds I forgot to breathe, then I felt my arms rising and going around his neck of their own accord to draw him closer. We weren't kissing so cautiously now, but much more intensely. Henry put one hand on my waist, the other went behind my head and buried itself gently in my hair. I closed my eyes. This was just the way kisses ought to feel, I was sure. My whole body was beginning to tingle when he suddenly let go of me and pushed me a little way off.

"Like I said, I've missed you," he said softly, reaching for my hand again to lead me on.

I couldn't work out how he could simply go on walking like that as if nothing had happened, while I was having difficulty in standing upright at all. It was as if the kiss had turned the bones in my legs into licorice. Very soft licorice. Luckily Henry was only making for the nearest bench, a few yards away, and I was able to make it that far. I dropped onto the bench beside him in relief.

He put his arm on the back of the bench behind me. "Almost as nice a view as in Berkeley, right?" he said, pointing downhill with his other hand.

"Mmmmm," I agreed. "We've lived in so many parts of the world—this one really isn't the worst."

"Better than Oberammergau?" he asked.

"What?" I moved away from him in shock.

He laughed. "Whether he'll come by way of Oberammergau or by way of Unterammergau or whether he'll come at all isn't certain," he said, but he said it in the German wording of the little folk song that was the puzzle I'd set as a barrier, about a boy called Hans going to see his girlfriend Liesl. *Ob er aber über Oberammergau oder aber über Unterammergau oder ob er überhaupt nicht kommt, ist nicht gewiss.* He laughed. "Are all German folk songs such tongue twisters? Dream Lottie wanted me to sing it, but then she said it was okay anyway. Hey, don't look at me as if you were horrified, Liv—did you really think I wouldn't work it out? After you gave me so many helpful hints? *Heut' kommt der Hans zu mir, freut sich die Liesl.* . . . Did you see that funny video on You-Tube, the guy in lederhosen with the mandolin? I've thrown myself away. . . ."

"Then you knew the answer all along?" I asked indignantly.

"Not all along. Only once I typed 'Hans' and 'nicht gewiss' into the search engine." He frowned. "Why do I suddenly get the feeling I'm that millipede you met in Hyderabad? I wish you could see your shocked expression."

I didn't have to. I really was shocked. And disappointed. And furious. "What's the idea?" I cried. "Pretending to me that . . . and then simply going behind my back and . . ."

Henry leaned back. "Why are you getting so upset? I only solved your puzzle. I thought you wanted me to."

"*Wanted* you to?" I glared at him angrily. "Have you lost

your marbles? What have you watched me doing in dreams? What have you done to me?"

"I haven't done anything," he said, sounding injured. "I didn't even go through that door."

"How else would you know about the millipede?"

"Lottie told me. She likes talking about you. I know that you hate to eat bananas, you stopped believing in Santa Claus when you were three, and you always start crying at the same place in *Finding Nemo*."

"Lottie?"

"The dream Lottie." He sighed. "I'm afraid we'll have to sit out that formation waltz if we don't want to make idiots of ourselves."

"So you haven't been visiting my dreams on the sly?" My fury was subsiding as quickly as it had developed.

He sighed again and shook his head. "No, I haven't. Ask dream Lottie. I was good and stayed outside the door waiting for you. But you never turned up." The look in his gray eyes was honest.

"Sorry," I said remorsefully. "And I'm sorry you were left waiting. It somehow all got to be too much for me. These dreams are so confusing. You begin to doubt your own sound human reason. And I hate it when they throw up more and more questions and there are never any answers."

"Oh yes? How about psychology and science?" he asked ironically. "Didn't you say there's an entirely rational explanation for dreams?"

I shrugged my shoulders. "I said it's about as-yet-unexplored fields of psychology. And to be honest, it's not the dreams that give me such headaches—it's not even mysterious creatures rustling in corridors."

"But?"

"But what *really* happened. And what hasn't happened yet." Now it was my turn to sigh. "People who seriously believe in demons give me a headache."

"You mean Arthur?"

I nodded. "You may not think that he wanted Tom Holland dead, but I'm sure he did. He thinks the demon cleared Tom out of the way for him. And the reason why he goes on with all this conjuring-up-demons stuff isn't because he's uncertain and scared. He goes on with it because he really *does* want to liberate the demon from the underworld. He's genuinely passionate about the whole thing—you must have noticed that yourself."

There was a flicker in his eyes. "I'll admit that he's changed since we've been playing this game. And the Anabel situation is wearing him out. But he's not a bad person."

No, maybe not bad, but possibly in the midst of going crazy. "Anabel hinted that she wasn't unfaithful to Arthur with Tom Holland, but someone else." I hesitated, but then I said it all the same. I simply had to be sure. "The Tittle-Tattle blog said you and Anabel got on well, and if it wasn't Tom . . ."

Henry's eyebrows rose. "Are you suggesting that I had a relationship with Anabel?" There was utter disbelief in his voice. "Do you really think I'm someone who'd get involved with his friend's girlfriend like that?"

Did I? No, not really. On the other hand, Anabel was incredibly attractive; what boy wouldn't be tempted? "All right, no," I admitted. "I do believe you. But you were on the same flight as us, and I thought . . ." Okay, maybe I ought not to do so much thinking.

"I helped Anabel move to Switzerland." He shook his head. "I was worried about her. She more or less went to pieces after Tom's death, and then there was what happened to her dog. . . ."

Children's voices came from somewhere; two little boys chased past us with a football and disappeared behind a group of trees. I watched them go.

"Arthur's your friend," I said. "And you think you know him well. But are you really sure of what goes on inside his head? The way he appointed himself head demon conjuror as if it were perfectly natural—what does he think will happen when that last seal is broken? Does he talk to the rest of you about it?"

"I . . . all Arthur himself wants is for this to be over at last," said Henry. But I realized that he wasn't certain.

He looked thoughtfully down at the city. Suddenly I was sorry we'd talked about it. We should just have gone on kissing. I hesitantly put out my hand and stroked his hair. I'd been wanting to do that for so long. Considering the way it stood out wildly from his head, it felt quite soft.

He immediately turned back to me.

"You have rather lovely eyes," I said softly.

A smile spread over his face. "And everything about you is rather lovely," he replied, and he would certainly have kissed me again if, at that very moment, Mia and Daisy Dawn hadn't suddenly been there in front of us, as if they'd materialized out of the ground.

"We're going to let the balloons go now!" said Daisy Dawn, and Mia bleated like a sheep. "Baaaa."

Henry and I didn't say anything to each other on the way back, but about halfway he firmly took my hand, and a strong, totally irrational feeling of happiness took me over. It had really been the best birthday of all time.

But without those black thoughts in my head, it would have been even better. Much better.

The sun was quite low in the sky, bathing everything in warm, golden light, and I remembered the Berkeley dream again. And how, that night, Henry had said, *It's in dreams more than anywhere else that you get to know people best—along with all their weaknesses and their secrets.*

Suddenly it was clear as day what I must do next. There was a perfectly good way of finding out what went on inside Arthur's head. I just had to steal something from him first.

And declare my abstinence from dreaming over.

28

DAMN. IT WAS A BLIND ALLEY. Arthur had secured his door with a four-digit code, just like the locker in school.

So far everything had gone smoothly. Admittedly it had taken half the week before I finally had a chance to snaffle some personal item belonging to Arthur, but then it was surprisingly simple: I'd borrowed a pencil from him in the library, and then I just "forgot" to give it back. He had been chewing the end of the pencil shortly before he lent it to me, and you can't get much more personal than that.

It was an almost solemn moment when, after so many days, I went through my green door and into the corridor again. The corridor itself lay ahead, quiet and peaceful. But I'd made up my mind not to let any invisible, rustling presences lead me astray. This was only a dream, and I had a mission. Also, even though I didn't know Arthur's door itself, I had a fair idea of where I'd find it. After all, Henry's door was right opposite mine as well.

The other doors had been playing their catch-me-if-you-can game again, but all the same I found Anabel's door quite quickly in a neighboring passage. Opposite her magnificent Gothic porch, there was a plain, smooth metal door without any decoration except for the letters hammered into its center, saying CARPE NOCTEM.

Even their doors matched in a curious way. There was something utterly humorless about them both. I shuddered when I remembered my dream meeting with Arthur and Anabel, and once again I wondered whether I was doing the right thing. I mean, they were a really strange couple—did I truly want to know what a character like Arthur dreamed about?

Well, maybe I never would. Because I couldn't get any farther anyway. It was infuriating. Four silly numbers! So unimaginative. I'd been expecting puzzles with all kinds of thrills and spills, maybe a doorkeeper with a curved sword or some such thing, but not a simple lock like that. I could have kicked the wall with frustration. It might have been possible to get through the metal with an oxyacetylene cutting torch, but to be honest I had no idea what a cutting torch looked like, so I couldn't dream one into existence. I was tapping various combinations of numerals in at random when someone right behind me said, "Try one seven zero four."

"Henry!" I spun around. "Are you nuts, scaring me like that?"

"I'm glad to see you, too." Henry was smiling at me. "One seven zero four," he repeated. "Anabel's date of birth. Get a move on." He cast a meaningful glance at Anabel's door behind us, and I realized that this was no time for a romantic reunion. I turned back to the numerical combination for the lock.

"Cool outfit, by the way," said Henry. "An elegant cross between Catwoman and a ninja warrior."

I blushed under my cat mask. To be honest, I'd tried turning into a breath of air first, and this was the best alternative. I wasn't good enough at dream changing yet to be a breath of air. However, at least Arthur wouldn't recognize me at once in this disguise if I turned up in his dream.

The lock clicked. One seven zero four did indeed turn out to be the right combination.

I cautiously pushed the door open, but I hesitated to go in.

"What did you steal from Arthur?" I asked, taking off my mask and dropping it on the floor. It suddenly seemed to me amazingly silly. And, anyway, I had company now.

"Nothing," said Henry. "We all drank each other's blood, remember? That's about as personal as you can get."

"Oh." Then my theft hadn't been necessary at all. And I'd been wondering what would happen if I let go of the pencil in the night—I was clutching it firmly as I settled down to go to sleep, and I'd been on the verge of fixing it in place with sticky tape.

I was still hesitating.

"Come along." Henry came over to me and opened Arthur's door wider. "Now to go in." He took my hand, and we went through the doorway together.

Next moment we were standing in the middle of a wide desert landscape, in a broad trench that looked like a riverbed where no water had flowed for a long time. The soil was reddish, dry, and dusty, there were stones and scree lying everywhere, and a few dried-up bushes and trees grew on the edge of the riverbed, along with giant cacti. I could see the outlines of mountains in the distance.

"Is Arthur dreaming a Western?" I asked, clambering over a rock and making for the bank. Although there was no one anywhere in sight, I was whispering.

"No idea," Henry whispered back while he looked all around us.

"I bet there are rattlesnakes here." I wondered whether to imagine myself a pair of good, stout boots. I'd forgotten to add anything like that to my Catwoman outfit.

At that moment we heard a strange rumbling sound, then a loud roar that filled the air as it came closer. The rock beneath my feet was shaking.

"Come on!" exclaimed Henry, taking my hand and leading me over the stones and to the bank, while the rumbling and roaring grew louder and louder. *Shit! Arthur must be dreaming of some damn earthquake, or an underground nuclear experiment, or a . . .*

"Tidal wave!" Henry shouted. The thundering was very close now, and all at once I saw it: a huge tidal wave surging toward us, a wall of water at least six feet high, and there was no escaping it. The mass of water carried away everything in its path: branches, stones, and in half a second's time it would carry Henry and me away as well. That half a second was just long enough for me to realize that we were going to drown.

But we weren't swept away by the huge wave after all. Instead, the rock under our feet suddenly rose several yards up in the air, growing like a stone mushroom. It was difficult to keep my balance, and I clung to Henry's hand. The water shot past us, swirling down the riverbed, but we didn't even get our feet wet.

"What on . . . ?" My heart was racing. The rock on which we were standing changed shape again, spreading out lengthways this time until it formed a bridge to the bank. Henry helped me over the bridge as the sound of the rushing water below slowly died away. The whole episode had lasted only a few seconds. As we reached the bank someone clapped, applauding us.

It was Arthur.

"Not bad," he said. He was standing motionless beside a dried-up tree and had never looked more handsome. "You're getting better and better, Henry."

Henry didn't reply, while I was trying to calm my pulse and breathing and think clearly.

"My apologies for the rough welcome, Liv." Arthur's mouth twisted in a smile that didn't reach his eyes. "I don't usually drown visitors. Only when they're uninvited."

Okay, so our plan of taking him by surprise had clearly come to nothing.

"I'm just wondering why my best friend is trying to slink into my dream on the sly." Arthur took a step toward us and looked penetratingly at Henry. "Would you please explain, Henry?"

"I wanted a few answers, that's all," said Henry, unruffled.

Arthur shook his head. "What did you think you could find out here that you couldn't simply have asked me?" He sounded injured.

"Oh, come on, Arthur! When did you last talk to me

frankly?" For a moment Henry said nothing; then he added quietly, "I'm worried about you."

Arthur gave a scornful snort. "Don't be so damn self-righteous, Henry! You of all people! I know what you get up to at night—don't think that escapes me. You've shown just now how well you've mastered the trick of it. But you were doing your duty, like all of us." He made a sweeping gesture that embraced the whole dream valley. "For this. For immeasurable power. For the granting of our hearts' desires." A shadow fell on his face. "Anabel is the only one who understands that."

Yes, of course, our perfect pair. Model students at the School of Demonic Invocation.

"Because you and the demon have Anabel's ex-boyfriend on your conscience. And her dog," I said. "Well, it's logical for her to believe in all that." A little too late, I caught Henry's warning glance. Okay, so it wasn't exactly the most subtle way of questioning a suspect. Sherlock Holmes would not have been proud of me.

Arthur narrowed his eyes. "Little Liv," he said in his arrogant way. "You're still too new to all this to have any real idea of what's at stake."

I folded my arms. When anyone called me Little Liv, I felt stubborn.

"Or maybe it's the other way around, and unlike you I'm still in possession of my sound human reason, and I'm not about to be totally confused by pentagram diagrams and the muttering of mysterious sayings." I darted an angry look at him. "So what's going to happen at the last ritual? What are you going to do on Halloween? Light a couple of black candles? Build an altar and slaughter a lamb on it? Or hey, while you're at it, don't you think a human sacrifice would be even more effective?" I'd talked myself into such a rage that I almost laughed, but a change in Arthur's expression stopped me. Something in his eyes had flickered up at my words, something dark and wild. . . .

All at once I felt sick to my stomach. Oh no! Had I by any chance hit the bull's-eye?

Nonsense. That simply couldn't be true. It mustn't be true.

"*Pugio cruentus*—the bloodstained dagger," murmured Henry.

Arthur nodded. "You have your answers, Henry. And in your heart you knew them all the time. It's just that you wouldn't look the truth in the face."

"You don't mean that seriously," I whispered.

Arthur wasn't taking any notice of me now. Only Henry seemed to count, so far as he was concerned. "Anabel is ready," he said. "She wants to make up for what she almost did. And she will go through with it to the end. For the sake of all of us!"

As he spoke, the landscape had changed, at first imperceptibly, then faster and faster, until the scenery around us was entirely different. Everything was greener and darker; the riverbed, the rocks, the red earth all turned pale, and instead grasses, ferns, and ivy grew thickly at our feet. The color of the sky had turned from radiant blue to an overcast gray.

Arthur's voice shook very slightly as he turned to a monumental tomb with two stone angels guarding it. "She's going to sacrifice herself at Halloween to release the Prince of Darkness from his shadowy spell." He raised his arm. "And it will happen here."

I stared at the angels without really seeing them. "But . . . you love Anabel," I stammered. "And she loves you. You can't really want her to . . . Can't you see how sick that is?"

I turned to Henry. How could he stand there so calmly when Arthur had just said he was going to make sure that his girlfriend—who was a friend of Henry's, too—killed herself for a demon who didn't exist?

Henry's gray eyes were fixed on Arthur. "You think you'd do it because all this is happening in a dream, right? You believe that because this is just a dream you could really go through with it."

Arthur nodded again.

I almost uttered a gasp of relief. A dream, of course. Anabel was only going to die in a dream. But—did that make it any less horrible?

Henry went up to Arthur, and now he was standing right in front of him. Beside Arthur the statue of an angel leaned against a gravestone covered with moss, and I saw other gravestones in the dense vegetation behind him. We were back in Highgate Cemetery again.

"You both think that's the way to end this thing without anyone coming to harm?" Henry was speaking very slowly, almost as if to a small child.

"It's the *only* way," cried Arthur. He was silent for a moment. Then he asked, "Can I count on you, Henry?"

Henry didn't answer at once. He and Arthur were staring into each other's eyes. It was as if they were fighting a duel with glances.

I swallowed. If Arthur and Anabel planned to complete

the ritual in a dream, they were counting on being able to wake unharmed from the nightmare they themselves had staged. But suppose they were wrong about that?

I felt for the gravestone beside me. These dreams were different. I had sensed Henry's touch on my skin distinctly, as well as every breath of air, the pressure of his hand, his kiss, and now I could feel the rough surface of the old gravestone under my hand. How would a dagger against your skin feel, a cut, blood flowing . . . ?

"But you can't do it," I said, and I realized that I was on the point of losing my nerve. "You have no idea what will happen to Anabel."

"She's right, Arthur. It's going too far," said Henry.

"You still don't understand, Henry. We have no option!" Arthur was looking both angry and desperate. "He leaves us no other choice, and we've sworn an oath."

"You always have a choice," said Henry forcefully. He put a hand on Arthur's shoulder. "We mustn't do this. *You* mustn't do it."

Arthur bit his lip. "Don't let me down now that it's serious."

"I won't," replied Henry gently. "We'll think of another solution. It's still almost a month until Halloween."

"Another solution," repeated Arthur, and there was something like a spark of hope in his eyes. For a second I had the feeling that everything would end well. Henry had all this under control. Or rather, he had Arthur under control.

But then I heard the growl. Right behind me.

I turned on my heel and stared into the empty eyes of a statue. It was a gigantic stone dog, lying on a plinth in front of a tomb overgrown with moss, in the shadow of an oak tree with ivy scrambling over it.

Another growl, and then one of the stone paws twitched. And slowly, very slowly, the creature raised its head.

"Henry?" *Okay*, I thought, *don't panic.*

"Stop that, Arthur," said Henry, but Arthur shook his head.

"I'm not doing anything." There was fear in his voice, the same fear that had taken hold of me. "It's not me."

At that moment the creature rose to its full height. When it growled, it bared a set of powerful fangs. Presumably we'd soon know what it felt like being torn to pieces by fangs like that in a dream. *Oh shit. We must get out of here fast.*

Arthur's door! Where the hell was it? My glance raced over the weathered crosses and gravestones. There—the metal door! Set into the wall of the monumental tomb, with the two statues of angels guarding it.

"Henry, quick! Over there!" I cried, and Henry reached for my arm.

"Get back, Liv!" He was looking up at the crown of the oak tree.

The dog crouched to spring, but before it reached us the tree came crashing down on it.

I didn't wait to see whether Henry really had trapped the animal under the treetop. I hauled him over to the stone angels. With an abrupt jerk, I wrenched the metal door open and staggered out into the corridor.

But Henry turned around once more. "Wake up, damn it, Arthur," he called to his friend, who was still standing in the same place, staring wide-eyed at the huge crown of the tree. "Wake up!"

Just as the door latched with a loud noise, I felt something warm and damp on my cheek. And the next thing I saw was

Buttercup's doggy muzzle as I felt her rough tongue lovingly licking my face. Dawn was already breaking outside the window. "Thanks for waking me, Butter," I murmured, trying to get my breath back as I snuggled close to her warm, soft coat. "I was just dreaming of a really bad dog."

And of a few other really troubling things.

"HI." HENRY MANAGED TO FOLLOW that up with "cheese," but he couldn't finish what he'd been about to say by adding "girl."

Complete with white tie and tails, he was standing at the Spencers' front door, and for the first time since I'd known him, he was at a loss for words. Or so it seemed. Behind him, the streetlights cast a warm glow on the gravel drive, and I wouldn't have been surprised if a coach drawn by white horses had come around the corner to take me to the ball. Huh! Cinderella had nothing on me.

Everyone had assured me that the dress suited me wonderfully, and when I'd taken a last look in the mirror just now I had a feeling that I would never be able to wipe the broad smile off my face. Idiotic as all those layers of tulle might look on the hanger, I had to admit that they made me into another person. A prettier person. And that shade of blue matched my eye color perfectly, exactly as Mom had said. Within two hours she'd taken about four hundred photographs of me ("To think I'd ever see the day!"),

Lottie had shed tears ("My beautiful elf-child!"), Florence had nodded with satisfaction ("Vera Wang is always a good choice"), and Mia had clapped her hands in admiration ("You'll be the loveliest sheep in the ballroom"). Only Ernest's reaction brought me down to earth a little, because he said I was the image of my mother. But I think he meant it as a compliment.

In the afternoon, Lottie had styled my hair with the curling iron and pinned it in place at the back of my head. I'd been surprised that it looked so good. There had been a minor panic when I couldn't find the little container with my contact lenses and was afraid I'd have to go to the ball in my nerdy glasses, but then it turned out that when Florence was tidying up she had accidentally put the container in the bathroom cupboard with the cleaning things.

But it was one thing to think I looked good, and quite another to see Henry's eyes shining. He looked pretty good himself in his tailcoat, even if his hair didn't quite match the formal evening dress; it was still standing out in all directions. However, we passed muster as we went by Mrs. Lawrence and Pandora Porter-Peregrin, who were on guard at the historic entrance to Frognal Academy. With the braziers and lighted torches outside, it could have competed with Downton Abbey this evening. Pandora and Mrs. Lawrence weren't admitting anyone who didn't conform to the dress code.

"Long skirts, white tie and tails," said Mrs. Lawrence unmercifully to a couple in a cocktail dress and a tuxedo respectively. "You can either come in after the official part of the ball or go home and change."

"The hardest door in London to get past," commented

Henry, who had reverted to his usual casual attitude on the way, and he made me laugh.

Who'd have thought, on my first day at Frognal Academy, that I'd be going to this silly Autumn Ball myself, just under five weeks after I'd stood in front of that poster? Then Persephone had told me brusquely, *Forget it!* And above all, who'd have thought I'd actually be having fun?

The ball committee had done a really good job. Not that creating the perfect Victorian atmosphere had been any big deal, because the Frognal Academy ballroom dated back to the time when the school was founded. The large bow window on the long side of the room gave it a distinguished look, and so did the murals and the stucco ceiling. The parquet floor was polished to a high gloss, and the huge chandeliers cast their light on the colorful flower arrangements and the shimmering dresses of the female guests, standing together in small groups. I was almost disappointed to find only a string quintet playing in a corner. With Florence's talent for organization, I'd have expected the London Philharmonic at least. But maybe they were on tour overseas at the moment.

As president of the ball committee, Florence received every couple herself. When it was our turn, she energetically steered us into the photography corner, which was up in a gallery. We tried to look as Victorian as possible in front of the camera, and I managed to do it at least once without bursting into fits of laughter. Jasper, who came after us, had no such problems. Very much Shaving Fun Ken tonight, he had a girl on each arm, and he'd probably left another in reserve in the girls' toilet. In other ways too he seemed to be in high spirits, particularly when he caught sight of his ex-girlfriend Madison.

"Poor thing," he said, meeting me at the side of the gallery. "This must be the saddest day of her life. She'll be looking at Nathan the whole time and thinking that she could have been here with me instead, if she hadn't been such a silly cow."

"Yes, sure," I said, and left Henry with Jasper as I faced the difficult task of climbing down from the gallery with my skirts intact, which depended on keeping my eyes on the steps. I'd almost done it when I bumped into a girl at the bottom.

"Anabel!"

It was indeed Anabel, looking delicate and wonderfully beautiful in a black and cream dress with a close-fitting bodice and a skirt as lavishly equipped with layers of tulle as mine. She seemed nervous and tense, and a little sad, just as she had in my dreams. No wonder: Arthur had his hand on her shoulder in a very possessive way. At least he had evidently awoken unharmed from last night's dream.

"Liv Silver," said Anabel, and her shining turquoise eyes looked me up and down. "Pretty dress. You and Henry make a fine couple."

"You know each other?" asked Florence in surprise. She was standing beside the steps with her clipboard.

"Well, no," said Anabel, smiling. "Or only from the Tittle-Tattle blog. Secrecy seems to take a particular interest in us, don't you agree, Liv?"

I nodded. "Are you all right?" I asked anxiously.

Anabel lowered her eyes.

"She's fine," said Arthur, answering for her, and he guided her up the steps.

Henry and I watched them go. "Have you spoken to him again? He seems kind of the worse for wear," I whispered to Henry. "And Anabel looks as pale as a corpse."

At the word *corpse*, Henry started. "I haven't had time to speak to Arthur; I had a few things to see about at home, then I had to find some damn patent-leather shoes, and . . ." He sighed. "Listen. Halloween isn't for another three and a half weeks. We'll have thought of something by then. But let's just think of other things tonight. This is a special evening. And we won't hunt any demons," he added, striking an attitude, and I had to laugh, because only now did I notice that he really was wearing his great-grandfather's medal. "By God, tonight we dance!"

"You got that out of a film," I said reproachfully, although I couldn't for the life of me think which one.

He shook his head, grinning. "Not that I know of."

One way or another, he was proved right. Because by God, we did dance. The dancing went like this: For the first hour only classical music was played, although not by the string quartet, which went away after the official photos had been taken, but from the stereo system (the recordings *were* by the London Philharmonic). The traditional opening waltz, led by Mrs. Cook the headmistress and a white-bearded teacher with a lot of pomade on his hair and beard, was only for hard-core ballroom fans and admirers of the Vienna Opera Ball.

Henry and I agreed that it was much more fun to watch the other couples lining up and then moving over the dance floor to the solemn sounds of Johann Strauss's *Homage to Queen Victoria*, including several bows and—the absolute highlight, at least for Henry and me—a moment when the men raised their partners in the air. We had to laugh at Grayson's expression of alarm just before he lifted Emily off her feet, but we also realized why Florence, with her talent for making the perfect decision on every occasion, had fixed it to get Callum Caspers as her partner. He might look as unimpressive as Secrecy had described him, but he danced very well indeed, maybe better than anyone else present. Unlike Persephone, who gave me a gracious wave in passing but then got the whole formation confused because at the sight of Jasper, as usual, she turned to a pillar of salt.

Anabel and Arthur weren't dancing. They were standing up in the gallery, holding hands and looking somehow distracted.

"Don't you think we should . . . " I began asking Henry, but he just shook his head.

Later we ventured onto the dance floor ourselves, and I felt a little sorry that I hadn't listened to Mom and taken dancing lessons ages ago. Henry surprised me with his ability to dance Viennese waltzes. Not that it did him much good with me. My dancing abilities, unfortunately, were confined to what Mom, Lottie, and YouTube had taught me. And I also had to keep murmuring "one, two, three, one, two, three" to myself so as not to dance out of time, which in turn didn't do much for communication with my partner. Cinderella would have done better in my place—but then, she was a naturally good dancer.

I was glad when Henry suggested we might fill in the time until the "real music" began by trying the much-praised buffet set out in the room next to the ballroom. We met Jasper again there. He had somehow managed to get tipsy, although there were no alcoholic drinks.

I had just helped myself to a puff pastry stick when Henry suddenly came up beside me, took the puff pastry stick out of my hand, and took my arm. "Hey," I protested, "dancing makes me hungry."

"Me too," he murmured, and led me around behind one of the pillars separating the buffet from the front hall. He put his hands on my shoulders, held me close, and looked into my eyes. "Do you know how damn beautiful you are, Liv Silver?" he asked, and then he began covering first my mouth and then my throat with little kisses. All of a sudden my appetite had disappeared. Who could have guessed that kisses would have such a surprising effect . . . ?

I positively melted into his arms. I've no idea how he did it, but when he kissed me nothing else mattered. My hand went to the back of his neck. I could feel the warmth of his skin. "Maybe we ought to forget about that demon and his silly obsession with virgin blood once and for all," I murmured.

"You mean so that you don't end up like your aunt Gertrude?" Henry drew back from me for a moment before holding me even closer. We kissed again, this time even harder. Then he asked, "You mean here and now?"

I didn't manage to answer, because at that moment Grayson came around the pillar. "Oh, here you two are," he said, looking at us with a frown as I hastily stepped back, hoping that my hair wasn't standing out in all directions like Henry's.

"I've been looking for you everywhere. Henry, Jasper's in there and on the point of picking a fight with Nathan. He just called him a *midget*. You must help me to sober him up a bit."

"That stupid midget." Reluctantly, Henry let go of me. "Is it okay if I leave you on your own for a while, Liv?"

"I was just . . . er, going to the toilet anyway," I said awkwardly.

"Right," said Grayson, and I couldn't help hearing the note of disapproval in his voice. "And splashing some cold water on your face wouldn't hurt, I guess."

What was biting him? Hadn't he been smooching far more heavily at Arthur's party the other day? And I hadn't said a thing about it. I gave him a cool glance, picked up my skirts, and walked away with all the dignity I could muster.

When I looked at myself in the mirror of the girls' toilet, however, I couldn't help agreeing with Grayson. I really did look as if I could use some cold water on my face. None of my lip gloss was left, and instead my cheeks were unnaturally red. I'd have liked to put a little powder on, but it hadn't fit into my bag, which was only a tiny little evening bag. Lip gloss, a tissue, peppermint drops, two ten-pound notes, and the front door key—that was all I could get into it. I hadn't even tried to bring my clumsy old cell phone with me.

The door of a cubicle in the toilets closed behind me, and Emily's face appeared in the mirror over my shoulder.

"Hi," I said, forcing myself to smile. I didn't particularly like her, and she might quite possibly be Secrecy, the most malicious person under the sun, but still, she was my future stepbrother's girlfriend, so I needed to at least take some trouble with her.

"Oh, here you are, Liv," she said. Not that she seemed particularly glad of that. She was wearing a plain black ball dress this evening. It would have been just right for a Victorian widow. "Grayson's been looking for you everywhere.

For some reason or other, he seems to think he ought to keep an eye on you. Well, I can't blame him—after all, you're going out with Henry Harper."

"What do you mean by that?" No, I didn't like Emily one little bit.

"I know how crazy you girls are about that sort." Emily opened her little evening bag and took out a lipstick. "Boys like Arthur, Jasper, and Henry—self-confident, casual, egotistic, superficial, and totally irresponsible. In fact, perfect examples of the classic heartbreaker. I'll never understand it."

"Goodness me, and I thought you were a girl yourself," I said. I was amused to hear her lumping Jasper, Henry, and Arthur all in together, when they couldn't have been more different from one another.

"Yes, but a girl with sense," said Emily. "And good taste. Grayson is the only reasonable one in that little circle. I really do wish he'd find other friends. Take Jasper, for example—he smuggled bottles of alcohol into the school today for himself and the girls he's with. Arthur and Anabel were with them too. With their relationship dying the way it is, they probably feel they have to get tipsy. Ball King and Ball Queen only last year, and today I somehow feel sorry for them." She made a contemptuous face. "At least, Anabel staggered past me, obviously drunk, and babbling something about, oh, I don't know what, but to give you her regards. I mean, how sozzled can you get? After all, she's going to be in London all weekend—she can say hello to you for herself."

I stared at Emily. All the alarm bells that had begun ringing faintly when she said that about the dying relationship between Arthur and Anabel were now going off at full volume.

"Where are they?"

Emily looked at me in surprise, probably because in my fright I'd grabbed her by the arm.

"Arthur and Anabel?" She shrugged her shoulders. "Gone."

"Gone?"

"They left just now. Anabel could hardly keep on her feet. She was so drunk that Arthur had to support her. She looked like a lamb going to the slaughter."

"What?" The words *lamb* and *slaughter* set off a wild association of ideas in my head.

"Anabel and Arthur have left the ball," repeated Emily patiently, as if I were a total idiot. "I can only hope that at least they had the sense to take a taxi."

The fright had gone straight to my stomach, along with the realization that we might have been on quite the wrong trail. And that we couldn't wait until Halloween.

Shit. Shit, shit, shit.

Suppose Arthur had been deliberately leading us astray last night? Suppose he'd had no intention of completing the ritual in a dream? Suppose he . . .

"Is there a new moon tonight?" I shouted at Emily.

"Well, I . . ." She sounded taken aback.

"When was this exactly? I mean, when did Arthur and Anabel leave?"

Emily stared at me. "Just now, as I said."

Oh no. No! I seized Emily by the shoulders and shook her.

"Tell Henry I'm trying to stop them! Tell him to forget all about Halloween—it's going to happen tonight. And for real! Tell Henry to . . ." I let go of her, snatched my tiny little evening bag off the side of the washbasin, and ran to the door. "Tell him to damn well think up something else!"

I took off my shoes so that I could go faster. Maybe I was on the wrong track, maybe I was the one going crazy, but if I was right, if the realization that had struck me full force just now wasn't merely the product of my imagination working overtime, then something terrible was going to happen tonight. And I had to stop it. Gathering up my skirts, I raced full speed ahead along the corridors, never mind what anyone else thought. *Please, please let them still be here*, I prayed silently.

But Anabel and Arthur had already left the school building. When I reached the entrance door, they were already out in the street and just getting into a taxi.

"Hey!" I shouted. "Anabel! Arthur! Wait!"

Anabel turned her head to look at me, but then she followed Arthur into the car and closed the door.

Damn.

I ran down the steps and crossed the school yard. Slowly, the taxi began to move away. Another taxi was waiting behind it, obviously intended for the elderly teacher who had opened the ball with the headmistress, because he was making straight for it. I couldn't stop to think of that now. I pushed him aside and flung the car door open.

"Young lady!" said the white-bearded teacher indignantly.

"I know I shouldn't do this, sir, but it's an emergency," I replied. I didn't wait for his answer but dropped into the back seat and said something that would never have crossed my lips if I hadn't been so desperate. "Follow that car, please. And fast."

30

I'D HAVE GIVEN ANYTHING TO WAKE UP.

But this wasn't a dream, in which I was crossing High-gate Cemetery in the middle of the night, barefoot, and wearing a ball dress. It was only too real. My silk stockings were in shreds, but to be honest I could hardly feel my feet. It must have been the adrenaline. Arthur and Anabel had a flashlight to show them the way along the overgrown paths, and that made it easier for me to follow them. They were holding hands and walking on as purposefully as if they had been here hundreds of times.

Was Henry on his way yet? Had Emily delivered my message to him correctly?

I'd hoped so much that I was wrong and Arthur was sim-ply taking Anabel home to sleep off her hangover. But my taxi had followed theirs straight to the gate of the cemetery, and when I'd seen them both disappear through the church-like entrance, I could no longer persuade myself that I was suffering from an overactive imagination. I went through the gate just after them.

And now I was running through the darkness, with no clear plan in my head. I only knew that I must keep Arthur from doing anything to Anabel. Did she really mean to sacrifice herself of her own free will, or had Arthur been making it up? I still couldn't imagine anyone—even Anabel—going so far as to get herself killed for this demon business, guilty feelings or not, and never mind the amorous tsunami.

In the darkness, I saw weathered gravestones and broken crosses, and the whole place seemed to be rustling. Rats, owls, werewolves . . . ?

I was breathing heavily. The cold night wind blew through the trees, and I realized that the slight noise I heard was my own teeth chattering.

I knew I mustn't panic. Henry would surely arrive soon. He could talk to Arthur. I'd realized last night how much influence he had over him. He'd persuade Arthur to change his mind, and together we'd rescue Anabel and—where had they gone? There! The beam of the flashlight moved over a tomb and showed me a door. I thought I knew the two stone angels on guard outside it.

In my fright, I stumbled over a root on the ground. If I hadn't put out my hands in time to save myself, I'd have hit my forehead on a statue lying on the plinth in front of me.

I struggled upright, and only then did I see where I was: This was the tomb where the scary stone dog had attacked us in last night's dream. It looked as menacing as ever now, with its empty stone eyes, but at least its paws stayed put. I had plenty of other problems, thank you very much.

Anyway, Arthur and Anabel didn't seem to have heard me. They disappeared into the mausoleum, and when the door closed behind them, I was alone in the dark.

Silence.

And no sign of Henry anywhere at all.

Oh God, what an idiot I was! I ought to have jumped Arthur from behind on the way here! He wouldn't have had a chance. Now, inside that tomb, it was going to be much more difficult.

I closed my eyes for a moment. Maybe I was simply over-reacting, and in my panic I'd just been following a pair of lovers who didn't want to be disturbed.

Yes, exactly. In this cemetery, by night. Inside a mauso-leum.

Because this was such a cozy place.

It was no good—I couldn't wait any longer.

If necessary, I'd deal with Arthur by myself. He might be tall and fit, but I was good at kung fu, and I had the advantage of surprise on my side. Okay, so it might be silly. It certainly wasn't particularly clever, to face up on my own to someone who was seriously expecting to liberate a demon from the underworld—and who didn't shrink from the idea of human sacrifice—but what choice did I have?

I stared at the shape of the sleeping stone dog beside me. Suppose Henry didn't turn up at all? Suppose Emily hadn't passed on my message? I could believe it of her, in view of what she'd said about Grayson's friends. And maybe she simply hadn't understood a word of what I'd been shouting.

I had to make my decision. Running back to the street in search of help wasn't really in the cards. By the time help came—if it came at all—it would be far too late. No, I couldn't wait any longer. Who knew what was going on inside that mausoleum at this very moment? Did Arthur have the nerve to draw pentagrams and declaim unctuous sayings in Latin? Maybe he'd go straight to the essential part, hoping to get it over and done with fast and painlessly.

I slowly put my shoes on again. They might not be much good for running, but in a fight they could turn out to be very useful.

My hand was shaking as I opened the mausoleum door, cautiously stole in, and looked around. It occupied an area of about ten to twelve feet, and the dim light came from candles placed in niches along the walls. Anabel was just lighting a torch, and Arthur was standing against the long side of the oblong tomb, looking at me. Not shocked, not even surprised, but as if he'd expected to see me there. The flickering light showed the outline of his perfect face.

"Liv," he said, taking a step toward me. I didn't wait for him to come any closer. His hands were empty and held no weapon, so I swung up my right foot and caught him just under the chin as I jumped. Still in the air, I turned at an angle of 180 degrees, and when I landed, my left forearm caught him in the stomach. I didn't have to kick his shin, because he collapsed like a felled tree. The ugly sound that had followed my first kick made me suspect that I'd broken his jaw.

Okay, I hadn't planned to do that. But it had been effective.

I was just thinking, with satisfaction, that the advantage of surprise had definitely worked, when something (an iron torch holder, as it turned out) came down on me. Only when my head hit the stone floor beside Arthur's, and everything went black before my eyes, did I realize that I'd made a mistake—I'd forgotten Mr. Wu's fighting principle number one: Tackle your most dangerous adversary first.

"I do like it when a plan works out," said Anabel as I returned to my senses. She'd stolen that from a movie too, and once again I couldn't remember what movie it was. My head hurt as if a small bulldozer was driving around in it—my whole body hurt, and now I could even feel the sore soles of my feet. I was lying on the hard stone floor, and someone—Anabel, I assumed—had taped my wrists and ankles together, but even without that, I wasn't sure I could have moved my limbs. Even opening my eyes hurt.

"Oh, good," said Anabel, pleased. "I was afraid you'd miss your own execution. Poor Arthur probably will, and I'm not ungrateful to you for that. I wasn't sure whether he would go through with this, anyway."

My throat was dry, so I could only croak, "You? Why . . . ?" That was all I could get out. Anabel had crossed my hands over my breast, and I could hardly breathe.

She bent over me and checked my bonds. "Why *what*?" Although the tomb was lit only by candles, the pupils of her eyes looked unnaturally small, and it occurred to me that she might actually *be* the demon. "Why do you have to die tonight?" she asked, laughing. "I wouldn't take it so personally if I were you. Although it's your own fault for being so nosy. I had a few other virginal candidates in reserve. They're not as rare as Jasper thinks." She seemed to be in high spirits. "But then you slipped into Grayson's dream. I don't believe in coincidences. I think that *he* showed you the way into that dream himself. And tonight your blood will bring him back to life."

No, she wasn't a demon. She was only a crazy girl who

believed in demons. But from my point of view that was almost as bad. Particularly because the book from which Arthur had read the ritual when I joined the circle was lying over there on the floor, and beside it was the hunting knife, with its blade shining unpleasantly in the candlelight. I glanced at Arthur, still lying motionless in the same place. How stupid could I get? While Anabel was coldly luring me into a trap, I'd knocked out the one person who might have been able to help me.

"The open cemetery gate . . . that was idiotic of me too," I murmured. "You were planning for me to follow you all the time."

Anabel giggled. "Hmm, yes, not very intelligent. But in case you wonder how I arranged for the gate to be open— well, night watchmen have dreams too. And if you have some personal item of theirs, you can easily find out what you need. For instance, where the duplicate keys are kept. These dreams offer so many opportunities." Anabel sighed with pleasure as she bent down to pick up the book. "This is Arthur's family mausoleum, by the way. All the Hamiltons who died before 1970 were buried here. I knew at once that it would be the perfect place for the ritual." Only now did I see that the round things in the niches—I'd taken them for stones—were really human skulls. "*Your* ritual! You should feel honored. It will be your blood that changes the face of this world, ushering in a new age. The Lord of Shadows will rise again to claim his rights in this world."

She was talking nonsense, but at least she was talking. I knew about that sort of thing from TV. As long as they could be kept talking, they didn't kill you. I really had to make sure that she didn't stop.

"You manipulated them all!" It was a shot at random. I felt something wet at the back of my head. Blood? "All that about virgin blood . . ."

Anabel laughed. "That was simple! They didn't understand the difference between innocent blood—*innocens*—and virgin blood—*virginalis*. It doesn't specify anywhere that you needed the blood of a virgin to break the first seal. That *would* have been a problem, because none of us had virgin blood, me least of all. And believe me, Arthur if anyone should know." She was coming toward me.

"But . . . but he was jealous of Tom. . . ."

"Yes, you bet he was. And more than horrified when Tom died. That was one of many lucky coincidences . . . although we agreed that there aren't any coincidences, didn't we?" With a sunny smile, she knelt down on the floor of the tomb beside me. "The boys have stopped trusting each other. When Henry came to lend me a hand in Switzerland, he seriously asked whether Arthur was treating me well. I'll tell you something—it's incredibly useful to look frail and be blond. They all feel they have to protect you."

I was fighting against my bonds, but crazy as Anabel might be, she was also thorough. Talking . . . I absolutely must keep her talking.

"And about your dog . . . ?"

"Lancelot, the dearest little dog in the world? *What's the matter with him?*" she said, imitating my voice. "The rat poison was really horrid. Poor dear, he suffered horribly. But I had to do it to keep the boys doing as I wanted. So that they'd see how serious it was and work hard to get a sweet little virgin like you into the circle." Her eyes were shining. "I'm almost sorry it will be over today. I've had so much fun," she went on thoughtfully. "Those boys are so good looking and so clever! Except for Jasper, of course. He's just good looking." She sighed. "I couldn't have found better collaborators."

Damn it, I wanted a way to turn all this around somehow. Unfortunately I couldn't think of one. I needed more time, not to mention superhuman powers.

"But mustn't you gather Henry, Arthur, Grayson, and Jasper together to complete the ritual?"

"Oh no—I really needed them only to break the first seal." Anabel leafed through the book. "Wait a moment—here it is: 'the Circle of Five, a circle bound by blood, wild, innocent, honest, brave, and free, will give the Lord of Shadows access to the first dimension.' I could have done all the rest of it without them, but it wouldn't have been nearly so much fun on my own. And now all I need for the last seal is your blood, virgin blood. And plenty of it. Or rather, *all* of it." She leaned forward again and laid her finger against my neck.

My throat felt tight with fear.

"It's somewhere around here . . . *Arteria carotis externa*," murmured Anabel. "You'll die quickly once I've cut it."

It couldn't be all over now, could it? I liked my life. Sixteen years wasn't very long. I didn't want to die yet.

I squinted down at myself. I couldn't move my hands, but if I managed to turn on my side, I could reach one of those torches with my feet. And with a little luck, then I could kick it toward Anabel. All those layers of tulle would surely burn like wildfire.

"One more thing," I said quickly, wondering what question to make up.

"I can understand that you don't want to die without knowing everything," said Anabel. She had opened the book at the place where the last seal held two pages together. It looked nasty. "But it's about time we finished all this." She got to her feet with a graceful movement. Oh God, no! Now she was holding the knife. This couldn't be happening.

"Anabel," I said pleadingly, and at the same time I tensed all my muscles. Now. I had to do it now, when she wasn't looking at me. When she bent to pick up the knife, I flung myself aside with a sudden movement, kicking out with all my might. But my kick wasn't enough to send the torch flying, only to give it a gentle nudge.

The torch fell over, but as if in slow motion, and stopped a good three feet away from Anabel's tulle skirts. So much for my good idea. Frustrated, I closed my eyes, while Anabel began laughing at my failed attempt.

And then I heard someone calling her name just as she began to scream, and I opened my eyes again. *Henry!* There he was at last. Couldn't he have turned up a minute earlier? Before Anabel had picked up the knife, screeching all the time like a woman possessed?

Only then did I see why she was screaming like that. It had nothing to do with Henry. The torch had set the book on fire—Anabel's sacred demonic book! She dropped the knife and flung herself on the floor beside me, trying to get hold of the book and beat out the flames with her bare hands. And all the time she never stopped screaming.

Henry threw himself at her, knocking the book out of her hand, and someone—it was Grayson—seized her from behind and pulled her back.

She was still screaming blue murder. It was an almost in-human sound. Her eyes were rolling, so that you could only see their whites. She was fighting back as hard as she could, but Grayson held her firmly.

Henry trod out the fire and then knelt down beside me. "Can't you be left on your own for a single moment?" he asked.

TITTLE-TATTLE BLOG

The Frognal Academy Tittle-Tattle Blog, with all the latest gossip,
the best rumors, and the hottest scandals from our school.

ABOUT ME:
My name is Secrecy—I'm right here among
you, and I know *all* your secrets.

13 October, 7 a.m.

Okay, you guys, let's forget about the democratic vote.
(You've been cheating anyway: How come there were 2,341
votes for Arthur Hamilton as Ball King when only 924
students came to the ball? I guess a few girls, madly in love
with him, made use of their right to vote up to a hundred
times. . . .) Of course, votes were also cast for Ball Queen,
but in my opinion the role of Queen goes to no one this year.
And as my opinion is the only one that counts, it's the
deciding vote. ☺

I mentioned the day before yesterday that Arthur Hamilton
is definitely up for grabs again, but now, at last, I can tell you
why: Anabel has changed her Facebook status from "in a
relationship" to "in the nuthouse."

But seriously, it's no laughing matter. Poor Anabel has been
diagnosed as a case of "acute polymorphic psychotic
disorder with symptoms of schizophrenia," and insiders
say she won't be discharged within the next few years.

They also say she's broken Arthur's heart. Really broken it—he wasn't seen in school all week, and no one has heard anything from him.

Even without their captain, however, the Frognal Flames have managed to extend their lead at the top of the league with a sensational victory over the Hampstead Hornets. Congratulations, guys!

And cheer up, Arthur. Other mothers also have beautiful daughters, and I'm sure I'll have something else to report before long.

See you soon!

Love from Secrecy

PS—Liv Silver, who had the bad luck to fall downstairs at the ball and get a concussion, is better again. She was at the game, and guess what? I think she and Henry Harper are definitely an item. At least, Henry scored a sensational eighteen points.

NOT MUCH HAD CHANGED in Amy's colorful dream world. The sky was violet blue, the sun had a laughing face, and soap bubbles were still floating in the air along with brightly colored butterflies. Today the carousel was turning to the tune of "London Bridge Is Falling Down," and Amy was sitting on a swing that was fixed to the branch of a huge chestnut tree and going back and forth of its own accord.

"In real life she hasn't quite mastered the trick of it yet," said Henry. "You have to push her for hours on end. But since the day before yesterday, she's been able to ride her bike," he added proudly.

I smiled at him and then looked up at the sun. The famous English weather had begun in London by now, and it seemed to have been raining for weeks without stopping, so it was good to see the sun in a dream, at least. It was early November. Halloween had come and gone, and nothing had happened. No demon had shown his face; no one had lost what was dearest and most precious to him or her; everything was all right.

Henry guided me over into the shade of a balloon tree, so that two rainbow-colored ponies could trot past us.

"How is Arthur?" I asked. He'd been back in school since a couple of days ago, but we hadn't spoken to each other yet. And as it was my doing that he'd had to go around with his jaw wired and splinted for three weeks, I didn't suppose he wanted to say anything very nice to me. For instance, "I'm sorry I handed you over to my crazy girlfriend."

Henry watched the ponies trotting away and shrugged. "As you might expect, I assume. We don't talk much these days. He does swear he'd never have let Anabel harm you, but I . . . I just can't forgive him."

He wasn't the only one. Grayson, too, had broken off contact with Arthur. He didn't want to talk about it, but on the first night after the ball, when I'd been afraid to close my eyes for more than a minute because when I did I saw Anabel coming toward me with that knife, he had come into my room as if it were the most natural thing in the world, brought an armchair over to my bed, and said, in his serious way, "You can go to sleep, Liv. Don't worry, I'll be here." Like a real big brother. Grayson had also helped me to give our family (and Emily) a plausible explanation for why they'd had to collect me from Accident and Emergency at the Royal Free Hospital on the night of the ball. Luckily Mom had immediately believed that I'd tripped over my long dress on the steps and fallen. And Secrecy had written it up in her blog as if she'd seen it with her own eyes. The wound on the back of my head had needed four stitches, and I had to stay in bed for a few days with a mild concussion.

Amy, over on her swing, began singing. Our presence

didn't seem to bother her—if anything, the opposite. Now and then she glanced at us and gave us a cheerful wave.

"Where did that book come from, anyway—I mean, how did it get into the possession of Anabel's family?" I asked.

"I assume it came from the estate of her mother. She left Anabel's father when she was in the clutches of a weird Satanic cult, and she took Anabel with her. It was months before the father and his attorneys managed to get custody of Anabel and take her away. The mother went into a psychiatric hospital. Three guesses what the diagnosis was. She died in the hospital a few years ago. Anabel didn't have any more contact with her, but she probably has memories of that time. . . ."

"How come you know all this?"

Henry didn't reply. He reached up to a branch and picked me a green balloon.

"Thanks." I held the balloon up and let it rise in the air. A few seconds later it was just a small green dot in the blue sky. Henry hadn't changed. He answered only the questions he chose to answer. But that didn't particularly bother me. We all need our secrets, and Henry obviously needed more than other people. I was just glad that it was over and no one had to believe in a demon anymore.

"I have something for you." Henry took a small black box out of his pocket and handed it to me. "Wait a minute." A red bow appeared on the lid of the box. "Better? Or would you rather have a blue bow?"

"No, red is fine," I said, undoing the bow. "Dream presents are so practical. You can give me an eight-carat diamond or the Koh-i-Noor without paying a penny or breaking into the Tower of London to get at the crown jewels. I'm thinking of giving you a yacht for your birthday. Along with a nice little Caribbean island . . ."

Henry grinned. "Open it."

With a sigh, I lifted the lid. "Oh," I said, and wondered for a moment whether I ought to feel disappointed. It was a small silver key, on a thin, black leather string.

"*Take the key and lock her up, lock her up, lock her up,*" Amy sang at that very moment.

"It's the key to my door," said Henry. "So you can visit me yourself."

"That's . . ." I was touched. "Does it fit all three locks?"

"No," said Henry hesitantly. "Only the middle one. But I'll just leave the other two unlocked."

I couldn't help laughing. "And if they're locked after all, then I'll know you're dreaming something you don't want me to know about, right?"

"Not very romantic?" He gave me a crooked grin.

"Yes, it is in a way," I said, putting both my arms around Henry's neck. "Thank you very much."

Henry closed his eyes before my lips touched his. Kissing him had lost none of its charm—I felt like I'd never have enough of it. Henry put his hands on my waist and pushed me back against the balloon tree, only to take a step away, breathing hard and shaking his head. "No, this isn't right. . . . Not really rated for viewers of all ages," he said, looking at his little sister. "Come on. Let's go this way."

He led me through the pink door and out into the quiet corridor. When he finally let go of me, I saw real color in his usually pale cheeks for the first time.

"I'm in favor of waking up right away," he said, rather

breathlessly. "I could be at your place in twenty minutes. In real life, I mean."

I smiled at him. "But it's the middle of the night."

"I could throw pebbles at your window. . . ."

"Or you could simply come to breakfast in a few hours' time."

"Yes, that's another good idea." Henry was stroking my hair and looking at me so intently that I felt slight goose bumps running down my back. "Do you know why I began believing in that demon?" he asked quietly.

I shook my head.

"Because my wish came true the moment I met you."

"You'd wished to meet someone with a stinking cheese in her bag?"

He didn't laugh at my joke, which admittedly wasn't very funny, but ran his forefinger around my lips. "You're like me," he said seriously. "You love puzzles. You like to play. You're happy to take risks. It's when things look like they're getting dangerous that you feel really excited." He leaned a little closer to me, and I could feel the warmth of his breath. "That's what I wished for. To meet someone I could fall in love with. You're my heart's desire, Liv Silver."

"How touching!" said a voice as clear as a bell behind us, just as our lips were only half an inch apart.

We stepped back and spun around in alarm. Anabel was leaning against the wall beside Henry's door. Her golden hair flowed over her shoulders in shining waves, her big blue eyes were gleaming. She looked beautiful, but at the sight of her all the butterflies that had been dancing in my stomach went away, and I had a queasy sensation instead. The last time I saw her, Anabel had been about to cut my throat with a knife. For real. And before that she had given me a wound to the back of my head and a concussion. Also for real. The shaved patch on my head reminded me of it every day.

"You're in the way, Anabel." Henry put an arm around my shoulders.

Exactly. So shove off.

Anabel twisted her lip scornfully. "You think you've won, don't you? You think that now you've burned the book and separated me from Arthur, that's the end of the story."

Right.

"Although the fact that we're talking to each other here in this corridor proves the opposite?" Anabel looked at us challengingly.

"No," said Henry calmly. "We think so because at this moment you're lying in a hospital bed in Surrey, stuffed full of mind-bending drugs and tied down for your own safety." He smiled sympathetically. "It's over, Anabel."

Anabel's lips twitched, and for a moment it looked as if she would burst into tears. But then she threw back her head and laughed.

"Oh, you're so wrong, Henry," she said. "In fact, it's only just begun."

CAST OF CHARACTERS

Liv Silver, has always had vivid dreams

Mia Silver, Liv's younger sister, specialist in all kinds of investigations

Ann Matthews, Liv's mother

Lottie Wastlhuber, Liv and Mia's German au pair

Ernest Spencer, the new man in Ann's life

Grayson Spencer, Ernest's son, twin brother of Florence

Florence Spencer, Ernest's daughter, twin sister of Grayson

Charles Spencer, Ernest's brother, a dentist

Mrs. Dimbleby, the Spencers' cook and household help

Henry Harper, loves dreaming

Arthur Hamilton, the best-looking boy in the Western Hemisphere

Jasper Grant, the dimmest boy in the Western Hemisphere

Persephone Porter-Peregrin, Liv's nightmare come true

Anabel Scott, Arthur's girlfriend, has had a tragic childhood

Emily Clark, Grayson's girlfriend, editor of the school students' magazine

Sam Clark, Emily's pimply brother

Tom Holland, Anabel's ex-boyfriend, dead

Secrecy, writes a blog—we'll keep her identity a secret

Princess Buttercup, mongrel dog; full name, *Princess Buttercup, formerly known as Dr. Watson*, one of the rare breed of Entlebuch Biosphere dogs

Spot, the Spencers' cat, looks like a sofa cushion

Callum Caspers, mathematical genius, Florence's partner at the ball

Brief guest appearances by various teachers (who wants to know their names?); *Amy Harper*, Henry's four-year-old sister; *Lancelot*, Anabel's dead West Highland terrier; poor *Hazel Pritchard*, who appears only in the blog; *Mr. Wu*, Liv's former kung fu teacher; the four malicious girls from junior high in Berkeley, California . . . and any number of anonymous shadows.

Author's Note

Hello, all you dreamers out there—if you've enjoyed the story of Liv Silver, you can look forward to another one, because, as Anabel rightly remarked, the story has only just begun. (Is that scary, or is it scary?)

In the next book there is another mystery for Liv to solve. Someone is living under a curse—good thing Liv doesn't believe in all that supernatural nonsense. Well, except for the dreams, but they are useful as well. It's amazing what you can find out at night. . . .

And maybe you would like to know whether Lottie and Charles will become a couple, or whether Mia will manage to marry Lottie off to the good-looking veterinarian in Pilgrim's Lane? And what Grayson and Florence's grandmother will say about the changes in the family when she gets back from her cruise around the world? And whether Liv and Henry will still be in love, or whether maybe Henry is keeping one secret too many in this second book . . . ?

Speaking of secrets, has anyone yet guessed the identity of Secrecy?

See you soon!

Sincerely,
Kerstin Gier

PS—What does your dream door look like? At the moment, mine is black and silver, with red owls and a really dangerous vampire lizard for a doorknob. ☺